Third Degree Yearn

BARTHOLOMEW SERIES
BOOK THREE

LANEY HATCHER

Copyright

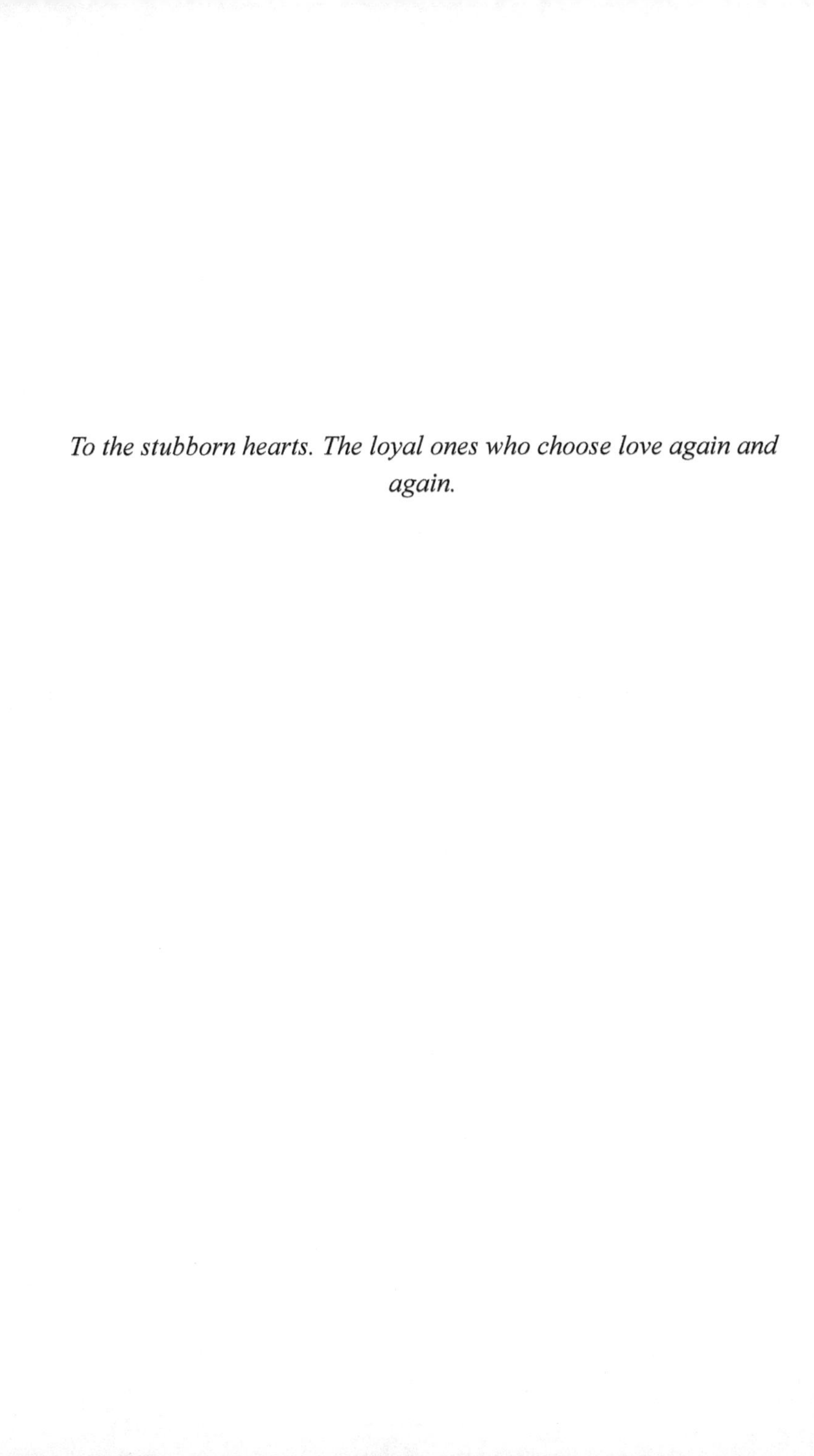

To the stubborn hearts. The loyal ones who choose love again and again.

One

GENEVIEVE

London, September 1863

"Gen, I need you to come with me. Hurry up now."

I startled a bit as my sister Emery came up swiftly behind me while holding a smiling baby Beckett.

Turning toward the intrusion, I ignored Emery and puffed up my cheeks, making Beckett laugh and reach for his favorite auntie.

My sister pulled her adorable two-year-old little cherub out of my reach and whispered frantically, amber eyes flashing, "Genevieve, I mean it. I need your assistance."

Frowning, I dropped the arms that had been reaching for my nephew and regarded my dramatic sister. Her husband, Augustus —Augie, to close friends and family—was approaching on the garden path with their daughter in tow and was nearly upon us.

I'd been speaking with our brother before Emery barged over and interrupted with her odd demand. Silas finally found his voice and

"

expressed his sibling offense, "I say, Em, you interrupted my story about the time I rowed—"

"—halfway across the Channel," Emery, Augie, and I all finished in unison for him.

Augie and I shared a knowing grin. Silas lived to entertain. I'd heard the story about the rowboat numerous times over the years. I assumed with our thirteen-year age difference, the eldest Bartholomew sibling had ample time to hone his craft for dramatic storytelling and general entertainment.

He scowled at us collectively for having not only interrupted but also for ruining the big reveal of his over-the-top tall tale.

Impatient, Emery looked briefly over her shoulder before stepping closer and demanding, "Gen, I really need you to come with me."

"Why?" I asked, crossing my arms over my chest. The early September day was fine indeed. I wished to remain out of doors in this lovely garden with the fountain bubbling happily at my back. I would even continue listening to my brother's ridiculous stories. That was how fine the day was in London.

Emery visibly cast about for an answer. She was terrible at lying or fabricating, or anything that deviated from her straightforward manner. I quite liked that about her, but I wouldn't admit it. That broke the sibling code of torture and mayhem. "Well," she finally attempted. "I need help with the children." She indicated Beckett on her hip before reaching back and plucking Reeve's little hand from her father's grasp. "See. Two children under the age of five. I am overwhelmed," she said with a beleaguered sigh. I rolled my eyes. "Please assist me in bringing the children inside."

My family was gathered today for a garden party at my eldest sister, Patty's home. It was a decidedly informal event for Bartholomews, former Bartholomews, and a few close family friends.

I wasn't sure why Emery was trying to lure me back inside the house. "But Augie is right there. He can help you with the children. What do they even need help with?" I leaned close to Beckett and puffed my cheeks once more. "They are absolutely perfect." I adopted a singsong tone for the baby's benefit and he giggled happily.

"Right, well," Emery tried again. "There is a surprise for you inside. I didn't want to tell you, but since you're being stubborn and pigheaded, I have to ruin the big reveal."

The deception was practically written across her face. I decided I'd play along. With a feigned gasp, I raised a hand toward my chest. "Truly? For me?"

"Yes," she hissed, all impatience. "Just come inside and you can have your surprise!" She reached forward to grasp my arm, apparently intent on dragging me from the garden and across the stone pavers toward the stairs and into the house.

"Is it for my birthday?" I asked brightly, just as her gloved hand clamped on the bare skin of my forearm. The day was so fair in the bright sunshine and the glorious autumn foliage I'd left my shawl indoors. My mother would be scandalized at the prospect of freckles, but they'd never bothered me.

Emery paused thoughtfully for a moment. "Yes! It *is* for your birthday."

Standing beside her mother, my tiny niece must have thought we were playing a game, because Reeve reached for my skirts and pulled me toward her as well, copying her mother's eager manhandling.

Augie frowned in confusion. "Genevieve doesn't turn three and twenty for another several months."

Emery huffed in irritation before shooting a glare at her husband.

"Oh, right! An early birthday surprise." Augie's claim was overly loud and manufactured.

My layered skirts were being tugged back and forth as little Reeve continued her game, laughing delightedly. I shot her a silly face that had my four-year-old niece giggling harder.

I shook my head at Augie's contrived explanation. He and Emery deserved each other. They were both incapable of subterfuge.

Sighing loudly, I decided that this had gone on long enough "All right, Emery. What is the meaning of all this? You're being difficult—even for you."

Her attention lifted from Augustus before snagging somewhere beyond. She turned back quickly to face me, eyes wide. "Nothing is going on."

I considered the direction of her gaze and glanced over her shoulder. Augie stepped up nearer to his wife and blocked my view. I raised on tiptoe and he, too, lifted off his heels and made himself larger. I was tall for a young woman, but my height could not compete with that of my brother-in-law, the duke.

The amusement that had been lingering as I'd entertained my sister's theatrics slowly vanished. Something was afoot. Emery was a distraction. Augie was assisting. And I was being wrangled.

Emery's hand tightened on my forearm and she tugged. I tugged back. "What are you doing?" I asked, incredulous. We weren't exactly in public, what with being surrounded by our family and close friends, but it was still a gathering at the Duchess of Cawthorn's home. Emery was being ridiculous. Reeve still hung on to my swishy golden skirts, pushing and pulling with her little arms.

"Please," Emery begged, yanking my arm toward her once more. "Just come inside with me." Tension and something else flooded her tone. Her bright brown eyes pleaded with me to just do as I was told.

My sister loved me. We'd been close all our lives despite our eight-year age difference. I respected her and looked up to her. And I trusted her implicitly. I didn't know why she'd walked over here and interrupted my conversation with Silas or why she was trying so very hard to get me inside the house. The strained face she was wearing now was one of protection with a good helping of fear.

What was going on here?

The only explanation was that something outside the house posed a threat. To me, specifically.

I loved my sister. I would follow her anywhere. But I'd learned to be stubborn and willful from her.

Jerking my arm back once more, I scanned the garden. Our friends Mary and Daly were conversing nearby with Daly's wife, all holding glasses of refreshment. I could hear Mary's loud laugh at something Daly had said. Turning my head, I noted Patty—my eldest sister and our hostess today—congregated near the gazebo with her husband, Miles, and their twelve-year-old daughter, Franny. Her little dog was jumping and circling them in her excitement. Nothing seemed out of the ordinary until I noticed a gentleman standing among them. Nearly hidden by the frame of the gazebo, a tall young man nodded intently to whatever Miles was saying.

As if sensing my attention, the man looked up. Our eyes met and something long buried startled awake—not like a slumbering giant, slowly stretching and reaching awareness. This was a jolt to my senses. Like being asleep one moment and painfully awake in the bright sunlight the next.

My surroundings muted themselves and time slowed as I stared in confusion at what could not possibly be true.

My mouth dropped open in shock as I took in all the changes of my former best friend. I didn't have a memory from my childhood that didn't involve Julian Moore in some capacity. When I'd known this man, he'd been four and rambunctious, seven and gap-toothed, eleven and my partner in crime. And when I'd last seen him, he'd been long-limbed and sixteen, and the undisputed love of my young life. From the nursery to our painful end and everything in between.

Now, Julian stood staring at me with no expression—no warmth in his gray eyes. No recognition of our lives spent together. No acknowledgement of sixteen years of friendship so thoughtlessly cast aside.

He was tall and broad-shouldered. The transformation from gangly teenaged boy to full-grown man was startling, and undeniably heartbreaking because I'd missed it all. I'd failed to witness the sharpness of his jaw emerging from his youthful boyish face. I hadn't been present for his body to grow and fill out upon its lean frame. I hadn't been there for any of it.

I knew if I opened my mouth to speak, my voice would quaver with the pounding of my heart. His name formed without sound, just a suggestion on my uncertain lips. "Julian."

I heard a muffled "dammit" from my sister's general direction. I was too distracted and thunderstruck to care. You could have knocked me over with a feather.

Or, as it turned out, with the strength of a small child.

Because my niece still tugged at my skirts. One moment my gaze was locked on to the blank expression of Julian Moore, and the next, I was falling—tumbling backward into the fountain behind me.

My arms cartwheeled, and before I knew it, I was completely submerged. Pushing my head quickly above the water, I sputtered and coughed forcefully. Once I got my hands under me, I pushed myself into a seated position.

Despite the warmth of the day, the fountain was cold—both the concrete beneath my bottom and the water covering me from head to toe.

I sat up amidst the voices of my sister and brother—Emery's profuse apologies and inquiries about my person overlaid with my big brother's attempt to control his laughter. I couldn't really be angry. If Silas had gotten pushed into a fountain by a four-year-old, I would have been doubled over on the ground. He was at least attempting to rein himself in with a valiant effort.

With a shaky hand, I struggled to brush aside the hair plastered to my face. And then before I could even try to stand with my heavy layers of skirts, Augustus was there, knee deep in the water and reaching for me. Proving once again that my brother-in-law was my favorite family member and far too good for Emery.

Augie helped me to standing and then handed me out of the fountain. I carefully raised one stockinged foot at a time—slippers floating somewhere behind me—and emerged as gracefully as possible into the suddenly chilly air and onto the stone pavers.

Emery rushed to me, mouth opening to continue her litany of well-meaning concern, but before anything had the chance to spew forth, I raised a staying hand. The warmth in my cheeks contrasted noticeably with the cool air. I fought both involuntary shivers and painful mortification. But I'd be damned if I showed it.

With my head held high and my dress plastered to my body, I bypassed my sister Emery, my brother, Silas, and Patty, who had apparently hurried over during the commotion.

I squelched and dripped all the way up the stairs and to the terrace doors without saying a word.

And I didn't once look toward the gazebo and the impassive face of Julian Moore.

The knock came at my door just as I'd finished dressing in warm dry clothes and before I had a chance to worry about my hair.

"Come in," I called, just loud enough to be heard through the barrier.

My eldest sister, Patty, entered from my sitting room and shut the door behind her.

I met her eyes in the mirror above my dressing table. My fiercely protective sister appeared troubled. Patty was, as always, impeccably attired in a fetching mint-green dress with delicate beading along the bodice and hem. Her pale blond hair was stylishly twisted at her crown with a long coil draped elegantly over one shoulder.

By comparison, I felt like a drowned rat—my own light brown hair hanging damp and frizzy around my face.

Patty crossed the wide expanse of my bedchamber. My parents spent the majority of their time in the country. So when visiting London, I stayed with Patty and Miles and their daughter, Franny, here at Cawthorn Hall. She'd decorated and reserved this guest suite specifically for me.

Now she came to my side and sat stiffly, joining me at the dressing table. "I had no idea he would be here."

I nodded to her reflection in the mirror.

"Emery feels terrible. She's mortified."

Shaking my head, I said quietly, "I'll speak to her later." I didn't wish for my sister to punish herself over an accident. She absolutely handled Julian's appearance in the garden very poorly, but I wouldn't forget the panic on her face as she begged me to come with her inside. Emery had been trying to protect me. I loved her for it. But still, I'd ended up in a fountain because of her.

Humiliation hollowed out the pit of my stomach.

Clearing my throat, I reached for the carved wooden box on the end of the table. The maids were thorough in my sister's grand home. Despite not having touched the container in quite some time, it was free of dust in all the elaborate, hand-carved grooves. I pulled it onto my lap and lifted the top edge. It opened easily on its hinges. Big enough to hold several hardback volumes, the box felt solid in my lap. Though it was years old, the fresh cedar scent assaulted me before I settled the top edge back into place and returned it to its position on the table.

Patty was patient. She gave me room to form my thoughts and she never demanded them from me. That was likely why I found it so easy to talk to her. She'd always been gentle with me, but not in a way that made me feel weak. Instead I felt respected and worthy of her time and attention. I finally managed, "What's he doing here?"

"He is here to acquire buyers for the horse farm where he's been employed since he left Laurel Park. Miles has been an investor for years, but I never made the connection. I didn't even know the name of the farm until recently. Julian has taken over much of the management of the property as his uncle is getting on in years. He's spending a portion of the season in London to make connections and entertain buyers. Miles asked him here today as a gesture of friendship for Julian's uncle with whom he's worked well over the years. I had no idea the stranger he'd invited was Julian until I saw him standing in our gazebo."

Who could have possibly made that leap?

Julian had grown up with me at our family's home in Hampshire. Born the son of our longtime housekeeper—Mrs. Belinda Moore —Julian and his mother came to live with us when Mr. Moore passed away unexpectedly from illness. Julian was educated alongside me and had been my playmate and closest friend for most of my life. But shortly after we turned sixteen—within a week of one another—Mrs. Moore decided it would be best if Julian apprenticed with her brother at his farm in Leicester. He'd been sent away, and I hadn't seen or heard from him since.

Until today.

"What are the odds?" I huffed a watery-sounding laugh. Perhaps it was left over from the fountain.

"It is quite unbelievable." My sister paused. I sensed she was struggling with the things she wanted to say. "I am so sorry, Genevieve." I closed my eyes against the pity and the pain. "You can stay here. I can send him away."

My eyes snapped open, wild and blue in the mirror before me. "Don't be absurd. You can't send him away just because he never returned my letters and I am apparently an emotional grudge-holder."

"Don't minimize his actions, Gen."

I wasn't minimizing them for his benefit. It was a self-preserva-tion tactic. Because if I sat here and let myself think about how my best friend went off and forgot all about me, I'd be in a heap on the floor—soggy once more, but for a different reason this time. I didn't want to think about how young and pathetic I'd been. How much I'd loved Julian and how I'd written to him for far longer than I should have. If I didn't minimize the past into the simplest terms, I'd recall the wooden box I'd had made specifi-cally to hold all the letters I hoped to receive from him until we could be together again. And I'd remember how it sat empty seven years later—a pretty ornament for my dressing table.

"I'm not," I said instead. "I'm a grown woman and he's a grown man and he's here on business. It would be silly to interfere with that because I got my heart broken when I was sixteen. He prob-ably doesn't even remember."

Patty turned from our reflections to look at me directly. "You're my sister, and if you don't want him in this house, I'll make sure he never darkens our doorstep again." Her voice held conviction and authority. My sister was a force. I nearly smiled.

But her words caused more than sisterly gratitude, more than quiet admiration. I felt panic—true fear that Julian would disappear from my life once more. I'd gotten but a glimpse before all hell broke loose out in the garden. He was *here*. Just downstairs in the dining room having luncheon with my family.

My curious nature was rather desperate to know what had happened over the years. And my pride wanted answers as well.

"He stays," I insisted, leveling a stare on Patty. I'd gotten my fierce independence from her, after all.

My sister sighed, but nodded her agreement. "Do you want to talk to him?"

"I do," I said. I could admit that to my sister. She likely knew. Patty had been the one to find me, weeks after Julian had left, miserable and grieving the loss of him on the floor of her childhood bedchamber. I'd hidden in there from my family—in the dark like a melodramatic adolescent. Part of me winced at how affected I'd been by the loss of Julian. We'd been bonded in friendship for so long. My sixteen-year-old self couldn't imagine my life without him. Not to mention the damage done to my youthful heart.

"I do wish to speak to him," I repeated. "But I'll follow his lead. No need for confrontation and accusations. It's too early in the day for that."

Patty smiled. "All right. But if you wish to leave, do so. I'll make excuses for you. You needn't worry about keeping up appearances."

I raised a brow. "I just fell on my arse in a fountain in your garden, Patty. I think that ship has sailed."

She covered her face with her hands and leaned into me. I wrapped an arm around her thin shoulders as she shook with laughter. "Oh, God. That really happened, didn't it?"

I huffed a laugh against her side. "It really did."

She finally straightened, blue eyes warm and focused on me. "We really tried, Gen. I sent Emery to distract you and take you inside until I could get Julian away from you."

I shook my head. "You should have sent literally anyone else. Emery has all the subtlety of a battering ram."

"She was standing closest to me!" Patty said in amused exasperation. "I didn't think you'd end up in the bloody fountain."

I snorted. "Next time send the cook to tell me there are fresh orange cakes. That'll do the trick."

My sister and I laughed at the unbelievable events of the afternoon. It was either that or cry. And I didn't want Julian to see any remnants of tears for him. I'd cried too many over the years. He didn't deserve to see the proof.

"Come on," Patty said finally. "Let's do something with your hair and go join the others for luncheon. I can at least promise orange cakes for dessert."

"See how easy that was? *That* is how one gets Genevieve Bartholomew to do their bidding."

Luncheon had just begun when Patty and I entered the dining room. Thankfully, our delay was not remarked upon. We took the open seats left for us, and I noted that mine was geographically as far from Julian as it could possibly be. He was placed facing me at the opposite end of the table.

With a hard swallow, I sat and unfolded my linen napkin, determined to control my stare and ignore the unobstructed view of the man who'd broken my young heart.

Emery tried to gain my attention with the force of her gaze alone, but I shook my head, indicating that she should wait until we were alone to bring up the fountain and her role in my soggy exit from the garden.

Silas and Miles kept the conversation going. The children were dining in the nursery. And I didn't hear Julian's voice once.

It was a particular kind of torture, waiting for him to speak, considering how his voice had surely changed—deepened and matured. I spent the majority of the meal bracing to hear it, my muscles and jaw clenched tight, warding off the likelihood he would speak.

But it never came. Eventually Emery and Augustus joined the conversation. And Julian . . . he simply observed—listening attentively with impeccable manners as he ate. We'd shared more meals than I could recall in our youth, relegated to the nursery and schoolroom of Laurel Park. I'd rarely troubled myself to use the correct utensil, not to mention breathing between bites. But Julian had always wielded the comportment of a debutante.

That hadn't changed on his end. Here and now, he took delicate bites, dabbed at the corners of his mouth with his linen cloth, and never once looked in my general direction. Oh, he smiled when appropriate. He remained an attentive spectator for Silas's story-telling. Though it was too far for my expectant ears to hear, he even nodded and spoke quietly to Augustus at his side. But Julian kept his eyes to himself.

The same could not be said for me.

I wasn't so much as stealing glances as I was hoarding them. I drank him in with my gaze—my mind attempting to reconcile the years of loss and withholding. Patty nudged my thigh beneath the table at one point when I'd been staring too long. I'd blushed and forced myself to focus on my plate until the next course was served.

But I'd been denied for so long, and my eyes longed to catalog seven years of changes while my mind made comparisons and fought to rectify this very new version of my former best friend.

"Genevieve?"

I started at the sound of my name coming from my brother-in-law's lips.

"Gen?" Miles repeated kindly, his hazel eyes were concerned, and he'd clearly been attempting to gain my attention for several moments.

My eyes darted quickly to Julian and then away. His stare was focused on his root vegetables.

"Yes? Apologies. I was woolgathering." The false brightness in my tone rang like a discordant bell.

"I was wondering if you planned to return to Laurel Park this week with your mother and father or if you'd remain here with us for much of the season."

It was a valiant attempt to include me in the conversation—in the most benign and least intrusive way possible. Both Miles and my sister knew of my plans to remain at Cawthorn Hall until the yuletide. We'd discussed it recently at supper—Franny seated beside me while Daisy rested at our feet. But my dear brother-in-law was attempting to give me an out. Announcing my return to my family's country estate would allow me a graceful exit from an awkward situation. I wouldn't need to be present while Miles entertained Julian and facilitated connections—keeping up his end of the gentlemanly and well-meaning bargain. I could bow out and spend autumn in the country.

But it would also give Julian the upper hand.

I'd never been very good at backing down from a challenge.

With a sweet smile for Miles, I confirmed, "I fear that you, Patty, and Franny must suffer my company a while longer. I wish to remain in town for several months at least."

Miles's expression was kind but knowing. He'd married a rather stubborn Bartholomew daughter himself.

"I am relieved to hear it, Gen," Emery stated loudly. "While I am sure Mama and Papa will miss your presence terribly in Hampshire, we'll be glad to have more time with you here in London." She speared a glazed carrot triumphantly from her plate before saying, "And it will give you time to entertain the offer from your Mr. Belham."

Before I had time to wonder what my interfering sister was playing at, a clatter of silverware from the other end of the table jerked my attention away from Emery's mischievous brown eyes.

"Apologies," Julian mumbled as he retrieved his wayward fork from where it had landed on the white tablecloth beside his dinner plate. His voice was quiet and controlled, and yes, deeper than I remembered from our youth.

Recalling suddenly my determination to control my gaze, I looked back to Emery—considering her absurd statement and her obvious intent. Her pleased expression confirmed my assumption and had me gritting my teeth in response.

If mentioning my passing acquaintance with Mr. Belham was some concentrated effort to provoke a half-hearted reaction from Julian, well, score one point for Emery Ward, Duchess of Kendrick. His reaction had been decidedly lackluster. I rolled my eyes at my sister.

Julian hadn't cared to return my letters or keep in touch following his departure for Leicester. Not one missive in seven years. He assuredly would not concern himself with whatever relationship Emery was implying between myself and *my* Mr. Belham. He wasn't *my* anything. She was ridiculous.

Emery was reaching for Julian's benefit and that was an embarrassing waste of time that had me scowling at my sister.

Had Emery forgotten that it was her effort that had left me dripping from a fountain this afternoon? Clearly her schemes were not welcome, and never in rapid succession.

As if sensing my mood and the threat to Emery's person, Patty steered the conversation away from my continuation in London. The meal concluded with the promised orange cakes, and I didn't speak again.

Following the meal, we all returned to the garden to enjoy the remainder of the mild afternoon before guests began taking their leave. The children joined us once more, and Patty stuck to my side like an elegantly persistent burr.

The sun was sinking in the sky, taking the warmth of the day along with it. Tightening my shawl around my shoulders, I watched Julian converse with Miles before being reacquainted with Augustus and Silas, who'd known him in youth. They ferried him around the garden and introduced him to close friends and even Augie and Emery's children.

Something spiteful tightened my throat as I watched my family offer smiling pleasantries to this man who'd changed me in so many ways.

It appeared that Julian himself hadn't remained the adolescent I remembered. The old Julian smiled easily and laughed often. Now, he was paraded stoically beneath the fall foliage, all stiff lines and firm nods. He looked like a marionette from the village fair—one with all his strings pulled taut. It was difficult to reconcile this new version with the boy I'd loved.

I was both eager and embarrassed at the thought of speaking to Julian. I deduced that he'd have to approach Patty eventually to thank his hostess before he departed. Julian was well-mannered. His imminent presence was inevitable.

Patty and Franny conversed easily about their upcoming visit to the country. I listened with half an ear as I occasionally tracked Julian's movements about the garden. I spent the time daydreaming—considering the first words we'd speak to one another. It wouldn't be permissible to embrace, but would he want to? Would I be able to read any affection on his face?

I spent the majority of my time immersed in my own imagination. This wasn't any different than how I typically spent my days. Only now, the characters of my story were Genevieve Bartholomew and Julian Moore. They had a rich backstory and emotional ties that crossed time and distance. But the character motivations were largely unknown. And, unlike in my own stories, I didn't know how this one would end.

Eventually, Julian and Miles broke away from a small circle of my conversational family members and began moving in our direction. I straightened and fought the urge to fiddle nervously with the curtain of fringe above my eyes.

I watched the gentlemen approach and considered a variety of smiles before deciding on placidly demure—close-lipped, no teeth—with a small helping of mysterious. It was all in the twitch at the corners of the mouth.

Finally Miles and Julian stood before Patty, Franny, and myself.

"I invited Mr. Moore inside for a drink," Miles said carefully. "We're going to talk business regarding the farm and the best use of Mr. Moore's time here in London. Augie has a few ideas, and we didn't wish to burden the other guests with our frightfully boring conversation."

"I see," was Patty's only reply.

Julian hadn't looked at me once. My twitching lips were growing fatigued.

Franny piped up, "It was lovely meeting you, Mr. Moore. I do hope to see you again during your stay in town." In a lovely display of etiquette, she offered him a genuine smile—several teeth on display—and a small curtsy.

"Thank you, Miss Franny. I enjoyed our conversation, and Miss Daisy, of course. I hope to see you again soon." Julian didn't smile, but his eyes softened as he spoke to the girl. After a nod of his hat, he turned to Patty and rattled off some unoriginal gratitude for her hospitality, but I couldn't hear the specifics over the blood rushing in my ears.

He wasn't going to look at me. Forget speak to me. I couldn't even get Julian's eyes to stray in my direction. My practiced smile died and pressure built behind my eyes.

Julian made to step around me and I heard Miles clear his throat but I couldn't look away from Julian's painfully impassive face.

It was as if I wasn't even there. A ghost from his past—one he'd excised neatly while I remained haunted.

The thought of going one more day forgotten by this man was too much to bear. If I stood here while he walked away from me again, I'd lose the battle with my emotions and hate myself for it.

So it was with little warning and a flagrant disregard for propriety that I blurted, "It's nice to know you aren't dead in a ditch somewhere, Julian. Welcome to London."

Truthfully, I'd known that Julian wasn't dead. He'd written to his mother over the years. Just not me.

Finally, vacant gray eyes met mine.

It didn't feel like I thought it would—having his gaze on me. There was little satisfaction gleaned from my outlandish statement. Julian hadn't reacted at all.

I didn't wait for a verbal response. With that out of the way and out in the open, I gathered my skirts and exited the garden. At least I was dry this time.

Patty reached out a hand as I passed but I smoothly sidestepped her well-meaning effort.

I held on to my anger for as long as I could. It carried me up the stairs and across the terrace. I sniffed forcefully as I moved up to the second floor. Just as I was turning down the corridor to the family wing, my fury abandoned me—as if being swallowed by a wave of grief and hurt and longing. My vision blurred as I opened the door to my chambers. I quickly shoved it closed and leaned back, feeling the smooth wood at my back. I breathed through the first of my tears, closing my eyes against this new version of the boy I'd once loved.

With realization came knowledge—no matter how painful or unexpected.

Julian had looked at me as if he didn't recognize me at all.

Two

JULIAN

Of course I recognized her.

Oh, Genevieve Bartholomew was different all right. The woman striding away from me in an indignant huff was nothing like the girl I remembered. Well, the indignant huff was reminiscent of the past. Gen and I had always been good at needling one another into low-level piques. Her temper had forever been like a firework—flaring bright and demanding attention. But it generally passed as quickly as it ignited.

There was something else behind the anger she still wielded to dramatic effect. I'd recognized the hurt in her eyes. And I'd ignored it.

Miles Griffin—the Earl of Basilton—cleared his throat uneasily as we all watched Genevieve exit the gardens and return to the house.

Some things had surely changed where the youngest Bartholomew sibling was concerned. The Gen I remembered had been wild and playful. I'd been her eager accomplice in all things.

Back then, she'd been just on the cusp of womanhood—her tall frame barely hinting at the person she'd become.

Now, however, Genevieve's figure was lush and womanly. Watching her emerge from that fountain with her dress clinging to her full bosom, the dip in her waist, and her rounded bottom had been a revelation. She'd grown and changed in my time away from Laurel Park.

Yet, it wasn't worth reflecting on.

Of course I'd felt a jolt at seeing her across the garden. That first surprised glance had loosened something wound tight. A foolish, hopeful part of the boy I'd once been had felt . . . *something* at seeing Genevieve again after all this time. But that *something* had wilted and curled in on itself before her head had even gone beneath the water.

Seeing her now didn't negate the past, but the truth remained. Our friendship would have faded away eventually. Just like my mother had said. Perhaps it was better that it happened all at once when I'd been sent from Hampshire—like a bandage being ripped from the skin. Her loss had been difficult. I'd been lonely for some time, but I'd eventually settled in at Brightleaf and earned my place there—in a way I could have never belonged in her world.

The fact that I hadn't received a single word from her after departing for Leicester mattered little in the grand scheme of things. Our friendship wouldn't have endured her debut in society anyhow. She would have moved on from the housekeeper's son. On to London and to her very bright future. Now she had two duchesses for sisters which assuredly opened nearly any door. And apparently a Mr. Belham eager for her hand.

"Why don't we gather Augie and Silas, and retire to the library for that drink?" Basilton finally managed.

I nodded my agreement before turning to bid the duchess a final farewell with the tip of my hat. Her frosty countenance had hardly thawed throughout the afternoon. I didn't remember Patricia Bartholomew well from my time at Laurel Park. She and Silas had been so much older than Gen and I. Patty was married and gone to London by the time we were in the schoolroom. She didn't seem to hold any special affection for the little charity case I'd once been.

I preferred it that way. The fewer reminders of the past, the better. I had a job to do here in the coming months. And if I failed in my efforts, I could lose everything. It was important to remember who I was now—not who I'd been.

After wishing the remaining guests well, Basilton wrangled the other two gentlemen in our party and we retired to the library on the main floor.

I wasn't precisely on the lookout for Genevieve, but one could never be too careful. The girl I once knew was quick to abandon her anger, but if faced with the opportunity to get even, she took it. Every time. I glanced discreetly around the expansive space just in case an angry woman lurked beyond the rows and shelves of books.

"Franny is a voracious reader," Basilton said by way of explanation, making a wide arm movement that encompassed the large room holding an unfathomable number of books. "And of course, Genevieve is here often. She's well versed in all manner of literature." Basilton's gaze faltered as he spoke of the latter. I didn't know if he was aware of my history with his sister-in-law, but after the odd exchange in the garden and Gen's ridiculous pronouncement about me not being dead in a ditch . . . well, he likely knew something was amiss.

I knew that Franny—Francesca—was Basilton's daughter in every way save for birth. He'd mentioned her many times on his visits to Leicester over the years. While the majority of his business had been handled by Uncle Phillip, the earl and I had been acquainted and friendly for some time. He'd spoken of his wife—Patricia Henney, a name unknown to me—and of a little girl taken from an orphanage and raised as their own. I knew what it was to be heralded into a family or shuffled along to a different one. But the twelve-year-old girl in the garden seemed happy and content.

Augustus Ward—now the Duke of Kendrick—and Silas Bartholomew filed in behind Miles as this impromptu meeting was apparently ready to begin. Basilton moved to the sideboard and retrieved several glasses.

Augustus approached me cautiously. I'd known Augie as long as I'd known Genevieve. Having been raised and educated alongside the Bartholomew daughters, it was through repeated exposure to Emery that I came to know her best friend and Bartholomew neighbor as well. They occasionally allowed little sister Genevieve and her tagalong urchin to participate in their fun and games. Augie and Emery had been close growing up, and it seemed that had worked out well for them—happily married as they were with two rowdy children.

"All right over here?" Augie said as he joined me by the window. It looked down into the gardens. The sun was setting and casting parts of the lush property in shadow. I wondered if it would be full dark before I could escape Cawthorn Hall and all these awkward reminders.

"Of course," I replied easily, warring with the urge to loosen the cravat around my neck.

"It's good to see you, Julian," Augie said, blue eyes earnest. "Your departure took us all by surprise. I know that both Emery and I were disappointed that we weren't able to wish you well in your life in Leicester." I offered no reply, unsure how to interpret the duke's statement. Why would Kendrick care to bid farewell to the son of his neighbor's housekeeper? "It must have worked out for the best because here you are, grown, successful, and looking to expand the farm."

I kept my face impassive as the man repeated the words I'd been saying since my arrival. Everyone thought prosperity and expansion went hand in hand. That wasn't always the case. "I'm eager to begin a very different kind of work here in London."

"And what sort of work do you normally do?" Silas Bartholomew asked as he approached the pair of us, crystal glasses with amber liquid held in both hands. He passed one to me with an easy smile. "I know I said it before luncheon, but who would have thought our paths would cross like this again? What are the odds of that? You were but a little tyke when I was off to university, but I still remember you and Genevieve scampering around the estate, causing mayhem and all manner of mischief. Aided, no doubt, by Emery and Augie."

I smiled at his reminiscing. It seemed the appropriate response and the one he expected. I wasn't here to remember the foibles of my youth however. "So, tell us what you've been up to at Brightleaf Farms, if this is your first visit to London."

I held the vessel in my hand, dragging my finger across the smooth, cut glass. Grounding myself and preparing to lie to everyone in this room—myself included. "The majority of my experience has been in horse training and overseeing their sale and purchase." I didn't tell them that I'd started out mucking stalls at sixteen for my uncle. Everyone had to work their way up, he'd said. Even the owner's relations who'd been sent to him quite unexpectedly. "My work with the animals and buyers has transitioned over the years as my uncle Phillip is no longer able to travel for business."

"So you're an expert rider, then?" Silas asked, expression open and genuinely curious.

I allowed a humble smile to claim my features. "I do all right."

Silas laughed good-naturedly and clapped me on the back. "Good man! We shall have to get you out on a horse—preferably one you hope to unload on the gentlemen of London—and parade you about in Hyde Park."

My stomach roiled as I considered what I'd need to accomplish in order to reach my goals.

"How long are you staying?" Basilton inquired.

"My plans should keep me here until spring."

Basilton glanced to Augustus before shifting on his feet. "Will you be staying here, then? You're more than welcome—"

"No," I replied, cutting off his uncomfortable offer of lodgings. "That won't be necessary."

"You should stay at Kendrick Manor," the duke offered seriously. "We have ample space. You could conduct your meetings there as well. You'll hardly notice the rambunctious children underfoot."

Silas snorted a laugh at Augustus's words.

"There is no need. I've rented lodgings for the length of my stay. I'm getting settled, I assure you." I also did not mention the simple boardinghouse in which I was staying. However, Kendrick brought up a good point about where to take meetings. I couldn't very well request that gentlemen and aristocrats meet me below my rented space in Mrs. Farnsworth's first-floor drawing room amid her twelve cats and pervasive scent of must and old things.

Augustus nodded, accepting my preference to stay where I liked. I didn't particularly wish to foist myself on the Bartholomews once again—no matter what titles they now possessed.

"So, what is your plan for gaining buyers and investors? How will you conduct your business while in town?" Silas said before turning to Basilton and Augie. "On top of riding in the park to show off the horses, gentlemen, we should take him to the club and introduce him to Drakefield's set."

Basilton nodded. "That is a good idea. Drakefield and his compatriots are always acquiring horses and carriages and whatever strikes their fancy. I believe they're still members of Tattersall's betting room. But they would be most interested in your thoroughbreds, Mr. Moore."

I frowned. I didn't like where this was going. Did they assume they would be planning out all of my own business for me? I was a grown man, and no one of consequence to the people in this room. Brightleaf Farms was my responsibility and I would handle it as I saw fit. Perhaps I would simply take out an advertisement in the newspaper and let the interested parties come to me.

Bartholomew and Basilton were going back and forth, dropping names of gentlemen in the market for horseflesh, those eager for equestrian show, and still more aristocrats in need of racing thoroughbreds.

Clenching my jaw against ungrateful and churlish comments, I noticed Augustus watching me.

"They'll talk themselves out eventually," he murmured around a small smile.

My jaw loosened a fraction as I prepared to interrupt their charitable endeavors where I was concerned. Those were no longer required.

"Gentlemen," I said slowly, the hand not holding my untouched drink raised in supplication. "While I appreciate your efforts, I assure you, I have this all well in hand. I simply came here today because of the earl's generous invitation." I hadn't realized I'd be bombarded by Basilton's extended family and our unexpected shared history.

Silas Bartholomew's eyes narrowed in confusion—as if he'd never been turned down for anything a day in his life. He was the heir to a marquess; perhaps he hadn't. "So, you don't want our help? Is that what you're trying to say? We wouldn't dream of overstepping, Jul—Mr. Moore. It's not as if you can simply take out an advertisement in the *London Post* and attract buyers. I wasn't aware that you had meetings prepared for your arrival, nor that you had acquaintances already in London. My mistake."

The silence was oppressive. I had none of those things, but I would be damned if I admitted it now. I cleared my throat and said evenly, "I appreciate your offer of assistance. Truly. And I am sure I will see you all in town this season. I should be on my way. Good day, gentlemen."

The three men were subdued in their farewells as Basilton relieved me of my glass. Bartholomew still appeared confused. Basilton was obviously conflicted, odd hazel eyes shadowed with concern. And Augustus looked so damned disappointed in me that I felt like I was once again a child in his presence.

The disquiet and irritation of the afternoon fueled my return to the boardinghouse in Lambeth. How dare they presume I required their help? It was that sort of innate belief that their mighty opinions were always welcome that made nobles so insufferable. I was hardly an acquaintance of those men, save Basilton. They'd known me as a boy. Having Bartholomew and Kendrick speak to me with such familiarity bordered on ludicrous.

I'd been out of their lives for seven years.

And for Genevieve to behave like a spoiled child . . . well, that was at least expected.

I thought back to her ridiculous statement. She well knew I wasn't dead in a ditch. I'd written to her for months with no response. Out of sight and out of mind and all that.

Upon recognizing her in that garden, I hadn't imagined our reunion would take such a turn. I wasn't foolishly expecting her to embrace me in greeting, but I assumed she'd be cordial. Perhaps happy to see me after all this time. Genevieve had been the center of my world for the majority of my life. The roles of playmates in our youth had transitioned to constant companions as adolescents. The Bartholomews had absorbed me into their fold because Genevieve had willed it so. I'd been present for family gatherings, meals, celebrations, and educated alongside Gen and Emery. I didn't have a memory from childhood without a Bartholomew in it, so entwined our lives were.

I shook my head against the barrage of memories and stomped my way into the foyer of the boardinghouse. Too late I realized I should have made my footfalls quieter.

"Oh, there you are, Mr. Moore!"

The grating and overly cheerful voice of Mrs. Amelia Farnsworth came from the large parlor off the main entrance.

With a wince and a bracing breath, I collected my manners and stepped into the room. "Good evening, Mrs. Farnsworth. I trust you had a pleasant afternoon."

The woman several years my senior stood awkwardly, tumbling one of her many cats off her lap in the process. She ignored the affronted meow and smiled brightly, brown eyes alight, teeth overwhelming the rest of her face. "I did, of course. Thank you. And I hope your outing was agreeable," she said breathlessly.

"It was."

She stared expectantly.

I stared back.

I didn't care to offer her any more information than she needed. I was a boarder, not her sweetheart. Truthfully she didn't need any encouragement. I felt uncomfortable enough in her presence. It was too forward and unwelcome. Mrs. Farnsworth had been constantly available since my arrival in London two days ago. She appeared whenever I was coming or going and felt the need to insert herself in my business at all times.

I cleared my throat over the awkwardness in the room, and finally said, "I believe I'll check in down at the stables before turning in for the night. Good evening, Mrs. Farnsworth."

The true reason I'd selected this establishment as my temporary residence lay in the well-tended stables on the property. I'd journeyed to London with four horses, and I'd needed lodging to ensure their upkeep. Those horses were a sampling of Brightleaf's fine stock. I needed them to remain in good condition to entice buyers to the farm and for the races they'd be running.

"Well, if you'd like to share supper, do let me know. I wouldn't be a very good hostess if I allowed you to go hungry." Her hands toyed with the ends of her dark hair and I fought a grimace at her suggestive tone.

"I appreciate your offer . . . of sustenance, but that won't be necessary. If you recall, I'm only here for lodgings for myself and my horses. I don't require meals in addition to your kind hospitality. Good night," I finished firmly.

In all honesty, I had considered the additional cost of regular meals during my stay, but quickly discarded that option after spending a quarter hour in Mrs. Farnsworth's presence. I got the unpleasant sensation that those suppers would lead to more than I was interested in. Her lingering looks and overt cheerfulness gave me the urge to flee. I didn't need a mistress or paramour while I was in London and certainly not one who lived beneath the same roof. That was just asking for trouble.

Changing direction, I exited the residence and made for the path to the stables.

"Ho, Charlie. How are they?"

The stable hand popped his head out of one of the stalls. "Quite well, Mr. Moore. I've brushed them all down since their journey and they're each settled in with a bucket of oats."

I'd bribed the young man to take extra special care of the two mares and two stallions who'd accompanied me to London.

As I made my way down the center aisle of the stables, Charlie's gap-toothed grin and smiling blue eyes lightened his features. He looked young with dirt smudging his cheeks, but he'd told me he was just small for his age and had just turned seventeen. He worked hard and seemed to enjoy the animals he cared for, temporarily in his care though they may be.

"Got a new friend, 'ave you?" Charlie said. I frowned in confusion. "You'd best return 'im to the drawing room. Mrs. Farnsworth would be distraught if one of her precious babies escaped. Not to mention the barn cat is a right foul tom. He'd tear that pampered feline to shreds for encroaching on 'is territory."

Following Charlie's line of sight, I found an orange-striped cat trotting after me into the stable. I stopped and he stopped, sitting down easily beside my right foot and gazing up at me as if awaiting further instruction.

"Oh. He must have slipped out behind me," I said. Although I was quite sure that no cat had followed me upon my escape from Mrs. Farnsworth.

"I can return 'im, if you like, sir," Charlie offered good-naturedly.

"No need. I'll take him back with me. I simply wanted to check in with you and make sure the horses were fed and watered for the night. And that you have everything you need." I glanced again to the cat who still regarded me solemnly. He let out a scratchy meow and I frowned.

"They're right as rain, sir. I'll take good care of 'em."

"Thank you, Charlie. Goodnight."

"Goodnight, sir!" the boy called before swinging back into the stall he'd been mucking.

"Let's go," I said to the cat and turned toward the house. I would enter through the garden and sneak through the kitchens to the stairs. Hopefully Mrs. Farnsworth would be distracted by other boarders.

The cat still sat staring at me.

With an irritated sigh, I walked back to the orange creature and plucked him up. He didn't squirm, merely remained limp and watchful in my arms.

"You better not have fleas," I grumbled as I walked back along the dusty path to the garden. A contented purr rumbled against my palms in response.

I carefully edged open the door to the kitchens. The cook gave me a startled glance from her position at the stove, but thankfully remained quiet. With a brief nod, I continued out and toward the hallway, depositing the feline on the carpet runner before I turned quickly for the stairs.

Cursing every creak and groan, I finally reached the third floor and the entrance to my room. Upon unlocking the door, I noted that the abovestairs maid had lit my fire for the evening. As I turned to shut out the world and the weariness of this day, I started as I saw the orange tabby sitting calmly before me, just inside the entryway.

Scowling, I poked my head into the corridor before looking left, then right.

Lifting the cat out of my chambers, I deposited him back in the hallway.

I closed the door firmly, then removed my jacket and boots.

Shaking my head at my own stupidity, I swung the door wide. The cat remained in the middle of the corridor. He gave another one of his creaky meows.

"What are you doing? Go back to your tufted pillows and madwoman in the parlor."

With that handled, I closed myself within the moderately furnished bedchamber once more. I began undressing. Nude from the waist up, I went to the ewer and basin and poured some cool water on a scratchy linen cloth.

I covered my face with the fabric and sighed deeply. I needed a plan. There was too much riding on my efforts in London in the next few months. I needed to acquire buyers for the Brightleaf stock—investors would be even better. But I didn't know how to go about it. I had the names of our current buyers and could pay calls and attempt to foster connections that way, I supposed. I wouldn't be taking out an advertisement apparently. And I wouldn't be relying on the Bartholomews and their spouses, regardless.

With quick and efficient movements, I pulled the cool cloth away from my face and began scrubbing over my arms. The splash of the water in the washbasin reminded me of Genevieve landing in that fountain. I allowed myself a small smile. She'd been mortified and angry—I could tell. But if the same thing had happened back at Laurel Park when we were adolescents, she would have been the first one laughing, sputtering water and unable to stand from the amusement of the situation.

My smile wilted a bit.

Something had changed in her—a great many things, in truth. I wouldn't be the one to know. But that carefree young girl who'd been quick to temper and even quicker to laugh hadn't be present in the garden today. A somewhat serious and confusing woman had taken her place.

Briefly, I wondered what had happened to alter her so deeply. Surely maturity and the rigors of womanhood couldn't account for such a drastic change. Was it so terribly taxing to be a wealthy debutante?

Some selfish part of me wondered if she'd been affected by our separation—by my abrupt departure from her life. I'd been sixteen and—admittedly—an idiot. I'd also been excited for the adventure of traveling and working with horses, visiting an uncle I knew nothing about. It wouldn't be until I was far from home that I realized how desperately lonely I was and how I'd taken for granted the consistency of Genevieve Bartholomew and her companionship. And in truth, I'd missed the lot of them. Her entire meddlesome family.

I wet the cloth with fresh water before wringing it out, remembering her farewell in the gardens of Laurel Park all those years ago. She'd hugged me tight and scrubbed quickly at her tears. I'd laughed and told her not to be so silly. She'd shoved my shoulder before kissing me quickly on the cheek, telling me I wouldn't even get the chance to miss her because she'd write to me every day.

Dragging the fabric roughly over my chest, I batted away the remembered disappointment. I needed to focus. I would sit down in the morning and make a plan. I would write letters and drop off calling cards, and achieve my goals without Basilton's well-meaning assistance.

And if I couldn't sleep that night, it was because of scratching at my door and not the wounded look on Genevieve Bartholomew's face.

I awoke the following morning with resolve, determination . . . and a cat across my chest.

Three

GENEVIEVE

Dear Julian,

I hope your journey to Leicester was uneventful with pleasant weather. But please do write back and let me know if you met any dashing highwaymen on the road north. I'll write more tomorrow and update you on all the things you've missed here at Laurel Park since you left this week. Mama is insisting I practice the pianoforte. Now that you're gone, she's making me take on your lesson as well. So, thank you for that.

More soon.

Yours,
Genevieve

"I wish we were in Hampshire," Emery complained from atop her horse—Beatrice Three. "If we were in the country, we could go riding and wear trousers and sit astride and no one would care."

It was a common grouse from my sister. She preferred life in the country for many reasons—just one of them being freedom with her wardrobe.

Truthfully, I didn't mind dressing and riding like a lady. Then again, I enjoyed the lack of formality we enjoyed at our family's country home as well. I was a complicated woman. I liked many things.

"Well, Mama would care," I corrected without glancing toward Emery.

"Mama wouldn't know," she argued, nudging Beatrice closer to my mare.

"Mama knows everything," Patty chimed in from my other side, her bearing and riding attire were flawless, as ever.

Emery and I snickered. Patty was right. Our mother did know all. And while supportive and caring, she didn't love her middle daughter's preference for snug-fitting trousers.

My sisters and I tried our best to go riding together when we were all in town and the weather was fine. Emery couldn't always get away because of the children, but she had Augie available today as well as her longtime lady's maid and friend, Gansey. A decade Emery's senior, Gansey was less of a maid these days and more of a guiding presence in Emery's household. She attended Emery when curing tongs were required but mostly joined us for gossip and tea on our days at Kendrick Manor and entertained the children because she loved them so.

In the fortnight since the fountain incident—as I was affectionately referring to it—the September weather had held nicely. The sun was shining today as we meandered about the park, away from the promenading masses. It was unlikely that the mild days would continue. So we'd put a good deal of effort into this outing together today.

I'd attempted to control my curious nature where Julian was concerned since that mad day at Cawthorn Hall, but I trusted my sisters. They'd never think me weak.

With a hesitant glance to Patty, I asked softly, "Has Miles heard from Julian?"

My best efforts had gone toward ignoring Julian's presence in town. Our paths had not crossed, and were unlikely to do so considering the sheer volume of inhabitants in London. However, that didn't stop me from looking for him while I was shopping on Bond Street or visiting the tea house or anytime I passed a gentleman with shining auburn hair.

It was inconceivable to think we'd been separated by time and distance, and now the only thing keeping us apart was stubbornness and hurt.

If possible, Patty's spine straightened even further as she moved sinuously with her mount. She'd taught Emery to ride a horse. And Emery in turn had taught Julian and myself. But I would never have the seat either of my sisters possessed.

Finally, Patty said, "No. Julian has not reached out to Miles directly."

I wondered at her odd phrasing, but before I could voice the question forming in my mouth, Emery asked, "Do you want to see him? Because it's okay to want to speak to him. He owes you an explanation."

Emery and I had spoken about the fountain incident in some detail. She'd apologized profusely, but we hadn't really discussed Julian's reappearance in our lives. I hadn't wanted to.

With uncomfortable emotion tightening my throat, I managed, "He doesn't owe me anything."

Emery turned her body my way with a fierce expression that reminded me of Patty. "He does. What could have possibly kept him from corresponding with you for seven years? There must be a reason."

Truthfully, I'd had those same thoughts. And I still had them. But the fact of the matter remained, he *hadn't* written. He hadn't visited Laurel Park again. It wasn't injury or miscommunication. It had been intentional, and I needed to finally accept it and move on.

I felt pressure behind my eyes and an uncomfortable stinging in my nose. How could something so firmly in the past still have such a hold on me? It wasn't natural or rational or . . . fair.

I should have forgotten Julian Moore long ago, but instead, my stubborn heart fought a losing battle with loyalty.

When I couldn't speak for the emotion spoiling the attempt, I shook my head instead.

Emery took a visibly calming breath. "You were the very best of friends. Constant companions. Inseparable. Seeing you apart was so rare that nearly all of my childhood memories of you have Julian in them as well." Did she think I didn't know that? "And then later, how much you loved—"

"Don't," I stopped any reference to the silly young woman I'd been. Thinking I'd marry the housekeeper's son was my own foolish burden to bear. I'd never confessed my feelings to Julian. Not beyond the pages of my letters, anyway.

I let frustration and humiliation force me away from the ledge of emotion I'd been staring over. I eventually managed, "We were just friends, Emery. Let it go. All friendships outgrow one another eventually."

Emery raised an accusatory brow. "I don't know about that. It worked out all right for me and Augie."

Of course she'd use that argument against me. She and Augie had been lifelong neighbors and friends and eventually they'd realized that they could be more. And now they were still friends but also blissfully happy in their marriage.

I fought the urge to gallop away from this fruitless conversation. I regretted asking about Julian at all. Why couldn't sisters ever do what you wanted them to do?

"Well, Augie never left you behind," I felt compelled to argue. Our situations were not the same. "Even at university, he didn't forget you. And he returned to Hampshire in the summer months and your friendship picked right up where it left off."

Julian had just left. And he'd taken our friendship with him. Actually, that wasn't true. It had stayed with me all these years, in an empty wooden box on the edge of my dressing table.

Patty cleared her throat pointedly. I didn't need to look in either direction to know they were having a silent conversation with their eyebrows.

"Have you had much time to paint lately, Emery?" Patty finally said, loudly.

Emery sighed, but obviously agreed to let the subject of Julian go. Thank God. "It's been difficult with Beckett so mobile now, but I have two current commissions that I'm working on steadily in my spare time away from the children."

Emery was a talented artist. She'd worked for years in secret and sold her paintings under the pretense that she was a man. But a few years ago, she decided to take her artwork in a new direction, and with it, Emery Ward, the artist, was born. She was married to Augie and a duchess by then, so her reputation had withstood the whispers. And she was so talented and sought after that her identity hardly mattered at that point. She still occasionally painted her famed landscapes of the English countryside as M. Barton, but those commissions were far fewer and farther between nowadays. She'd eventually confessed to her family—myself included—her connection to the pseudonym, but it was not widely known. And it was that point that I was actually interested in discussing today with my sisters.

"I'm sure that will improve as my nephew grows," Patty assured her.

"And at this stage of your career, you can pick and choose the work you want to do. Isn't that true?" I asked, warming to the subject of Emery's accomplishments.

Emery shot me a look. "I suppose. But I still enjoy painting. And I recognize that it's important to have something for myself. It's easy to get lost in the perils of motherhood. It can be isolating, at times."

"That's true," Patty agreed. "I remember feeling like I had no idea what I was doing when Franny came to live with us, and despite Miles's steadfast loyalty and constant presence, I sometimes felt alone in my struggles."

Emery nodded knowingly. "You can lose yourself. For a while there, I felt like I was Reeve and Beckett's mother and nothing else. I need my artwork to keep something all my own. Just like I need time with Augie to nurture our relationship as husband and wife. And I need these outings to ensure you all feel my sisterly devotion quite keenly."

I met Emery's smile with one of my own—a peace offering. We only argued because we cared. And she only prodded at old wounds because she hated the hurt I still obviously held.

And while I didn't have children to fully understand the depth of her reasoning, I could comprehend the concept of keeping something entirely for oneself. Patty had encouraged me long ago in my writing, and I'd fostered my love for it for many years.

Now it was a career I was able to share with London—in some capacity.

"Speaking of work, do you have your next installment of *Detective Barton Owensby* prepared, Genevieve?" Patty asked.

Emery's eyes lit with our new topic of discussion. "Oh! Do tell us which Mr. J. shall be maimed this week."

I shook my head, smile widening. It was a running joke that the only victims in my stories were male with names starting with the letter J. I'd started toying with the Detective Owensby narrative when I was new to writing—just after Julian's departure. You could say I'd felt inspired to vent my teenage frustration in a very dramatic way. And the habit had persisted as I'd continued writing my favorite mystery and adventure character. It was too late to turn back now, even if the living, breathing inspiration was now suddenly back in my life.

I swallowed around the painful reminder of Julian's presence in London.

"You know, if you were a good sister, you'd allow us to read your serial early," Emery complained before I could respond.

This was an old argument. "No special treatment. You must find out along with everyone else if the good detective finds James McEllen's murderer while avoiding capture from the notorious gang of highwaymen." Their expectant stares intensified. I laughed. "I'm not telling you! You'll have to read it in the issue on Thursday next."

"Rude, Genevieve." Emery pouted. Patty snorted her amusement.

My weight shifted atop my horse for a few steps before I voiced what I'd been considering for a while now, "You know, I've been thinking. And I could use your advice. Both of you."

Emery sniffed. "I don't know if I'm feeling particularly generous after your refusal of advanced knowledge regarding my favorite detective."

I flashed her an unrepentant grin. "Well, I hope you find it because you're well-versed in the topic at hand." My sister's false ire faded and she and Patty both looked genuinely curious. Nerves had my hands tightening on the reins and my gaze on the path before us. "I think . . . I want to reveal that I'm the writer behind *The Thrilling Tales of Detective Owensby*. I want people to know that I'm G. Everett."

Silence met my pronouncement. It took me a moment to notice that my sisters' horses had halted in their forward progress. I turned my dun mare and returned to them.

I'd been publishing my adventure serial for nearly four years with the *London Post*. My weekly installment was the newspaper's answer to the obscenely popular penny dreadfuls circulating like gossip in a ballroom.

Right after I'd turned eighteen, Patty had asked after my writing. I'd given her a few short stories I'd been particularly proud of, and with my permission and her encouragement, she and Miles had consulted their editor friend at the *Post*. I presumed they were intent upon his advice as far as which publishing houses might be open to working with a young girl. But Mr. George Shepard had given us a different option and now—years later—I continued writing under a nom de plume for the newspaper. And circulation had just reached forty thousand.

Very few people knew of my career in publishing: Emery and Augie, Patty and Miles—of course. Mr. Shepard had been my only contact at the paper until his retirement last year. That was why I was now acquainted with Mr. Aaron Belham. He'd been amenable to the arrangement, and by that time, my stories were popular with the public. Thus, Mr. Belham was my newly appointed editor and printed my writing while maintaining the secrecy that Mr. Shepard had instilled.

My parents didn't know of my success at a career I genuinely loved. I'd decided to withhold the truth from Silas as well. Bless him, he was just too friendly and personable. I loved my rascally brother but he couldn't keep a secret if his life depended upon it.

Lady Mary Lovelace, Patty's best friend—and now a friend to us all—knew of my writing as well. And that was the limit I'd placed on the secrecy surrounding *Detective Owensby*.

My horse stepped easily into the space between my sisters and I faced them both.

"May I ask why you'd like to reveal your identity?" Patty asked simply. Her blue eyes were curious.

I sighed, struggling to put into words the turbulent feelings that settled like a weight upon me. "I don't know." Attempting a laugh, I continued, "Perhaps I'm just tired of G. Everett getting all my accolades."

My sisters shared a look.

I rolled my eyes. "All right, I don't know how to explain it. I feel dishonest—especially with Silas and Mama and Papa. Well, Mama will likely be scandalized, but Papa might enjoy knowing the truth."

"Papa would definitely want to know, and he'd be proud of you, too, Genevieve." Emery's words were earnest. She shifted uncomfortably in the saddle as we remained stationary on the path. "And Mama would accept your choices. She nearly fainted dead away when she found out I was M. Barton and her friends had my paintings in their drawing rooms all across London. But once she recovered from the shock—and the hurt from the secrecy—she enjoyed the novelty of having a daughter who was sought after for her artwork. And she was thrilled that some of my comportment lessons had finally stuck. But telling Mama and Papa does not mean you have to tell the world."

I nodded. I knew that. I just couldn't vocalize the pressure I felt at carrying this secret, day in and day out.

"How did you feel, Genevieve? When you found out the truth about Emery?" Patty's question had me considering. I'd been fifteen and dramatic enough to refuse to speak to Emery for her deception. That hadn't lasted long. I'd mostly been in awe of my sister and her abilities. It was a rare thing to see a woman harness her future, and Emery had done it unapologetically with a willful spirit and a hidden talent. I'd been awash with pride. Frustration, yes. But also pride.

Instead of answering Patty, I said, "I know there will be hurt feelings from our family and close friends. I anticipate whispers from society and for my name to appear in the gossip rags."

"Do you think it will impact your future? For making a sound match?" Patty's next logical question landed flatly between us.

"Perhaps." I shook my head in frustration. There was no right answer when you warred with yourself.

"And what will your Mr. Belham have to say to that?" Emery grinned.

I resisted the urge to knock my sister from her horse. Barely.

"Stop calling him that," I snapped. "I don't know what you were on about announcing his nonexistent intentions at luncheon the other day when you well know that Mr. Belham and I have a working relationship. And that is all."

Mr. Belham was my editor and my point of contact on Fleet Street now that Mr. Shepard had retired to a life in the country. Mr. Belham and I had a passing flirtation at best. No offers of courtship—or marriage—had been expressed. We'd danced together a handful of times in my last two seasons. It was all very innocent.

Thank the lord our mother had not been among our numbers for Patty's garden party weeks ago. Mama would have needed no assistance whatsoever to encourage a match with Mr. Aaron Belham. One would think Emery could be more sympathetic as our mother had badgered her about marriage for years before she'd wed Augie.

She appeared unrepentant now, however. Perhaps I *would* push her from atop Beatrice Three. "I'm just suggesting, perhaps *he* will not want the truth of your authorship and your position in society revealed."

I hadn't considered my editor's opinion on the topic nor the need to acquire his permission, but mayhap my meddlesome sister had a point. I hated when that happened.

Patty reached forward and gently touched my knee. "We're not trying to upset you," she said with an annoyed look at Emery. "We only want you to consider all the ramifications of revealing the truth. And then decide what you can stand."

Patricia—the Duchess of Cawthorn—had been subjected to society's demands as soon as she'd married an old duke four times her age during her debut season. Her horrible five-year marriage had changed her greatly. So when she was widowed and free to live the life she wanted, she made sure to make it count. Patty and Miles and Franny were an unconventional family, but she lived with her decision and actively chose happiness. And I respected her for it.

I softened my features and ignored Emery's teasing. "I was rather hoping having two duchesses for sisters would afford me some good will and latitude where gossip was concerned. Surely I can weather any associated scandal."

Emery snorted a laugh. "You know, Patty, I don't know where she gets her sense of self-importance."

Patty's smile deepened. "Not from me."

"Probably Silas," they both finished. And we all laughed.

"But tell me truthfully"—I looked between them—"what might happen? Beyond soothing Mama and Papa. And mollifying Silas."

Emery shrugged. "You may be right. I couldn't say. We've rather used up our allotment of scandals and novelty between my painting career and Patty's family outside the norm."

"But all of that was years ago," I argued. "Hardly cause for gossip anymore. There hasn't been a Bartholomew scandal in ages."

"Perhaps you're right," Patty agreed. "If you feel strongly about it, and revealing your identity as G. Everett would make you happy, then you should."

Emery's wide smile turned mischievous. "Maybe it's time we stirred things up a bit."

Sometime later, the sun turned the corner on our afternoon ride. Emery left for home, and Patty and I made our way to the stables behind Cawthorn Hall. Mama and Papa were back in Hampshire and I was staying in residence with Patty and her family. This had been my practice since my debut at nineteen.

I mostly enjoyed the atmosphere of London. The dancing and the gowns didn't hurt, either. I was a fair combination of Emery's love of the country and Patty's penchant for remaining in town. The baby of the family, I was adaptable and easy to please for the most part. I often jested that I inherited the best parts of each of my siblings and simply discarded all the troublesome bits, making me everyone's favorite Bartholomew.

Patty cleared her throat as we turned down the drive toward the mews. "We are hosting a dinner party on Friday."

"All right," I said when she failed to continue.

She looked uncomfortable. "You needn't attend."

I frowned in confusion. "Why wouldn't I—"

"Because Julian is on the guest list," she finished quickly, as if believing if she got the words out fast enough, I might not register the blow.

My breath gusted out of me just the same. "Oh."

My thoughts were in a tangle, but we were silent as we approached a groom and dismounted. He took the horses and led them away as we shook out our skirts and turned toward the house.

Clouds were gathering on the horizon. Either the sunset would be dramatic and lovely or we'd be in for some foul weather shortly. I felt a bit like that. As if a dinner party with Julian could go either way.

Patty finally met my gaze and slowed our progress through the garden. "Miles feels horribly conflicted. He—of course—feels loyalty to you, but he's heard around town that Julian has had little success in enticing buyers for the farm. He wants to help as an investor for Brightleaf but also as a friend to Julian's uncle and to Julian himself."

Guilt churned as my sister attempted to placate me. I felt just as dramatic as that potential sunset and shamed by the awkward position I was putting my brother-in-law in with his business and his wife.

"Patty, that's silly. Miles needn't feel at odds with the simple decision to invite Julian to his home. Just because I am staying here—"

"It is your home, too, Genevieve," my sister cut in firmly.

I smiled at her assertion. "You and Miles have welcomed me with open arms over the years. And I am grateful. But I'm not selfish enough to think I deserve your single-minded focus and allegiance."

However, it was nice to know that Miles had considered my comfort. But I could be mature about this. Julian and I could surely remain civil for the length of one dinner party. We needn't cut Miles in half.

"Are you certain?" Patty asked, worry in the stern line of her brow and the set of her shoulders.

I grasped her warm hands firmly. "I am. Julian may very well be in our lives for the time being. I am no longer sixteen. I assure you, I am fine. I will behave myself at dinner." I mustered up a winning smile for my dear sister.

She sighed, unconvinced. I'd never been good at outmaneuvering any of my siblings. "Come on. Let's get inside before we get rained on."

It didn't matter if Patty believed me or not. The fact of the matter was this: I would have to survive seeing Julian again. I wouldn't hide in my bedchamber or take supper in my rooms. I refused to retreat. A gathering in three days' time would go swimmingly. I'd will it so.

And if I started planning what I'd wear—the low-bodiced pale blue gown that made my eyes glow—to said gathering as I climbed the stairs to Cawthorn Hall, it was only in preparation. It was armor I'd need to survive the encounter.

Four

JULIAN

To say that I was irritated to be back in the dining room at Cawthorn Hall would be an understatement.

The weeks since arriving in London hadn't been entirely fruitless, but they'd yielded few results. The majority of my letters and calling cards had gone ignored, and it was nearly impossible to congregate with titled and moneyed gentlemen without an introduction into their circles.

Miles Griffin had been the only one willing to help. While I might have been prideful and determined, I was not an idiot. Accepting assistance from the Earl of Basilton might be the only way to acquire a steady stream of new business—something Brightleaf Farms desperately needed. My future as the head of business depended on the success of this trip to London. My uncle's health was declining, and had been for some time. My work was mostly with the horses—training and overseeing their care as well as other jobs required of a somewhat large operation. I hadn't realized how important Uncle Phillip's annual trips to London were until he'd been unable to travel. For three years, he'd downplayed and minimized the loss in sales until I'd confronted him about the farm. That conversation had been difficult, but we'd decided that with my future well established as Brightleaf's overseer, I—as my unmarried uncle's only real heir—would journey to London in his stead.

Only I hadn't realized how difficult it would be to get my foot in the door. Any door.

"And how have you been enjoying our fair city?" Silas Bartholomew asked from his position opposite me. Perhaps I was imagining the smugness behind his jovial expression, but something told me that if we were better acquainted, he would be crowing "I told you so."

"The weather has been mild," I answered noncommittally.

"Very true." Bartholomew's smile was indeed smug. "By the end of October, however, it'll be endless gray and rainy drizzle for your trouble."

I nodded and fought the urge to roll my eyes. Leicester was still England. I knew our weather patterns.

The conversation flowed around me for the most part. The evening meal was not truly what I'd been invited for. Basilton indicated that we'd convene following supper for cigars and drink, and I'd have abundant opportunity to talk to the other gentlemen in attendance about Brightleaf and our quality stock.

In addition to our hosts, Silas Bartholomew was once again in attendance, as well as the Duke and Duchess of Kendrick, and a constantly smiling Genevieve was seated on the other end this mahogany monstrosity. Honestly, did the Bartholomew siblings take every meal together?

The Earl and Countess of Drakefield were joining us in an attempt to slowly introduce me to the appropriate set in town for my needs. Plus, I gathered that the Bartholomew ladies got on quite well with the countess. I'd heard nothing but laughter from that end of the table.

In contrast, Silas Bartholomew had yet to shut up down here.

I looked up as the women erupted at something the countess said. My eyes snagged briefly on Genevieve. Her face was aglow with amusement, cheeks flushed and smile a mile wide. She'd never been subtle with her emotions. If she felt it, Gen wore the evidence right there for all the world to see. Apparently not everything about her had changed.

I cleared my throat and turned my attention back to my plate. It wouldn't do to let my gaze drift toward Genevieve's bodice and all the ways she *had* visibly changed over the years. I blinked to focus on the fish in delicate white sauce instead of the blue of her gown—the color of a cloudless summer sky—and how her eyes brightened as a result. I didn't need to be looking to recall the way her neckline skimmed low. Who'd let her wear a gown so scandalous anyhow? It was practically indecent.

Shifting restlessly in my seat, I acknowledged that I was being ridiculous. I've never entertained such odd thoughts of Genevieve in our youth. Although admittedly, at sixteen I hadn't yet been interested in the soft curves possessed by women. That had come later.

In penance for my wayward imaginings, I forced my attention on the conversation before me. My focus remained on making a good impression on Drakefield. I didn't allow my gaze to wander to Genevieve again.

~

"Oh, I'm happy to buy some horses from you, Mr. Moore. I know Basilton has been in business with you for some time, and I trust Miles's good opinion." Drakefield was sipping whiskey in a tufted armchair in Basilton's well-appointed study, the rich colors and opulent fabrics a good indicator of wealth. I was a little surprised by Drakefield's easy acquiescence. "Why don't we go for a ride Sunday in the park? And you can bring one of your fine stallions for me to get a feel for and I'll bring some of my close acquaintances with deep pockets."

This felt too easy. Despite my suspicion, I nodded my agreement. "Of course. I'd be happy to. I have a well-muscled chestnut with just the right amount of spirit."

"Sounds like a winner." Drakefield tipped his glass up in a salute before downing the contents. "Well, gentlemen, that's it for me tonight, I'm afraid. I'll see you at the club, I'm sure. And, Mr. Moore, I shall see you the day after tomorrow. Let's say eleven o'clock."

And with that, the tall man shook hands with everyone in the room and took his leave. I stared after him, quite dumbfounded not knowing how to interpret the ease with which everything had gone this evening. Part of me was relieved—for myself and for Brightleaf. And another part twisted bitterly. Drakefield had only given me the time of day because Basilton had willed it so.

Kendrick approached and sat on the adjacent sofa. The earl joined him. And Silas Bartholomew sat down right beside me. I discreetly inched a little closer to the arm of the chaise to afford myself a bit of space.

"He means Hyde Park, you know," Augustus offered, ignoring Silas as he attempted to pass him a cigar.

"I assumed," I answered even though I'd been too distracted at Drakefield's easy agreement to even think ahead to our meeting in two days' time.

"Just be your straightforward self. Drakefield likes that," Basilton commented. "He's a decent sort. And bring a fast horse. If you can impress his friends, your business will be well in hand."

Ignoring my wounded pride, I finally gave voice to my other concerns, "But are they likely to remain loyal? Will they buy one horse from me and consider our business finished? I am here to acquire customers, yes, but I'd also like to establish connections and foster loyalty."

Selling one horse was fine, but these gentlemen likely had connections already in London—probably Tattersall's regular auctions. Aristocrats needed horses for sport and hobby as well as to pull their fancy carriages. I wanted Brightleaf Farms to stop begging for patrons every year. If I could convince these men that I could supply them with all the horseflesh they'd ever need, *then* my business would be well in hand.

"Difficult to say," Basilton replied. "Their return business would likely depend upon how pleased they are with their initial purchase."

"If you left a lasting impression, I think that would entice future business as well," Silas offered around a mouthful of cigar smoke.

"Two of the thoroughbreds I brought will be participating in the Royal Ascot in the spring," I admitted. The annual horseraces in Berkshire should provide ample opportunity to impress, should my mounts perform well over the course of the four-day event.

"That would do it," Silas said, looking impressed.

Positive exposure at one of the spring season's most popular events could be instrumental in acquiring new buyers. I'd utilized my uncle's contacts and acquired jockeys. The popular races would be my final attempt to provide the future Brightleaf Farms so desperately needed. Word of mouth only got you so far.

"You should consider staying with us as a guest," Kendrick said seriously. "We have ample space to accommodate your horses. You could come and go as you pleased. There's no need to remain in a boardinghouse for months. Save yourself the expense."

Bitterness twisted something in the pit of my stomach. Augustus was presuming familiarity once again. It was bad enough these men had accomplished in one after-dinner conversation what I had been unable to do on my own after weeks of effort. My irritation flared hotly at the injustice of my circumstances.

The thought of dealing with that Farnsworth woman for many long months was admittedly wretched. I'd followed leads on several advertised rooms for rent, but none of them boasted appropriate accommodations for my horses. I would need to endure the relentless landlady and all the cat hair—as both owner and persistent feline continued their pursuit.

It would never sit well to accept charity from the Duke of Kendrick, much less any other man in this room. They still thought of me as the little boy who'd needed to be taken in so long ago.

While I appreciated their kindness, I could still resent it.

So it was with some effort, I managed to loosen my jaw and respond, "That is generous, but I'm quite comfortable with my current situation."

Augustus's blue eyes widened and I knew my tone had missed the mark for politeness, landing somewhere between clipped and irritated.

Finally he nodded and held up his hands in easy surrender. "As you wish."

The duke briefly met Bartholomew's gaze before he stood and went to the sideboard to pour himself a drink. After so much wishing away the easy acceptance of the Bartholomews and their spouses, it was a bittersweet ache to realize I'd actually accomplished it.

Silas opened his mouth—to say what, I didn't know—and I decided I'd had enough helpful interference for one evening.

Relinquishing my untouched glass to the low table in front of me, I stood quickly. "I should take my leave. Basilton, thank you for your hospitality once again."

"Think nothing of it," the earl replied around a tight smile as he rose to standing.

Silas left his cigar burning in the tray as we all maneuvered back to the parlor so I could offer my gratitude to the duchess and bid all the ladies farewell.

"That was fast," Emery said by way of greeting.

Genevieve and Patty turned at her pronouncement. They stepped back to allow our entrance.

"Yes," I responded before turning to the Duchess of Cawthorn. "I'm afraid I must be on my way. I appreciate your generosity, Your Grace."

Emery interrupted before Patty could stare an angry hole through me, "But how did the meeting go? Will Drakefield take some horses off your hands, Julian?"

Must this family intrude upon my business at every turn? Even the women knew of my struggles in town.

I could feel heat climbing my neck beneath this uncomfortable cravat.

Kendrick moved close to his wife and said simply, "They're taking a ride in the park on Sunday to discuss things."

"Perfect!" Emery exclaimed, as if that solved all my problems. Her genuine, well-meaning excitement had a strange tightness lingering in my middle that warred with my irritation. "We shall all go," she continued happily. "Julian, I'm sure you recall, but I am quite the horsewoman. Give me one of your mounts to ride and I shall turn every head in the park."

The heat beneath my skin continued its upward progress and I chewed helplessly on my words. I didn't know how to respond to her ridiculous statement with anything less that prideful hurt and incredulous anger. I'd always liked Emery Bartholomew. Truthfully, she had been like a sister to me in my youth with her genuine warmth and gentle teasing. But the only words I had for her right now would cut like knives.

Augustus made to interject but it was Genevieve who got there first. "Emery, don't be silly," she said, her blue eyes knowing and never leaving mine. "I'm sure M—Mr. Moore wishes to conduct his business without you inserting yourself"—Emery made to argue—"no matter how well-meaning your intent."

Years had passed, but there was the girl who fought my battles and read all my expressions. Despite her obvious irritation with me, Gen had inserted herself on my behalf. Gratitude battled with self-righteous indignation, and I felt a hollow open up inside me.

My gaze stayed locked on Genevieve as I finally managed to speak for myself, "I do appreciate the offer, Your Grace. But we wouldn't want Drakefield and his friends to feel inferior to your obvious expertise."

I turned away from Gen's perceptive stare and watched Emery's smile widen, pleased with my flattery. "Well, if you insist. I apologize for overstepping." I shook my head, ready to offer false platitudes, but she continued, unperturbed, "And stop with all the 'Your Grace' nonsense. I used to tease you when hair started sprouting on your upper lip at fifteen. I'm quite sure you can dispense with the formality. If I hear one more honorific, I might just get a bar of soap for your mouth."

Genevieve snorted a very unladylike laugh before muffling it behind her gloved hand. Her eyes were bright with amusement, however, forever giving her away.

The flush on my cheeks went absolutely nowhere.

Oblivious to my embarrassment, Emery went on, glancing between those assembled, "Do you remember that time Mama overheard Gen swearing and washed her mouth out with that awful French soap that smelled like freshly tilled dirt?"

Genevieve's earlier amusement died abruptly when my eyes snapped to hers. It was my turn to snort out a laugh. I knew we were recalling the very same memory. We'd been eleven or twelve years of age and I'd overheard the stable hands cursing. When I'd reported back to Gen the words I'd heard while visiting the horses, I'd dared her to say them, knowing she would.

Even then, the challenge had been too difficult to resist. We hadn't known that the marchioness was in the corridor, just outside the schoolroom.

Genevieve's eyes narrowed at my obvious attempt to withhold laughter. I quirked a brow that might as well have had "dare" engraved upon my forehead.

"Well, it was Julian's fault. He dared me to say it," she blurted, unable to help herself. I fought the urge to cackle. She was already in a mood. It wouldn't do to tease her any further—she'd likely punch me in the stomach like that time we were thirteen and I'd told her she'd looked like a fancy poodle after her maid had attended to her hair for over an hour with curling tongs.

I bit my lip to contain my mirth, and her blue eyes tracked the movement. She swallowed hard and said no more.

"I was certain you'd heard it from Emery," Augustus deadpanned, drawing Genevieve's attention. His wife whacked him lightly on the shoulder.

"The grooms were foul-mouthed at Laurel Park," Emery said by way of explanation.

"That's where Julian heard it, too," Genevieve admitted, glancing back to me.

"Well, you didn't have to accept the dare," I said magnanimously.

"What now? A Bartholomew resist a challenge?" Silas laughed. "Not likely."

Genevieve ignored him. "You're right. I should have just ignored you."

My mouth twisted. "It wouldn't be the first time."

The ensuing silence and stares from nearly everyone were oppressive.

Genevieve frowned with her entire face—light brown eyebrows pulled low as her nose scrunched and her mouth turned down. "That is rich, coming from you," she practically growled.

"And what is that supposed to mean?"

"It's just like old times," Emery murmured, wide-eyed.

I realized suddenly that Genevieve and I were the center of attention. Our bickering on full display and so reminiscent of the past that my chest constricted. It was so easy with these people—to fall back into remembered behavior.

The past was long gone, however, and I needed to focus.

Emery looked on unabashedly. Augustus was solemn, as always, but watchful. Patty appeared ready to spirit Gen away from my dastardly machinations. Miles regarded us warily. And Silas—of course—appeared endlessly entertained.

"Perhaps we should send them to bed without supper," Bartholomew offered congenially.

Emery chuckled at her brother and took up his mantle, "Or we could lock them in the schoolroom until they can get along with one another."

"That's not a bad idea, Em," Augustus mused.

Genevieve was still staring at me, breathing fire. Her blue eyes were shards of glass, and I could suddenly see her resemblance to the Duchess of Cawthorn—or at least the inspiration. "You know what? I think that is an excellent plan. Come along, Mr. Moore. Let's have a word."

My former friend stalked toward me and I took an involuntary step back. Her smile was satisfied and a little mean. She continued forward and grasped my arm, dragging me toward the corridor.

"Gen, wait," Patty called, concern lining her aristocratic face. Basilton placed a hand gently on her shoulder.

"It's fine, Patty," Genevieve called without looking toward her sister. "I'll be back shortly. I promise not to kill him."

"Oh, good," Silas murmured. "There's not room for a body in Patty's garden."

"No maiming either!" Emery added helpfully just as we turned the corner and exited the room.

I could have planted my feet. I could have refused to be led. But the truth was, Genevieve obviously had something to say, and there would be no rest until she'd gotten her way. And perhaps I had a few questions of my own. So, I allowed myself to be manhandled down the corridor and to the front of the house, her grip severe on my arm.

"I can walk without a lead," I said tersely.

She huffed a frustrated sound. "I'm not so sure you won't disappear again if given half a chance."

I was getting a little tired of her snide remarks. She was the one who'd forgotten me. I didn't know why she was pretending otherwise.

My back was up by the time we entered the receiving room just off the foyer. The fire was banked but Genevieve released me to go light a lamp on the mantel. But she didn't approach me with her task complete. She simply remained stubbornly across the room while I'd halted just over the threshold.

Eventually she turned and we faced one another. Her severe expression had chipped away since we'd left the others, and now she appeared contemplative and more in control of her anger.

"Well," I goaded. "Say what you so desperately needed to say."

Her pink lips parted but no sound emerged. I raised my brows in response, waiting for her to gather herself. She'd dragged me here without a plan, it seemed.

Genevieve looked down at her feet suddenly. "I've thought about this moment for so long and so often, and now I can't figure out what I want to say." Her voice had gone soft. The bravado and confidence that had led me unflinchingly down the hallway seemed to have fled in the face of my attention.

Frowning, I took a step closer in order to hear her better. "What have you thought about?"

Genevieve's chin rose and I noticed two slashes of color painting her cheekbones. "About what I would say to you. How I'd yell, demand answers. The way you would grovel and apologize for abandoning me. I thought the first time you saw me, I would be cool and unaffected." A bitter laugh twisted her features, and for a moment I thought she might cry. "The fountain incident really saw to that."

My confusion warred with the lingering adolescent urge to comfort her. I stepped closer, the sound muffled against the rich carpets beneath my boots. "Genevieve, I don't understand why you're so upset."

And just like that, her features rearranged themselves. Her vulnerability and emotion hardened like ice freezing over. "You—you don't understand?"

"We were children. And I left. I was never going to be able to return to Laurel Park. It was never going to be the way it was."

"So you severed our connection straightaway? Why bother promising to write? You should have told me goodbye and told me it was for good. Then I wouldn't have spent years waiting."

I shook my head, disbelieving. "I did write to you, Genevieve. For months. But I never received a reply. I don't know what else you could have been waiting and hoping for."

"I never received a letter from you, Julian. Not one. I wrote to you for *years*." She hissed the final word, fisting clenching helplessly at her sides. "And I didn't stop. I continued on—far longer than I should have. Far longer than I'm proud of."

How is this possible?

My thoughts were a chaotic jumble as I realized her anger and hurt were vibrating on the surface of her skin. Her eyes were pleading, desperate.

So I forced myself to remain calm no matter how much I wanted to demand she explain herself. What did she mean? She wrote to me for *years*?

Despite my efforts to maintain control, I could feel my heart racing along the precipice of some horrible realization.

Approaching slowly, I stepped around the furniture and moved closer. Genevieve hadn't abandoned her position by the mantel. "I'm telling you the truth. I never received any correspondence from you. Did you post your letters from the village?"

She shook her head. "No, from Laurel Park. Your mother insisted it was easier for her to send them off together."

Our eyes met and held.

I always sent Genevieve's letters along with those for my mother, in the same envelope.

Ah, Christ.

I fell over the edge of painful comprehension and had to look away.

I couldn't stare into her turbulent blue eyes, full of pain and confusion and utter disbelief. Not knowing what I knew now.

It was quite clear what my mother had done now that I had all the pieces. She had never approved of my friendship with Genevieve, nor my familiarity with the Bartholomews. She was a hard woman with little use for the aristocracy. They paid her wages. She didn't see the point of them choosing to educate her son or welcoming him into their household, but upon my father's death, shortly after my birth, she'd needed the help.

My mother had resented the Bartholomew family all my life. I didn't know how to explain that to Genevieve, so I said nothing. I couldn't stand here and admit that my own flesh and blood was the reason for this misunderstanding between us. There were so many things I could never explain. Not to this woman who was valued and loved by her parents and siblings—whose fierce devotion would never seek to hurt her.

Yet I supposed, in her own way, my mother thought she was doing what was best.

"I don't know that it matters, Gen," I said gently despite the rapid pace of my frantic heart. Could she not hear it beating so loudly?

"Even if every letter you'd sent had been delivered, how would the outcome have been any different? Our lives were on two very different paths. Those paths were destined to diverge at some point."

Genevieve's skin paled and she took a step back—away from me. "That—that's not true. You can't know that."

"I was the housekeeper's son," I reminded her.

"You were my best friend," she implored, voice rife with emotion, demanding I listen, incredulous that I didn't understand. Genevieve's eyes became impossibly bright, the blue of a summer's day shimmering across the surface.

"You were my—" She cut herself off abruptly.

Eyes narrowing, I scrutinized her suddenly panicked expression. "I was your what?"

"Nothing," she said, clearing her throat.

I made to protest, but she cut me off. "You're right. It's too late now." Voice flat, her gaze finally slid away and she stepped around me.

While I believed what I'd said about our differences was true, I still didn't want her to leave like this. I would gladly take that righteously indignant hellion towing me down the corridor over the despondent young woman seeking escape.

With my hand outstretched, I caught her arm gently above her elbow as she passed by. Her skin was cold above the edge of her gloves.

Genevieve's reaction was violent. She jerked from my grasp so forcefully that I startled.

With both hands raised in surrender, I met her wild stare. "Gen," I breathed.

"I have to go," she murmured in the growing space between us, her voice rough and uneven as she backed away. That same feeling that she was about to cry gripped me. Knowing that it was because of me had me forcing a tight swallow.

I was left alone staring after the woman who'd been my closest friend and greatest ally for the majority of my life.

It had been a long time since I'd felt the absence of Genevieve in my life. I'd grown up and worked hard and moved on. I'd put Laurel Park and the Bartholomews behind me after a time.

But now I felt Genevieve's loss as fresh as those first lonely weeks in the stables at Brightleaf Farms. Seeing the woman she'd become and the person I'd missed out on knowing was a bitter pill to swallow—made even more uncomfortable by the knowledge that my own mother was a driving force in our separation.

The Genevieve-sized hole in my adolescent heart gave a painful thump, making itself known. A wound I'd thought had long since healed felt suddenly jagged and raw as she stormed away from me.

Five

JULIAN

The little stone cottage sat lonely at the end of a lane.

She liked it that way.

Three years ago, before my uncle's health had declined, when Brightleaf Farms was a well-respected and popular horse yard and stud farm, I'd saved enough by then to purchase my mother a small cottage and facilitate her departure from Laurel Park.

She'd wanted to return home to the village of her youth, before she'd met my father and been spirited away to Hampshire. I didn't take it personally that she didn't wish to be close to me in Leicester. I could understand the wish to return home.

The small village sat a half-day's ride out from London, eight miles beyond the well-traveled coach road north. I'd visited exactly once over the years. My mother hadn't set foot in Leicester during my time there. She and her brother were not close. And, in truth, she and I hardly corresponded.

My mother was of the belief that parents did their duty in raising children, and once those children were of age, they were either well-equipped to lead their own lives or they weren't. It was no matter to the mother and father. They'd done their job.

And true to her conviction, I'd had a roof over my head and food in my belly all throughout my youth. My mother hadn't been a source of affection, but that was all right. I'd had the Bartholomews for fanciful things like companionship.

The clouds hovered ominously and I expected my return trip on horseback would be soggy at best and miserable at worst.

I'd removed the ginger-striped cat from around my neck before the sun had even given thought to rising. And I'd saddled Brutus for the journey. While all the horses from Brightleaf were mine to various degrees, the big black stallion with a gray muzzle was the horse I sought most often. He wasn't a racehorse or a workhorse but I'd seen him born just like all the others. There was something about our personalities that matched, and I knew Brutus the best of any of them. And I thought perhaps he understood me in return. He'd never be for sale, in any case.

I approached the cottage and noted the smoke rising from the chimney. The small plot of land was in decent shape, but the fencing could use a new layer of paint. I'd mention it to the gardener I kept employed—Mr. Godfrey—to tend to the small property.

I saw the curtains shift as I dismounted, but my mother didn't emerge from the house. I brought Brutus around to an old lean-to on the rear side of the yard that would at least keep the rain off of him. I'd stop at an inn along the coach road on my way back to London this afternoon for a bit of supper for myself and my horse. I could not imagine this awkward visit would take long.

With a steadying breath, I made my way to the kitchen entrance and knocked lightly. It took longer than I expected for my mother to appear, and when she finally opened the door, I realized how much she'd aged in our years apart.

Belinda Moore had married my father as a young woman but decades went by and they were never blessed with a family. As such, they were beyond surprised when she got with child just after she turned four and forty. She'd been the housekeeper at Laurel Park for nearly a decade at that point, a bit young for the position but extremely efficient. I imagined the unexpected surprise of an infant arriving during middle-age was less than a joyous occasion—at least it had been for my mother. And then my father had passed shortly after my birth. She'd been forced to move with me to Laurel Park. The maids had helped, and the Marquess and Marchioness Northcutt had been sympathetic and accommodating. They'd had a new babe of their own. Genevieve's mother had been quite adamant that my mother have assistance where I was concerned. Thus my familiarity with the Bartholomews was born.

"Mother, how do you do?"

"Julian," she greeted simply and led the way into her front room.

Looking at my frail, unsmiling mother with hair gone gray, it was difficult to remember a time when she'd been young and spry. If she had been, I'd never known that version of her. Mother had always been rigid and exacting. It had been confusing as a child to see the indulgent marquess with Emery and Genevieve. And while a bit fanciful and flighty, the marchioness had doted on her daughters quite lovingly.

I'd always just accepted that my mother was who she was, and Genevieve's mother was very different. It wasn't until I got older that I realized perhaps those differences were because of each woman's conflicting position in society. Bitterness and resentment had turned my mother's heart. While the Marchioness Northcutt enjoyed a life of privilege.

"Didn't know you'd be comin'." Her words weren't accusatory but there was an impatient edge there.

"I apologize for arriving unannounced," I offered. "I'm in London for the season. For Uncle Phillip and the farm."

She sat in a floral-patterned armchair by the fire and pointed to a small worn sofa, indicating I should sit.

I noticed the kindling and peat were low near the hearth. "Would you like me to bring in some firewood while I'm here?" I did want her to be comfortable and not strain herself, but I was also stalling for time. I didn't know how to broach the subject of her deception years ago. Genevieve's stricken face hadn't abandoned me since our conversation last night. I wanted answers but I had no idea how to begin this conversation with a woman I hardly knew how to talk to.

"Naw, it's not necessary. Mr. Godfrey will be over tomorrow morning before church. No sense in doing his work for him and paying him twice."

I nodded and finally sat gingerly on the edge of the sofa. Looking about the small, tidy cottage, I noted the crocheted blanket on the back of her armchair and the teacup on the nearby table. I wondered if my mother was happy here, occupying her own space and answering to no one for the first time in her life. Looking at her lined features and the pinched frown that had imprinted itself after a lifetime, I didn't know if my mother was capable of being happy in the traditional sense. She'd always viewed life as a perpetual disappointment that one must merely endure. I hoped at the very least, she was content.

"What's brought you this way?"

Her abrupt question jolted me from my wonderings. I ignored it and asked instead, "Are you well, Mother?"

Her gray eyes—so much like my own—narrowed in confusion. "Well enough, Julian. What's this about? Is your uncle dead, then?"

"No, Mother," I rushed out. "Uncle Phillip is having some mobility issues, but his mind is sharp. Both his will and constitution are strong."

She said nothing. No wish for her brother's improved health. Neither did she ask after mine. When I couldn't find more than impatience on her stony features, I allowed disappointment to direct my words, "I've been in London for several weeks now. I've become reacquainted with the Bartholomews. The children are all in town for the season."

She sniffed but didn't offer a reply.

"They all seem to be under the impression that I left for Leicester at sixteen and put them out of my life for good." My mother had told me in her short, barely legible correspondence that there was no word from any of the Bartholomews. That they'd hardly noted my departure.

I'd carried that bitterness right to their doorstep and clung to it tightly at the dinner table this past Friday.

She watched the fire and maintained her silence.

"Why did you withhold the letters I wrote them? And Genevieve's letters, Mother."

I knew. I *knew* her answer would change nothing. But I wanted the truth confirmed, my suspicions along with them. And I wanted to see her face when she told me. If nothing else, to banish the haunted expression of Genevieve Bartholomew from my mind.

"What difference did it make?" Her voice was unrepentant. "You had a new life to keep yourself occupied with. It was pointless to concern yourself with the goings-on at Laurel Park."

Her answer shamed me. It was the same one I'd thoughtlessly given to Gen the evening prior. The one that had stilled her arguments and leached the color from her face. My stomach hollowed uneasily.

Mother continued, "That was the whole reason I sent you. To give you a future. You were already too soft and growing used to the finer things by the day."

I swallowed. "And Genevieve's letters to me? You what? Destroyed them when you lied and told her you were posting them along with yours?"

My mother sighed sharply, a dismissive and exasperated sound. "That girl." She paused to shake her head, the movement twisting her frown neatly into place. "She didn't need the encouragement. She'd had your attention for long enough. And the ideas and ridiculous notions she fancied . . ." Another disapproving shake of her head.

Frowning in confusion, I questioned, "What notions?"

With a frustrated breath, she heaved herself from her armchair and stomped off toward her bedchamber. I sat stunned until she returned a moment later laden with bundles of paper in her arms. Three heavy stacks were deposited on the sofa beside me, aged envelopes bound together with twine.

"I don't understand," I admitted as I carefully retrieved one set of letters.

"That fool girl had it in her head that she was meant for you." A humorless huff followed. "The daughter of a marquess and the housekeeper's son. I saved her the heartache in the long run."

I thought about the utter shock on Genevieve's face when she'd seen me in the garden of Cawthorn Hall weeks ago. The resentment and the anger she'd wielded afterward. And then last night. The way she'd wilted when I'd brushed aside our years apart in the dim light of that drawing room.

I wasn't sure my mother had spared Genevieve anything.

I hadn't known that Genevieve fancied me or saw a future for us. We'd always been close friends. But she'd never indicated she hoped for something more in our time together at Laurel Park. I rifled through my memories, looking for anything to indicate that Gen wanted more than friendship, but all I could see were the hazy memories through the lens of a distractible sixteen-year-old boy. I'd been obsessed with horses and an idiotic adolescent half the time.

My thumb flipped through the edges of the second stack of letters. There were a hundred here or more in this set alone. "But why keep them and bring them with you from Laurel Park?"

"She used to watch to make sure I took them off to the village, even tried to go with me or follow me on my errands. I caught her checking the grates for burned papers left among the ashes. It was easier to put them in the bottom of my trunk and leave them. She knew better than to search the servants' quarters. She stopped writing them just before I came here. They were still in the trunk. Hadn't thought about 'em in a long time."

The thought of Genevieve on her hands and knees sifting through ashes looking for proof of my mother's deception had my throat feeling oddly tight. And the image of her waiting for word from me—for years by the look of the envelopes I held in my hands—had me swallowing roughly around that tightness.

No wonder she'd been angry.

The ink had faded and smudged in some areas, I noted. There were so many letters.

I wrote to you for years. And I didn't stop. I continued on—far longer than I should have. Far longer than I'm proud of.

And I'd stopped including my short missives to her among my mother's letters after a few months.

She hadn't given up on me for a very long time.

Disquiet settled around me. I had to get out of this house.

I gathered the three bundles and stood. I'd gotten what I'd come for and quite a bit more.

The constriction in my throat went nowhere and I had to swallow several times before I thought I might be able to speak, so heavy was the shame weighing my tongue.

Reprimanding my mother for her actions would be pointless. She'd never understand the damage she'd done—how she'd hurt Genevieve. Our friendship had always been a sore spot for her anyhow. I'd brushed aside the snide comments and the forced time away from the Bartholomews on my mother's days off with the rest of the staff every Sunday. It had always been her way. I'd simply accepted it.

"Perhaps Genevieve's adolescent heart had been misguided. But the Bartholomews were good to me, Mother. They treated me like

I was one of them. They never asked or implied that I should earn my keep, working in the gardens or the stables."

The marquess had been the one to inform me about procreation. The marchioness had taught me how to dance. I had been educated alongside Gen in reading, maths, Latin, and French. We'd taken nearly every meal together—with the exception of Sundays—in the nursery and then the schoolroom. And Emery had taught me how to ride a horse.

"You were not one of them," my mother said roughly.

"Believe me, I knew my place. You reminded me often enough."

I'd been making excuses and trying to minimize the familiarity the Bartholomews had shown me during these last few weeks in London. They'd done nothing but welcome me into their homes and encouraged me in my efforts for the farm. I'd thought ungrateful, unpleasant things and diminished their efforts at every turn. Between all of us, I was the only one who'd been poorly behaved.

The scraping claws of humiliation and grief raked their way across my middle.

"Your hardness about them made me resentful. They didn't forget about me because I was out of sight—as you attempted to orchestrate. But you forgot, Mother. You sent me away. And I imagine I wouldn't hear from you now if I simply stopped sending you letters."

My mother didn't respond, just stared into the fire with a bitter frown.

With a sharp nod and a final glance, I left the oppressive silence and the lonely cottage behind.

Removing my satchel from the saddlebag on Brutus, I tucked the stacks of envelopes carefully in the bottom. I leaned my head against the horse's firm shoulder and attempted to quiet the thoughts racing through my mind.

I was turning over memories and sharpening the edges of every one.

Brutus finally released a breath through his lips and flicked a dark ear back in concern. I straightened and took in the misting rain that had been threatening for most of the morning. We should arrive back in London late that evening after a meal and rest at an inn along the way.

With one last glimpse at my mother's cottage, Brutus and I took off toward the main road eager to return to town and the people there awaiting our return.

~

Dear Julian,

It snowed last night. I woke up to a blanket of white. Augie and Emery let me traipse around with them until I couldn't feel my feet from the cold. Augie and I joined forces and threw snow at Emery. She fell down laughing and dragged Augie with her. I would very much like to throw a snow-ball at your face. Why haven't you written to me, Julian? I've seen the letters that come addressed to your mother, written in your own hand, sitting on the front table in our foyer. It's been nearly two months. Have you forgotten me already?

Yours, in the snow,
Gen

Dear Julian,

I'm happy to report that Bramble delivered her colt last night. I know she was always your favorite despite you claiming you had no favorites. I went out to check on her in my dressing gown before the sun was even up because one of the grooms said it could be any day. And when I got to her stall, I could have sworn there was a black deer within. Ha! The colt was sitting there so sweetly and Bramble was standing nearby watching as if she had no idea what to do with him. I ran to get one of the stable hands so they could check the colt over. Both mother and baby are doing well. I just wanted you to know.

Yours,
Gen

Dear Julian,

Not much to report these days, I'm afraid. I'm leaving for London soon to stay with Patty, and only wanted to write a quick note of farewell. I imagine life in town would seem boring to you. That's why I don't send you letters when I'm there. I know it sounds silly, but it feels disloyal that I should enjoy London while also loving Laurel Park so. Regardless, I just wanted you to know I would be away for several weeks. Not that it matters. I haven't heard from you once in all these months. You don't care whether I'm in the town or the country.

Yours,
Gen

Dear Julian,

I am a writer. Patty advised me to keep something for myself, and so I have. I write stories about adventure and mayhem, Jules. Can you believe it? It's a secret I carry so that I can have something for myself. In a world where nearly everyone has expectations of me, I needed one thing to remain entirely my own. Perhaps I should not have told you my secret. But I suppose it doesn't matter. It's been years now. I feel safe in admitting the truth to you. And not because you're so trustworthy or loyal, but because you're not really *there at all. You're a ghost, and oddly enough, I am the one still living. The one who cannot let go.*

Gen

~

Three hundred and eighty-two.

That was how many letters Genevieve had written over three and a half years.

She'd written nearly every day that first year. And then once per week the following year. Then the correspondence was less frequent but generally dated once per month.

She'd stopped closing her letters with "Yours" after I'd been gone for a year. I checked the dates and registered the change.

Some missives were long, others were short. Most were details about life at Laurel Park—the things I was missing, visits from her sisters and brother, the animals and the land we'd roamed all our lives. She'd written to me about a ruined treehouse she'd found in the woods and visiting the hillside we'd played on as children. Sometimes her words were angry and imploring. Occasionally she scratched through half the letter and then simply signed her name. A few of the longer ones were stories about a detective and a highwayman. Genevieve had always been a gifted storyteller. She could make up silly songs that rhymed at the drop of a hat, too.

"Here's another one for the I-hate-Julian pile," I told the orange cat. His ear twitched in my direction otherwise he remained curled up on the end of my bed, long-since bored of this new game.

It was late and I was drunk.

Brutus and I had returned to the boardinghouse just after ten o'clock—late enough to avoid Mrs. Farnsworth. I'd carefully removed the letters from my satchel and stared at them for ten minutes before untying the twine that bound them neatly. The ginger cat had watched me pick up the first one and start reading.

Half an hour later, I'd poured myself a drink and then I'd kept right on pouring, hating myself a little more with every line I read.

"Oh, another detective tale. This one was short but it was good." No response from my feline friend. I smoothed the paper and put it in the shortest stack of papers.

I didn't really know what I was doing beyond punishing myself. I couldn't admit to Genevieve that I'd confronted my mother and was now reading her years-old letters. She would probably kill me. These missives were very plainly written by a sixteen-, seventeen-, and eighteen-year-old girl—one who was angry and bitter and heartsick. They weren't silly or anything so simple as that. But after a time, they had very clearly transformed into something beyond letters to a long-lost friend. She'd been writing them for herself there at the end. Her words felt raw and personal, and something she assumed would never see the light of day.

And tucked between the pages, scratched along with the ink, were the wishes of an adolescent heart. I might have missed all the signs of her devotion as a boy growing up alongside her, but reading her words now, I could see very clearly how she'd had hopes and dreams for us . . . together. I didn't know how to feel about that.

Dear Julian,

I woke up from a dream that I cannot quite recall, the edges blurry and just beyond my reach. But my cheeks were wet and I knew somehow that it had been about you. I think I hate you most days. Except for the days I don't.

Gen

I exhaled a shaky breath, adding the note to the appropriate stack and taking another drink.

"Tell me what to do, cat." I rubbed a hand across my bleary eyes, knowing I'd regret all my decisions in the morning when I was supposed to trot out two horses for that ride with Drakefield.

I startled and removed the hand covering my face when I felt the cat land lightly in my lap. "What? Do you finally have some wisdom to impart?" I slurred the words and slouched down in my armchair, crossing my arms over my chest.

I wondered what it might have been like to receive these letters years ago—the way I was meant to. Well, Genevieve likely wouldn't have sent all the hateful ones if I'd been responding. But there was something about the truthfulness of them, the naked honesty written out in her delicate script.

What would it have been like to know that Genevieve fancied me? Even more than that, she'd wanted a life with me.

I considered what it felt like to have her attention on me now—even burning with anger and frustration. This new, full-grown version of Genevieve was all fire and ice. The pull between us was still there. I didn't know if a connection like ours could be snuffed out, even by time and distance.

And I wasn't blind to Genevieve's beauty. She'd always been eye-catching. It was different now. Looking too long felt like admitting defeat.

We had been comfortable and honest in a way that only true friendship allowed. I thought of Emery and Augie and how their easiness had transformed to the happily married couple they were today.

My mind returned to Genevieve's defeated response in that drawing room. The way her face had paled. How she'd said it was too late. She'd jerked herself away from me. I could see it now for what it was . . . self-preservation.

I sighed deeply, helpless and confused by my drunk and disorderly thoughts.

The cat regarded me solemnly with his strange golden eyes before letting out his creaky meow and climbing up my crossed arms to sit snuggly against my chest. His purr rumbled against me and I thought I didn't deserve the comfort.

Six

GENEVIEVE

Julian,

I kissed James Madigan after the village festival today. I just wanted you to know that. He tasted of licorice candy and smelled like hay and I cried the whole way home thinking it should have been you.

It should have been you.

It wasn't you.

Yours,
Gen

The offices of the *London Post* were bustling.

I typically did not wait so long to deliver my pages. In fact, I'd never come so close to the deadline for printing. My weekly delivery of the *Detective Owensby* serial was always made two evenings prior to the printing deadline.

However this week, the words had not come quite so easily. I'd wavered on the best way to resolve the good detective's current case. I'd almost consulted Patty and asked her opinion, but in the end, I'd decided to solve the problem on my own, hence the delay.

Yesterday, I'd sent off a quick note to Mr. Belham explaining my tardiness and assuring him that the pages would be well in hand before six o'clock this evening.

With the current articles going to print, the office was far more active than when I typically handed off my pages. Assuming a quick exchange, I'd bid my maid remain in the carriage and ventured through the busy offices on my own.

At this point in my career, Mr. Belham rarely had notes or changes for my weekly serial. He read my updates and expressed his love of the story which was very kind but at times made me feel awkward. That was the one instance when it was easier to be the anonymous writer behind Detective Owensby. I'd rather over-hear someone discussing the latest installment on a street corner than have Mr. Belham praise my abilities with a pen and paper. Strange how a compliment could turn a rational, confident indi-vidual into a rambling mess who smiled with too many teeth.

Regardless, I was here at five forty-two in the afternoon braving the curious stares in the *London Post* offices. With a quick knock on Mr. Belham's door, I offered polite nods and cautious smiles to those around me.

"Come in," called my editor from within.

I opened the door and left it wide as I entered. "Good afternoon, Mr. Belham. I do apologize for the delay."

He stood quickly and offered a genuine smile in greeting. "Lady Genevieve, how do you do?"

Mr. Belham was at least a decade my senior and successful by any standard. He had friendships with high-ranking aristocrats and was often found on guest lists throughout the season despite his lack of a title. He was wealthy, from a respected family, and his influential position with the newspaper made him consistently well-received. And as my sister Emery loved to remind me, I could do a lot worse in the suitor department.

But Mr. Aaron Belham had not specifically applied for the position. And I didn't necessarily *want* a suitor. It wasn't that I didn't wish to marry someday. I did. Mostly. Being fortunate enough to have two duchesses as sisters had afforded me some latitude where expectations were concerned. There was no rush to marry for the sake of familial connections or the need to make a smart match. Silas liked to jest that I could wait until I was his age to marry and no one would complain about it save our mother.

I wasn't explicitly waiting on a love match to materialize. That would have been ineffectual and foolish. Regardless, I wasn't rushing myself. I was happy writing and living a life with my family for the time being.

"I am well, thank you," I said, finally meeting Mr. Belham's warm brown eyes.

His tall form came out from behind the desk, and I instinctively raised the sheaf of papers between us.

Despite his work keeping him indoors, Mr. Belham appeared quite fit and well-muscled. His shoulders were a strong line beneath his jacket. The patterned waistcoat he wore emphasized a trim waist and narrow hips.

My gaze snapped up to his. I hoped I hadn't been looking too long. "Here are this week's pages. Again, I apologize for the necessary extension of my usual deadline."

"Oh, think nothing of it." He took the papers and placed them offhandedly on the desk behind him.

I frowned. Having been relieved of my burden, I wasn't quite sure what to do with my hands.

"Your appearance is timely indeed."

"Well, yes"—I fidgeted—"I knew the deadline to print was looming and—"

"No, no," Mr. Belham interrupted. "The paper is fine. And your serial is in no danger of being excluded. I wouldn't hear of it. I only meant that in my busy schedule this afternoon I haven't yet taken tea. Would you care to join me down the street at Stratford's?"

I blinked slowly, somewhat surprised by the invitation. I could suddenly hear Emery's voice in my head calling him *my* Mr. Belham and I fought the irritating intrusion.

Recovering valiantly, I smiled and nodded. "Of course. That sounds lovely. My maid is awaiting my return. She can join us for the outing." I was the sister of two duchesses, but I still required a chaperone for a visit to a tea room.

Mr. Belham's smile was bright on his handsome face, the little lines near his eyes crinkling agreeably. "That sounds most delightful." With a smooth grab for the papers on his desk, Mr.

Belham held out a hand toward his office doorway. "I'll just pass these off to my assistant and we can be on our way."

"Oh, should you not review the pages before they go to press?" He *was* my editor after all.

The smile he wore didn't dim. It merely changed shape, appearing indulgent and amused, as if he were stopping himself from ruffling my hair or bopping me on the nose. "Of course I'll read about my favorite detective. I shall just find out about his latest case along with everyone else. Wouldn't want to spoil the fun."

I nodded despite the odd feeling that gave me in the pit of my stomach. Did no one review my serial before it was printed in a major periodical every week? Could I write whatever I wanted, then? Almost immediately, my unease shifted to curiosity as I gave further weight to the idea of revealing my identity as G. Everett.

My smile came much easier as we maneuvered our way back through the offices and down the stairs to the street. I summoned Posey, my maid, and then we were off to Stratford's.

The tea room was on the first floor of a popular hotel. We walked through the main lobby as afternoon light filtered in through large windows. Mr. Belham's happy expression never faltered as he escorted me to where we were eventually seated amid the sounds of quiet conversation and porcelain teacups and gleaming silver cutlery. Our table was lovely, with fresh flowers and white table linens. The scent of fresh tea and fragrant jam settled warmly over me as I took in the room at large. There were several patrons enjoying a light repast at the twenty or so tables filling the space. I was familiar with the service here as I'd frequented Stratford's with my sisters and our mother when she visited London.

Posey was seated nearby and I ensured she had her own refreshment for the duration.

"That's thoughtful of you," Mr. Belham said with a warm smile and a glance in Posey's direction.

"What's that?" I asked as I draped my napkin across my lap and straightened in my chair.

He clarified, "Your consideration for your maid."

Oh. I considered arguing the point. Saying it was merely common decency on my part. But that would just draw more attention to me. And it would make me seem even more odd to assert my radical beliefs than to just simply have them.

Growing up, our household had not been terribly formal. Emery wore trousers when she went riding at Laurel Park. Her own lady's maid was still one of her closest friends. And then there had been Julian. My family had done more than simply tolerate the housekeeper's son. We'd all cared for him. My father used to take him hunting and riding. Mama doted on his fine manners and chatted with him often. Julian took meals with us and attended celebrations and gatherings.

I was, of course, aware of how maids and servants were treated in less hospitable households. But that wasn't the way of things for the Bartholomews. That wouldn't be changing just because I was in public with a gentleman.

I swallowed down the words that longed to be free. "Well, I'm just thankful I'm able to spend the afternoon with you, Mr. Belham. Posey affords me that opportunity. Have you been terribly busy at the paper?"

My swift change of subject didn't bother my companion. He spoke at length about his eventful workday and the demands on his time. The tea service arrived and we prepared our respective beverages while I selected a crustless sandwich as well.

"But despite my many responsibilities, I find I'm able to create a balance between my home and work." Mr. Belham's brown eyes were expectant.

"That's lovely to hear," I replied noncommittally, knowing where this was going and doing my utmost to keep my voice even. "Balance is important in one's life."

"I agree," he replied seriously as he adjusted the handle of his teacup, moving it a quarter turn. "And priorities often change over time."

I nodded around my sip of tea. I had a feeling I was the horse and Mr. Belham thought I looked particularly thirsty.

"For example," he led on, gaze warm, "as a young man, I prized my career and position above all else. And now, as a man of nearly five and thirty, I find things shifting and my priorities leaning more toward family and the future."

While relieving the silver serving tray of a seed cake, I smiled. "I could not agree more. Family is such an important part of my life. I don't know where I would be without them."

If Mr. Belham was disappointed by my obtuse response, he didn't show it. He smoothed his hand along his dark mustache before asking quite plainly, "And what of your feelings on the future?"

Perhaps he wasn't as unobservant as I thought. I wasn't ready for this discussion, and certainly not so openly. But perhaps it was time I gave more consideration to Mr. Aaron Belham and the potential there. He was obviously working up to something— something involving me. Just because I was enjoying tea with the man or entertaining the idea of this ambiguous future he was alluding to, did not mean I had to marry him.

However, one could argue that I'd been stagnant in my personal relationships for far too long. What I'd said about family was true. I valued my brother and sisters and their husbands, my nieces and nephew. I loved my parents and the life I'd created around all of them. But that was mostly where my socializing ended. I interacted well with the friends and acquaintances of my family, but I didn't really have any of my own.

An association with Mr. Belham would be something that I could claim for myself, at the very least. Just because I couldn't envision a future with the dark-haired editor didn't mean I was opposed to the notion. Perhaps I just needed time to warm up to the idea of it.

Unbidden, an image of Julian flashed in my mind and I worked to banish it.

Finally, I gave Mr. Belham a coy response to his subtle digging. "The future, in general? Or mine in particular?"

His laugh was bright and turned the heads of a few matrons sitting nearby. "Always so clever with a turn of phrase." And then he leaned forward and said in a low, conspiratorial tone, "I suppose that is the risk one runs when conversing with a talented wordsmith."

My smile was tight, strained by all the inconvenient feelings that accompanied my secret profession. I wondered briefly what Mr. Belham would think of my idea to reveal the truth behind G. Everett. Would he support my career? As my editor, would he be opposed to my desire for acknowledgement? Would he want an ambiguous future with a woman who was a known writer?

When my eyes finally managed to return to the man before me, I noticed he was watching me. The laughter had bled away into something comfortable and steady. His warm gaze had gone soft and lingering. He looked very solemn and fond all of a sudden.

My palms grew damp inside my gloves. For some reason, I was uncomfortable with Mr. Belham's obvious attention. My natural inclination was to be . . . hesitant with him, and I did not know why.

Julian's serious face chose that moment to intrude in my thoughts once more.

I probably only felt odd about an association with Mr. Belham because for so long my heart had belonged to Julian. It wasn't Mr. Belham's fault. And it wasn't mine, either. Through consistency and habit, my feelings had remained loyal to someone who never even wanted me. My heart hadn't yet accepted its freedom despite me having turned the key and opened the cage door wide. It would simply take time to adjust. I was sure that this lingering awkwardness with Mr. Belham's attentions would resolve itself over time.

And it wasn't as if I had been waiting on Julian. Theoretically, if I had been—which I definitely hadn't—the mystery of Julian was now solved, thanks to our coincidental meeting in London, all these years later. I could move on. Julian was my past.

Replaying our standoff in the front room at Cawthorn Hall, I fought a wince at my emotional state. So he'd never received my letters. It was no matter. Clearly, it was a blessing in disguise. Julian had been so dismissive. He'd brushed aside our friendship, the end of which he'd called inevitable. The missing letters wouldn't have changed anything for him. Any of my foolish, lingering hopes had died a quick death at that.

I could trust that Julian was telling the truth. In our extensive history, he'd never been a liar. And his expression had been honest and open that night. Julian had been confused by my anger. I'd been so consumed by his perceived dismissal for so long, the absence of those feelings had left me hollow.

Beneath that resignation, however, had been relief. Julian hadn't received my letters—by some fortune or turn of fate. He'd never learned of my adolescent devotion nor my resentful ramblings.

This was a good thing. I needn't feel embarrassment or expectation where Julian was concerned. I needn't feel anything at all.

Yes, our paths might cross while he was visiting London. Miles seemed invested in his success with the farm. But I could shrug off that painful heartbreak as if it had never happened. Because as far as Julian was concerned, it hadn't. I could simply paint the past with nostalgic brushstrokes and recall our years of friendship fondly. There was no reason to make things strained and awkward. Truly, a crisis had been averted.

I took a final sip of lukewarm tea and relinquished my cup to the table. Mr. Belham was looking at me expectantly.

"I'm so sorry," I blurted, having no idea what he'd been saying. "I was woolgathering. What was that?"

Unaffected by my rudeness, Mr. Belham smiled. "It is quite alright. I wasn't saying anything important. Your creative mind was likely overcome. I imagine your stories and ideas strike whenever they fancy, no matter your surroundings or whom you're having tea with."

My laughter was a touch forced, but he wouldn't know it. "I do have an active imagination that cares not for time and place. That is the truth."

"Well, I'm afraid I must return to the office. There is a paper to put out, after all." He seemed so regretful. I should be grateful for his kindness and attention. Mr. Belham knew my secret and didn't seem to mind. He was making an effort. The very least I could do would be to return the favor.

I smiled politely and brushed a hand along my skirts. "Yes, of course. Thank you for accommodating the delay in my schedule. And for the invitation as well."

"It was my pleasure. Will you be attending Drakefield's event next week?"

"Yes." I nodded. Drakefield's wife was one of Patty's friends and we got along well. I was looking forward to the ball. The season wasn't in full swing yet, so the gathering shouldn't be overly crowded which would be nice as well.

"Perhaps you might save me a dance," Mr. Belham suggested, his face hopeful and kind.

"Of course, Mr. Belham. I look forward to it." A knot formed in my throat, but I managed to swallow it down, reminding my heart —once again—that it was unchained to the past and free to live a life without the ghost of Julian Moore.

"Mr. Moore is joining us for supper!"

Franny's greeting left something to be desired as she bounded through the open doorway to my sitting room wearing a jubilant expression.

Her words caused an annoyed pang, but I buried it. It wasn't

Franny's fault that my feelings surrounding Julian were so complicated.

"Is that so?" I said, attempting to meet her smile. I set my writing aside and placed my pencil in the drawer of my desk, focusing my attention fully on the little girl who was like a sister to me.

Although, these days, it was easy to see the young woman she was becoming. With dark hair and striking hazel eyes, Francesca still wore the innocence of youth. Perhaps most twelve-year-old girls were more interested in fashion and gossip, but Franny was sweet-natured and tender-hearted. She loved reading and caring for her dolls and any animal that crossed her path. Her faithful spaniel Daisy trotted at her side nearly everywhere she went. The pair settled easily on the patterned sofa of my sitting room while I looked on in amusement.

"Yes. Papa invited him after they went boxing together today with Uncle Silas. He hasn't told Mum yet. I'm not so sure she likes Mr. Moore very much," Franny added thoughtfully.

"Your mother is just protective. She's still getting to know Mr. Moore," I tried to explain. I couldn't exactly say that Patty resented Julian on my behalf. My sister was fiercely loyal. Perhaps I needed to have a conversation with her about her frostiness toward him. I had confided in my sisters following my last conversation with Julian. They knew about the letters.

Franny frowned. "I thought Mr. Moore was raised at Laurel Park. Surely Mum knows him well enough."

My throat tightened instinctively when I thought of that time and how very long Patty had been absent from our lives. At a dozen years my senior, Patty had left home at seventeen for her first season. She'd made a fine match by society standards but had been miserable with an uncaring husband, a duke old enough to be her great-grandfather. Patty's life had changed so much that even after she'd been widowed, she'd felt the need to remain in London and away from her family for much of that time. It wasn't until I'd been nearly fifteen that Patty had reconnected with all of us in earnest. And now, despite it being many years later, some wounds were still tender. I didn't like to consider all the time we'd missed together.

Clearing my throat, I attempted to explain, "Patty left Laurel Park when Mr. Moore was but a small child. Her memories of him as an adolescent are very few. I'm sure your mother is simply reacquainting herself with him."

"What a happy surprise to have him back in all your lives," she said sweetly, stroking Daisy's floppy brown ear.

I nodded, but said nothing. I wasn't sure I'd be able to lie.

While Julian's arrival had been undoubtedly a surprise, I could not call it happy. That had been *one* of the emotions I'd experienced when first spying him across the back garden, but too many others had crowded for attention. All the anger and bitterness, the swirling confusion had coalesced and flooded any happiness I'd felt. But perhaps now that we'd spoken and addressed the letters he'd never received, I could loosen the hold on my complicated emotions. I hoped I could find that easiness with my former friend. It would be nice to know Julian again, even briefly, for his time here this season.

Perhaps the dinner would provide an opportunity to show Julian that I wasn't the hysterical female I seemed. I could be pleasant, and act as if he was any other guest of my brother-in-law. Or even better, I could strive for indifference, which seemed to be his aim since reacquainting himself with the Bartholomews.

"Oh, and Mary is coming to supper, too!"

I smiled at Franny's announcement. "That is wonderful news. She and Silas can keep us all entertained."

The little girl smiled happily. Lady Mary Lovelace was Patty's best friend. They'd known each other for many years during Patty's time in London. She was loud and outspoken and endlessly supportive. We all enjoyed Mary's company. And she and my brother lived to bicker with one another. It generally provided excellent entertainment for whomever was seated nearby.

Hours later, Franny's guest announcements had come to fruition. We were all seated in the opulent dining room of Cawthorn Hall. I was listening in as Mary and Silas argued over their root vegetables, occasionally stoking the flames of irritability by agreeing or disagreeing when appropriate.

Eventually their banter receded and Silas announced, "Well, Mr. Moore, it seems your business with Drakefield is progressing. I heard the outing in the park went well and you'll be attending the countess's upcoming event."

Julian cleared his throat, his gaze snagging briefly on mine, and admitted quietly, "Yes, I've accepted the generous invitation."

Silas looked like he was waiting for a more thorough and informative answer, but Julian had always been uncomfortable with being the center of attention. His shyness made for concise and efficient conversations—the quicker to move things along and take the focus off himself. It was in direct opposition to my brother's overall conduct. Perhaps that was why Silas looked so confused.

Smoothly, I diverted, "Silas, do you have any travel plans in the near future?"

With my brother distracted and lamenting his need to remain in England for the foreseeable future, Julian was free to enjoy his meal. He caught my gaze, lips tilting briefly in gratitude.

Supper concluded without further incident and we eventually moved to congregate in the drawing room. Franny trotted off to bed after a cheerful "goodnight" for everyone.

Julian's eyes continued to find mine. Or I would look up from my conversation with Patty and Mary to find him watching me curiously.

"What's happening there?" Mary murmured.

"Hmm?" I replied offhandedly, turning my attention to the woman's curious dark brown stare. Mary was a decade my senior and striking in her appearance. Perhaps not traditionally lovely and sought after in some social circles, but her tall, lean frame wore her impeccable manners well. Her wild red hair, on the other hand, was forever out of control—spiraling away from whatever coiffure she'd attempted on any given night.

"Don't *hmm* me, missy. What is going on with you and the quiet and solemn Mr. Moore'?"

"Nothing," I said too quickly. Her auburn brows snapped high on her forehead. "Nothing," I repeated after a long breath. "I think he's simply treading carefully."

"Is that what you want?" Mary asked easily, no consideration for my obvious unwillingness to discuss my complicated relationship with Julian. Thank God Emery wasn't here this evening. She and Mary often joined forces and were overwhelming in their straightforward honesty.

"She doesn't have to answer that," Patty said, followed by a sip of her sherry.

Mary cast her friend an exasperated look. "Of course she doesn't *have* to. I just thought she might want to address why they've been staring and making squishy faces at each other all evening."

Patty rolled her eyes and I answered with a flat, unamused stare.

Then we all turned in unison to look across the room at the space occupied by Julian, Miles, and Silas.

Unfortunately Julian chose that moment to glance my way. His gray eyes quickly broke off when he found my attention already trained on him and returned to Miles and whatever he was saying.

Mary made a smug humming sound before taking a sip from her glass.

"No need to sound so superior," I groused.

A satisfied smile claimed her features. "It *is* a trial always being right."

With one last aggrieved huff, I left Patty and Mary behind and went to join the men. I didn't know what to think about Julian. But I knew I couldn't attempt to figure it out from across the room and with Mary's commentary as accompaniment.

"Sister! Welcome. Were you growing bored with only Lady Mary for entertainment?" Silas said in his permanently jovial way.

The men widened their circle and allowed me entrance. I stood between my brother and Julian and kept my gaze fixed firmly on Silas.

"Patty was there too," I acknowledged.

"Well, she hardly counts. Patty is too serious and exacting to be a source of entertainment," Silas argued.

"I find I disagree with you," Miles said without offense. "I'm charmed by her constantly."

Silas made a sound of mild disgust. "*That* is what marriage does to you."

I smiled at my brother's ridiculousness.

Miles snorted a laugh. He was forever easygoing, and had learned the best way to deal with Silas over the years. "In fact, I think I shall join my lovely wife." Miles glanced my way quickly before turning back to Silas, "Come on. You can keep us entertained."

My brother looked between Julian and myself quickly before clapping Miles on the shoulder. "Excellent plan. Be good, children."

I watched the men make their way across the room before inviting Patty and Mary to join them on the seating arrangement by the fire.

When I pivoted around to face Julian, I found his gray eyes already waiting. Instead of polite or cautious conversation, I blurted, "Why are you staring at me?"

He looked startled. "I'm not staring."

"You are," I argued.

"I am not."

"If you're worried I'm going to yell at you again or burst into tears or something . . . I'm not."

"I know that," he said with a frown.

Silence descended for a moment. I couldn't decide if he truly believed his claim. After our last encounter, perhaps he thought

I'd be an emotional mess and was being cautious and watchful as a result.

Finally, I said, "I'm being cordial. There is no reason for things to be awkward while you're in London. And we—we—we cleared the air, so to speak." For some reason I had to look away. Despite our conversation surrounding the missing letters, I didn't feel as if we'd truly put the past behind us. But I wasn't about to admit the disquiet and grief I still carried about our lost friendship. Some things could never truly be recovered, and remained even more difficult to discuss.

"Cleared the air?" he questioned.

"Yes," I said, finally managing to meet his knowing gaze. "Cleared the air. And there is no reason we cannot be friendly while you're in town. Our paths will undoubtedly cross. No need to be strange and stare at me like I'm a wounded animal."

"I'm not being strange. Jesus, Genevieve, I haven't seen you in seven years. Am I not allowed to look?" Julian seemed incredulous, like I was being completely unmanageable when I thought I was behaving admirably and maturely.

He was looking now. We both were. I was cataloguing every change to his handsome face—the sharpening of his jaw, the hollowing beneath his cheekbones. But some things remained the same—the wisdom in his cool, gray eyes, the freckles sprinkled lovingly across his nose and cheeks, the way his dark auburn hair swept across his forehead when I know he wanted it to stay brushed away from his face.

"You're allowed to look," I said quietly.

A sound from the other side of the room broke our stare, and we turned to find an audience watching our exchange with rapt attention. They all noticed and looked away quickly, heads going in all directions, save ours. Mary and Silas recovered first and started speaking, drawing the others into conversation.

I sighed. That was all I needed—everyone invested in my relationship with Julian. I loved my family and they meant well, but they were nosy and opinionated. I should know. I was one of them.

With the moment broken, I finally shifted my attention back to Julian. "So, you're attending Drakefield's ball next week?"

"I suppose." He sounded resigned to his fate.

"It won't be horrible," I encouraged. "The season hasn't truly started. The guest list will be moderate. And you'll have ample opportunity to chat with Drakefield and his friends to suit your needs." It would be an excellent opportunity for him and his purposes for Brightleaf.

Julian nodded, as if he expected as much but still didn't enjoy the idea of attending a *ton* event. "And you'll be there?"

"I will."

"Good," he said finally.

What does that mean?

"Good," I echoed, like an idiot.

I could see him preparing to leave. He glanced toward the door and shifted on his feet. He was about to say farewell and wish me a good night. I knew it like I knew he needed a distraction at dinner. Too much attention was on us—on him—and he needed to escape and gather himself. He'd been that way in our youth, needing quiet and calm following a social situation.

Before he had the chance to leave, I decided I needed some sort of reassurance. I didn't want all of our exchanges to be fraught and awkward. "Can we be friends, Julian? Again? I don't want things to be uncomfortable. I could be an ally for you—like Miles."

"Like Miles?" he questioned.

"Yes. I can help with your efforts for the farm, offer counsel . . . I can be a friend."

Julian regarded me seriously as if he were considering every ramification of my proposal. Perhaps an offer of friendship held secret paths and scenarios that could lead to his imminent demise.

Something had changed. I didn't know what, but this man was different than the one I'd first spied in my sister's garden. He wasn't even the same one telling me he'd never received my letters. Julian's bitterness and hostility had softened. It was subtle, but perhaps our previous conversation had changed something for him, too.

But when the silence continued, I swallowed uneasily. "Or, if you'd prefer, I can steer clear. I can—"

"We can be friends again, Genevieve," he interrupted my attempt to backtrack. "Of course we can."

I nodded, feeling small for some reason.

"You're already sniping at me and calling my behavior strange," he said with a smile in his voice. "It'll be just like old times."

Just like old times.

I felt pressure behind my sternum and fought the urge to place a hand there.

He didn't know the half of it. Old times weren't simply bickering in comfortable friendship. Old times were me loving a boy who didn't know it. Old times were my heart slowly breaking when I'd been left behind.

Yet, this *was* a good thing. Julian's agreement would mean smooth and easy interactions. I could manage a friendship between us now. It was not as if he was the same boy I'd once loved. For that matter, I was not the same fanciful girl any longer. Why should my heart be in danger now?

I would be better prepared this time. I would be mature and realistic. I would not allow my imaginings to run away with themselves. That was what my writing was for. And speaking of my work, I'd decided to give Mr. Belham a chance just this afternoon.

Everything would be fine.

It did not matter that Julian was all grown up and exceedingly handsome. I could ignore his soulful gray eyes and his endearingly floppy hair and his strong male body with the hard line of his shoulders and the firmness of his thighs in those breeches.

"Now you're staring at *me* and being strange," he mused, looking far too smug and irritating, casting me forcibly out of my inappropriate thoughts.

My wandering gaze snapped to his and I mustered a vicious sort of smile. Julian's focus dipped momentarily to my lips.

I ignored the tightness in my chest and echoed his sentiment, "Just like old times."

Seven

GENEVIEVE

Dear Julian,

Where are you? What is going on in your life that you could have forgotten me so thoroughly? Did Leicester assign you a new best friend upon your arrival? Are you even reading these letters? Do you burn them or throw them out? Perhaps you have a carved wooden box and yours is full while mine sits empty on my dressing table. I sometimes imagine what it would be like to finally receive word from you. The darkest part of my heart fantasizes about removing your fictional letter from the correspondence tray and chucking it directly into the nearest grate. But the more realistic part of me knows I never would.

Gen

. . .

The following morning was gray and dreary and there was a letter waiting for me at the breakfast table.

"What's this?" I asked Patty, turning over the envelope in my hands.

Patty's blond brows lowered in confusion, but it was Miles who spoke, "I found it on the table in the foyer this morning. Perhaps it arrived very late or very early. I thought I'd save Mr. Pitch the trouble and deliver it to your place at the dining table."

It wasn't particularly unusual for me to receive correspondence but neither was it typical. This bit of mail hadn't been posted. There was nothing save for my name in slanted script across the front.

I placed it carefully beside my plate and served myself some bread with a generous helping of butter while the three of us listened to Franny discuss her current lessons and her French tutor whom she suspected was a former spy.

My gaze caught on the curve of the G in Genevieve and I had to force my attention back to my family. I didn't wish to be a rude breakfast companion.

I made it halfway through my second cup of tea before I retrieved the envelope and lowered it to my lap before carefully breaking the seal. I could hear Miles speaking about our upcoming visiting to Laurel Park but the sound of his voice faded beyond notice when I unfolded the paper within and read the opening line.

Dear Gen,

I believe I owe you a letter.

My eyes scanned quickly down the short missive, skipping over everything in the middle, until I reached the signature at the bottom.

Yours,
Jules

On instinct, I folded the paper closed, cutting off the words. It felt like an illicit secret to have this letter at the breakfast table among my family. I didn't know why but I wanted to gather the note close and hide in my bedchamber before I opened the page again.

When I looked up, Miles was still speaking, Franny was sneaking bacon to Daisy beneath the table, and Patty was watching me.

I smiled brightly.

She stopped stirring her tea and frowned.

Well, perhaps too brightly.

I took a hasty sip from my teacup before standing. Miles stopped speaking and everyone stared my way. "Thank you for a lovely breakfast. But I have some writing to do and I would like to get an early start."

"But you didn't eat your bread," Franny said.

I smiled. "Right." And picked up the bread from my plate and started shuffling toward the door before calling, "I'll see you all later!"

They all regarded me as if I were mad, but I didn't care. I was moving swiftly down the corridor and toward the stairs to the family wing. I could not say if I passed the butler, Mr. Pitch, or anyone else. My surroundings were blurring behind Julian's slanted scrawl. *I believe I owe you a letter.*

My pulse was pounding out a warning through my veins.

Don't get too excited, Genevieve.

This means nothing, Genevieve.

It's just a letter, you idiot.

But my heart didn't know that. It knew that seven years ago, a young woman had written hundreds of letters and never received a reply. But today, a response was waiting in her hands.

So I gave my willful heart a bit of rein and welcomed the rapid beat.

Rushing into my suite, I closed the door and moved closer to the window. The curtains were open and gray light filtered within. I unfolded the paper and ignored the buttered bread I still held as well.

Dear Gen,

    I believe I owe you a letter.
    Many of them, I'm sure. But we can start with this.
    London isn't nearly as unbearable as I imagined. When we were young, I always hated the place that took you away from Laurel Park for weeks at a time. Town felt like another person I had to share you with—a more sophisticated friend who could make you smile with its fine things and

happy memories. I grew up hating London because it felt like a thief, stealing bits of you until it would take you away entirely.

I am stubbornly surprised to find that I enjoy London after all. While I miss the farm and the horses and the comfort of my routine, I find myself energized by the bustle of life in town. There are so many people. So many things I never could have imagined in my simple way of life. I wonder what your reaction would be to Leicester and Brightleaf Farms. But then, you've always loved the country.

Perhaps we're both these complicated creatures who find ourselves enjoying contrary and opposing forces. Or perhaps we simply love a different side of the same coin.

Yours,
Jules

I read through the letter twice more, tracing my fingers along the dark ink before I moved toward my dressing table. I set the bread aside as I lifted the edge of the carved wooden lid. For so long the cedar scent had been a painful reminder. I fought the ache of those memories, and I placed the letter in the box on the edge of my dressing table, empty no more.

I added a note to the box the following day. And the next. And the next. I'd received one letter every day since our dinner and conversation at Cawthorn Hall—since we'd decided to be friends again. Six letters filled the once-hollow wooden box.

All week I'd been distracted, anticipating his correspondence. Here I was, seven years later, still waiting on Julian. But now, the notes were arriving regularly.

I wondered why Julian was doing this. Did he feel it was necessary to mend something strained and jagged between us?

I never would have asked this of him. Albeit cautiously, I was content to simply start anew in our friendship.

The letters *were* all friendly in nature. Julian wrote about all manner of things in his straightforward and dry-witted style.

I should have been preparing for the Drakefield ball this evening, but instead, I pulled out my favorite correspondence thus far and held it along with the letter that arrived just this morning.

Dear Gen,

It seems I've acquired a cat. Not like the barn cats who wanted nothing to do with us at Laurel Park. But a very persistent cat that wants to be something more. The way Daisy is loyal and fond of all of you.

Well, the boardinghouse where I'm staying has many cats. The proprietress is obsessed—and that is frankly the kindest word for her—and has at least twelve cats under her roof. They typically remain on the main floor, but one of them has taken a shine to me. This orange-striped menace. I still don't know how he finds his way into my room every night, but I awake each morning with a ginger scarf around my neck or a purring hat atop my head and nearly always with cat hair in my mouth.

I find myself conversing with the little monster half the time. And he has a truly horrific yowl. It's as creaky as the door to the larder at Laurel Park. I know you remember. Made it damn near impossible to sneak treats out from under Mrs. Pennyworth.

Anyway, I can't imagine why this ginger cat prefers my company to all others, but it looks as if he'll be my roommate for the foreseeable future. It pains me to say it, but I know you'd love him.

Yours,
Jules

With a smile straining my cheeks, I shuffled the next page forward and reread this morning's note.

Dear Gen,

I feel I must introduce you to the horses I brought with me to London. Two of the four will be racing in the Royal Ascot in the spring.

Brutus is my favorite horse. Don't tell the others. He's the one I consistently choose to ride and he's been with me for years. He and I share a similar temperament and perhaps that's why we get on so well.

Cinder is one of the racing thoroughbreds. She's a four-year-old mare, very dark gray, and absurdly fast. She is eager and willing to work hard, and for that reason, you have to keep her in check or she'll run herself into the ground in her determination. I watched her being born, and it was indeed like seeing an awkward black fawn rising on shaky limbs among the straw bed.

Lark is another of the horses taking part in the races. He's a six-year-old chestnut stallion and runs just for the sheer joy of it. If you keep a horse just ahead, he'll stay interested in the spirit of the chase, and before you know it, Lark has surged ahead and every other horse is behind you. I'm eager to see what he can do with a trained jockey on his back.

And then there is Graceling. You would absolutely adore her. She's willful and incredibly opinionated. Perhaps we should go riding and you can try her out. If anyone could handle her, it would be you.

I'll see you tonight,
Jules

I'd meandered over to my dressing table while I reread the passage. Catching sight of my happy expression in the mirror, I quickly folded up the correspondence and placed it in the wooden box. With renewed inspiration, I crossed to my desk and made a few notes to myself. I wasn't brave enough to write back to Julian. I didn't know what all of these letters were about, but somehow I just knew that I shouldn't draw attention to them. The truth was, I didn't want them to stop.

Instead, I scribbled my intention to give Detective Owensby a cat in the next installment of the story. The good detective deserved some companionship. He'd been alone long enough.

A knock on the door to my rooms had me covering my notes and placing them in the drawer below my desktop.

"Come in!" I called.

Posey entered with a quick curtsy. "Good afternoon, my lady. Shall we prepare for the ball?"

She held curling tongs in one hand and I fought the urge to grimace. My thick hair typically fought the battle against stylish measures and lost.

However, I pasted on a bright smile and told Posey to do her worst.

After what seemed like endless dressing and grooming and curling and powdering, I arrived at the Drakefield event along with Miles and Patty. Emery and Augie would also be in attendance, as well as Silas. I didn't know when Julian would arrive, but I forced myself to take a deep breath in order to avoid spinning my head in every direction to seek him out.

As the ball had drawn closer this week, I'd grown more and more nervous. I didn't know what the letters meant nor if we'd address them when next we spoke. But the swooping tension in my middle told me I needed to gain control of the situation. Nearly a week of mounting strain meant that I could hardly still my fidgeting when faced with the prospect of Julian's eventual appearance tonight.

I'd been forcefully reminding myself to lower my very eager expectations when I spotted him in the crowd. His auburn hair gleamed in the candlelight and drew my eye. Julian looked every inch the polished gentleman—his gray-striped waistcoat was fashionable without being ostentatious. And his tailored black jacket accommodated his wide shoulders while his dark trousers hugged his muscular thighs. Julian was speaking with Drakefield and several other gentlemen. He hadn't noticed me and seemed absorbed in the discussion.

I didn't realize I'd stopped walking until Patty threaded her arm through mine and said softly, "Come. I see Emery and Mary talking to Tabitha. We'll join them."

Nodding, I allowed my sister to guide me around the dance floor, passing the musicians and the candelabras and the elaborate flower arrangements to where the Countess of Drakefield was holding court.

Tabitha Mooneyham was a contradiction. She was a petite woman nearing forty years of age. Her lovely features remained unlined save for the signs of a lifetime of joy creasing the delicate skin near her eyes. Tabitha was quiet and soft-spoken and yet she told raucous stories and inappropriate jokes that entertained nearly everyone, save for the staunchest of matrons. Mary and my sisters had been well acquainted with the countess for years. She'd been kind to me as a result.

"My darlings! How lovely of you to attend." Tabitha greeted Patty and myself in turn with genuine enthusiasm. "I was just telling Mary and Emery that the key to a pleasant event is to schedule it before the start of the season."

We all laughed as a footman bearing a tray of refreshment offered us glasses of champagne.

"It's true," she asserted happily after a sip from her glass. "There is nothing quite like being able to breathe in a ballroom without getting your skirts crushed by two hundred guests. I find I am not the hostess I once was, ladies. I've lost my patience for entertaining the masses. I find I'd simply rather entertain myself."

"I'll drink to that," Emery agreed.

While the ladies continued extolling the virtues of less crowded events, I brushed a hand down the waist of my pale yellow gown. My skin felt warm and tight. I sipped my champagne and noted how the bubbles burst brightly along my tongue. When I could fight the pull no longer, I glanced to the group of well-dressed men standing opposite. They were still conversing and Julian hadn't looked away from those assembled.

I was relieved that he'd been included on the guest list this evening. It meant that his efforts with Drakefield's set were going well, and that meant good things for Julian and the farm. Seeing him included in their conversation now, nodding along and chiming in to whatever was being discussed, only increased the odds of his success.

What felt like an hour later, Emery and Augie had gone off to dance. Tabitha was circulating and greeting her guests. Mary was in search of the ladies' retiring room. Silas had yet to make an appearance. And that left only Patty standing sentry at my side.

Drakefield was moving between circles with Julian in tow, making introductions. He hadn't looked in my direction once.

Disappointment settled its weight upon me, stooping my shoulders and dragging my gaze to the wooden floor beneath my jeweled slippers. I didn't know why I was being so dramatic. Nothing had really changed. I'd received a few letters. Julian and I were friends again. That didn't mean he was obligated to approach me just because we were attending the same event. He was busy. Jules had an agenda, the success of which depended on his ability to gain access to certain social circles here in London. There was no point feeling rejected or some such nonsense.

"Would you prefer to leave?" Patty's quiet voice drew my attention to her concerned face.

"No, of course not. Don't be silly," I said around a smile my lips couldn't quite commit to.

I felt ridiculous. Here I was getting my hopes up, and reading too much into those letters. Perhaps it was a kindness that I'd never received responses from Julian all those years ago. They would have done nothing but encouraged my fanciful imaginings, when Julian had been right all along. Our lives had diverged down two very distinct paths. I would have been broken-hearted no matter what.

"I think I'm just in a foul mood tonight. I'm sorry, Patty."

"*You* needn't be sorry," she replied pointedly with a glare aimed in Julian's direction.

I sighed and followed her angry stare. "My expectations are foolish and entirely my own."

She said nothing.

I sighed again. "Patty, I need you to give Julian a chance." Finally, her scowl lessened and she turned to face me. "I know you are my fiercest supporter, but there is no blame to be placed. Jules doesn't deserve your ire for my benefit. It's misdirected and noticeable. Even Franny has remarked on your dislike for him."

Patty appeared contrite at the mention of her daughter. "I will do better. I can't promise friendliness, but I will make an honest effort."

Sisterly warmth and devotion filled me up. "I'm not asking for much. Simply allow your facial features to relax in his presence. No need to sear the flesh from his bones."

She allowed a small twist of her lips. "Well, if you're sure."

"Quite sure," I replied with a grin of my own.

I caught sight of Drakefield introducing Julian to an elderly earl and his three sons. Julian's handshake and smile were polite but I could see the weariness behind his eyes. He'd done quite a lot of socializing this night. I couldn't imagine he was used to participating in so much conversation.

These were the appropriate thoughts of friendship. Seeing someone you cared about and worrying over them. Not the nervous flutter I'd experienced when I thought of encountering Julian tonight. And certainly not the eager expectation brought on by the letters I'd received. I'd invented intentions where there were clearly none present.

I should focus on being a good friend to Julian, and stop my ridiculous imaginings.

A figure stepped in my field of vision, blocking Julian from view.

"Your Grace. Lady Genevieve, good evening. I hope you both are well," Mr. Aaron Belham greeted with a warm smile and a short bow for both Patty and myself.

"Yes, thank you, Mr. Belham." I smiled. "I trust you are enjoying yourself tonight."

"Indeed, Lady Genevieve. I was hoping I could steal your dear sister away for a dance." He said this to Patty who spared me a quick glance before inclining her head.

"Of course, Mr. Belham. While I can surely spare Genevieve, the decision is hers, I'm afraid."

I fought a smile. Patty didn't appreciate high-handed males.

"Right you are, madam," he replied with his ever-present smile, unbothered by her subtle rebuke. Turning to me, he held out an elegant gloved hand. "Lady Genevieve, would you do me the honor of joining me for the next dance?"

So quickly it could hardly be noted, my gaze flickered to Julian—still absorbed in his conversation—before I mustered up a genuine smile for the handsome man who actually sought my attention. "Nothing would please me more."

Placing my hand in his, Mr. Belham led me to the dance floor as others rushed to take their places. Experience made my steps precise as the music guided our movements. My partner maintained his pleasant expression. My face must have been arranged in some semblance of agreeability because no one frowned or shouted in alarm. I couldn't really say. I found I was distracted and unfocused. And I did not want to consider why.

Our dance finally ended and Mr. Belham delivered me back to Patty who was now joined by Emery and Mary. Pleasantries were exchanged all around, and Mr. Belham excused himself without promises to call or see me soon. Perhaps my inattention was more obvious than I thought. Or mayhap he had no intention of growing our acquaintance.

"Gen, are you all right?" Emery asked, pulling me out of my internal musings.

"Yes!" I replied brightly, taking in her worried frown. "Did Silas ever manage to make his grand entrance?" I asked, hoping the change of topic would divert my perceptive sister.

Mary rolled her eyes. "Ah, yes. Your brother finally deigned to grace us all with his presence. He's talking with Drakefield and the others now."

And sure enough, my eyes found Silas laughing jovially across the way. He was with Drakefield and Miles and Augie. And standing shoulder to shoulder with my brother, was Julian. He wasn't laughing so openly but his face remembered the shape of a smile. I was standing too far away to know what they were saying, but I saw Silas slap Julian affably on the back. I just *knew* he was trying not to roll his eyes at my brother's theatrics.

My sisters were listening as Mary complained about Silas. He didn't even need to be within earshot to irritate her. Under normal circumstances, I found their battling to be endlessly amusing, but tonight I simply felt tired, my foolish heart a little bruised.

I'd let my active imagination build up this entire evening, only to have Julian, once again, forget I exist. Shaking my head ruefully, I thought about the moments until Patty and Miles would be ready to go back home. In a short while, I'd get out of these shoes and this dress and take a deep breath for the first time all week. Perhaps I'd write for a while upon our return. I did my best writing at night when the house was silent and my thoughts had room to emerge.

I was well within my own thoughts when I glanced up. Musicians still played as the sounds of one hundred guests spoke and moved about the ballroom. But it was difficult to focus on anything but the way Julian Moore was watching me. It seemed I'd finally caught his attention, and the weight of it kept me rooted to the floor.

My heartbeat sped. I could feel it in my throat, and I knew instinctively that if I attempted to speak, my voice would waver with the pounding of my heart.

Julian's intense focus pinned me in place, those gray eyes answering a hundred questions while asking a hundred more. While I couldn't claim to know every part of this man, at one time I'd known him better than anyone. Julian's stare was an acknowledgement—one I'd sought all night long. His letters had found their way to me with purpose and meaning. I could see it all over his face.

And I had no doubt what he was reading on mine.

I'd mourned the loss of Julian for years. Devotion didn't just die because you felt like you had. I'd taken my pain and my anger and my love and poured it into hundreds of letters that had gone undelivered.

The prospect of their reply now felt dangerous and unwieldy. But it also made the fearless, foolish young girl I'd once been awaken.

She slowly unfurled from where she'd been tucked carefully away in a carved wooden box.

Eight

JULIAN

After so much socializing at the Drakefield event the evening prior, I was reluctant to make plans with Basilton. But Miles seemed to think I should remain relevant in the public eye rather than retreat the way I wanted.

So, I'd grudgingly saddled Brutus mid-morning and brought Graceling with me to Cawthorn Hall. The temperamental mare could use a bit of exercise, and truthfully, I'd wanted Genevieve to see her.

When I'd written to Gen about the horses and mentioned that we should go riding, the invitation had been offhand and vague. It was true that I wanted the horse and the woman to be acquainted, but there had been no forethought behind it.

But when Basilton had invited me to go riding in Hyde Park today with him and Miss Francesca, I found I wanted to include Genevieve and introduce her to Graceling. She might be busy or uninterested in joining us, but I liked the idea of spending time with her—attempting friendship as we'd agreed.

I couldn't say what compelled me to pull out pen and paper every morning, and start my day with a letter to Genevieve. It was true that I owed her a response—many of them. But sometimes it felt easier to talk to her this way, with my thoughts neatly organized on the page. When she wasn't standing in front of me with her light brown hair and her enormous blue eyes, I could think rationally. I could see beyond her anger and her bitterness and ignore the hurt and the unease she wore so openly.

So the letters had continued.

I hadn't known what to say last night at Drakefield's. Truthfully, I'd been so consumed with introductions and polite conversation that I could do little more than glance in Genevieve's direction all evening. And the possibility that she'd draw attention to the letters I'd sent in the last week seemed mortifying.

I wasn't ready to explain why. Hell, I didn't understand it myself. And I definitely could not admit the truth of our past—that my own mother had deceived us both and that all three hundred and eighty-two of her letters were sorted and carefully concealed in my rooms at the boardinghouse. It would strain everything between us again, perhaps to the point of breaking.

Genevieve was newly back in my life. When I cast aside the undeserved bitterness, I could admit how much I'd missed her. At one time, she'd been the most important person to me. Having her back while I was in London would be a good thing.

I could ignore all the changes. Pay no mind to the way she'd looked last night in her glowing gown—all curvaceous lines and soft skin. I could even overlook the odd tightness I'd felt when she'd been dancing with that grinning buffoon.

My thoughts would remain friendly and we wouldn't discuss the letters. I could stop sending them whenever I felt like it.

With the sun on my face, I approached the stables behind the grand Mayfair manor, unsure if I should wait there or pass the horses off to a groom while I went up to the house. But the decision was made for me when I saw Basilton and Franny walking out with their mounts. The earl guided a brown stallion and Franny led a smaller dun pony who snuffled affectionately at the girl's dark curls.

Franny smiled at my approach and Miles waved a hand in greeting.

Just as I pulled Brutus to a stop in the yard, Genevieve emerged from the stable. "Am I riding her, then?"

That was it. No greeting. No welcome. And the overwhelming familiarity of it nearly made me smile. So much had changed between us, but some things were just the same.

"If you can handle her," I stated, knowing it would earn me a scowl. "I suppose you're welcome to try."

Genevieve's eyes narrowed at my words and I fought another grin as she approached.

"She's gorgeous!" Franny called as I dismounted.

It was true. Graceling was a striking dappled gray with a pale mane and tail to match. She stood sixteen hands and drew attention wherever she went, but the horse was a menace. She took to certain people and snapped at others. Her willingness to work was determined by who was on her back and she was only growing more particular with age. I wouldn't let the young girl near the horse until I could gauge the mare's reaction to our company this morning.

I'd teased Gen in my letter about being able to handle Graceling, but something told me that she and the horse would suit.

Before Gen reached us, I walked around Brutus and made to check the girth on Graceling's saddle, but to the horse, I whispered, "Be good, Grace." It was a fool's hope that she would listen, but I had to try. Genevieve was likely too stubborn to ignore the challenge the horse presented. And I didn't want Gen to get bitten or thrown for her trouble.

Graceling flicked her ears in Genevieve's direction as her boots brought her closer. The horse raised her head and regarded the woman standing before her in a riding dress and dark blue cape.

I moved to stand next to Miles and Franny while the two got acquainted.

"What are they doing?" the girl whispered.

I kept my eyes on Genevieve but replied, "Getting to know one another. Graceling is an acquired taste, I'm afraid."

"That's alright," Gen said from over her shoulder, "so am I."

The mischievous grin she shot me had a sudden bolt of heat traveling down my spine. Some depraved and confused part of me wondered just what those pink lips would taste like.

Shaking off that inconvenient imagining, I watched as the mare extended her nose toward Genevieve, apparently having deemed her new acquaintance acceptable. Genevieve stroked her gently before giving me a triumphant grin.

"It seems you have been found worthy," I said. But it was my answering smile that claimed, *I told you so.*

Her gaze caught on my smug grin before rising to meet my eyes, and there it was again. The same as last night. The prolonged awareness in her stare, the intensity of which acknowledged something more happening between us.

The letters.

A secret.

A confession.

Written in ink and signed by my hand.

I swallowed and fought the urge to look away. But Basilton chose that moment to say, "Good, now we can be on our way and get Mr. Moore in front of the masses."

Genevieve blinked and I cleared my throat.

"It is a surprisingly fine day for riding," Franny proclaimed as her father assisted her in mounting her horse. The sun was indeed shining on this October day. "Gen, where is your bonnet? You know Grandmother will have a fit if you arrive at Laurel Park next week with evidence of the sun on your skin."

Genevieve rolled her eyes. It was an old argument between the marchioness and her daughter. When we'd been young, Gen had been wild and willful, saying she liked my freckles and wanted the sun to give them to her too. If her nurse tied a bonnet beneath her defiant little chin, Genevieve would rip it right off her head as soon as we were out of doors. Later, it became a small rebellion that fondly exasperated the marchioness, and it brought a smile to my face remembering it now.

The sun never did give Genevieve an abundance of freckles, not like the ones that persisted across the bridge of my nose and the tops of my cheekbones in the warmer months. Her pale English skin had simply turned a rosy shade of pink during our adventures in the forest or the wildflower field behind Laurel Park.

With a happy sigh, Gen said, "I'm not wearing a bonnet, Franny. And a hat will just fly off when you and I race together."

The young girl grinned.

With a few more affectionate strokes down Graceling's neck, Genevieve finally turned to where I was standing. "Well, are you ready?"

I nodded despite the odd feelings swirling within. The memories and the reminders were competing with the strangeness of joining this unusual family unit for a Saturday stroll in Hyde Park. I knew that Basilton was invested in the success of the farm. And I even knew that his efforts leaned more toward kindness than financial gain. But I still felt ill at ease parading myself and my horses around to impress these aristocrats. The discomfort could be tied to many things: accepting aid from Miles and the rest of the Bartholomews, the sort of pain that only came from rigorous social interaction . . .

And perhaps even the realization that I wanted to be here—spending time with Genevieve, getting to know her once again.

"So, how did your socializing go with Drakefield? Any interested parties from all those introductions?"

I shot Genevieve a look but she kept her gaze studiously forward. I wondered at all she'd noticed the evening prior.

"Drakefield's support has been beneficial. I have meetings set up early in the week with several gentlemen interested in buying. And I'm to be a guest at his club the day after tomorrow so I can continue my efforts."

Our horses walked side by side as Miles and Franny pulled ahead of us. The well-dressed crowds were out enjoying the mild weather in the park. Families congregated for picnics, and gentlemen and ladies promenaded in an effort to see and be seen.

I suppose I could count myself among the latter. My presence here was to make a name for myself as the guest of the Earl of Basilton. The public spectacle had the added benefit of engaging curiosity, which seemed important here in London.

I offered a nod and a tip of my hat to the gentleman approaching in the opposite direction. We'd been introduced last night but I couldn't remember his name.

"That's Baron Oglethorpe," Genevieve whispered just as the young man in question noted our presence.

His eyes lit in recognition and he brought his horse closer. "Mr. Moore! Good to see you out and about."

"Lord Oglethorpe, good day," I greeted with a quick glance to a smug-looking Genevieve.

The baron smiled happily. "And, Lady Genevieve, how do you do?"

"I'm well. Thank you, my lord," she said, beaming in his direction.

Pleasantries were exchanged as well as comments on the agreeable weather before Oglethorpe bid me to call on him soon to discuss business.

When we were on our way down the gravel path once more, I turned to find Genevieve already looking my way, a knowing grin twisting her lovely pink lips.

I forced myself to meet her blue gaze. "Thank you for the save."

"I could see the panic on your face." She chuckled.

"Well, I knew it was Ogle-something."

"So close," she teased. "It's a good thing you have me."

"It was one name, Gen. I wouldn't go that far."

She raised one dark brow in accusation. "Perhaps I'll ride on ahead with Franny and Miles and let you fend for yourself."

We stared at each other, and just like old times, I rolled my eyes at her challenge and capitulated. "Fine. Stay. Whisper in my ear and keep me from embarrassing myself."

Genevieve's arrogant expression faltered just a bit and her cheeks went pink before she focused resolutely on the path before us.

I replayed my words. Having her close, whispering in my ear might not be the best course of action. Now I was thinking of her lips again. I shifted uncomfortably in the saddle.

"What is it like in Leicester?" Genevieve asked suddenly. "Your life there."

I didn't know how to answer that. Her tone held accusation. I could hear it in the way she approached the edge of politeness without going all the way over. She wanted to know if I was happy in the place that had stolen me. The answer was as complicated as the question.

Clearing my throat, I finally settled on, "I've always enjoyed the countryside. It's beautiful there. And I like training and caring for the animals. It has been a challenge with my uncle's health and so much responsibility falling on me unexpectedly. But that's part of why I'm here."

I thought of all the things I hadn't said: that Leicester wasn't home the way Laurel Park had always been and how my life at

Brightleaf consisted mainly of work from sunup to sundown. It felt like a betrayal to the farm and my uncle to admit such things.

Genevieve watched me closely, but in the end, simply nodded.

"Did Miss Francesca say you were returning to Laurel Park soon?" I wondered at the comment back at the stables. I had been under the impression that Gen was remaining in London for the season.

"Oh, yes. We're all traveling back to Hampshire to visit with Mama and Papa before the season is fully underway. They insisted upon a small birthday celebration for me." She said this shyly, as if unwilling to remind me of the day. It was difficult to forget. We'd shared celebrations growing up as our birthdays were but a week apart. Apple cake for me and blancmange for Genevieve. I hadn't had apple cake in years. "And Miles has a building project he wants to review with his land manager before work begins at their country estate."

I nodded.

"But we don't leave for another week," she rushed to added, hands tight on the reins. "Perhaps you'll join us for supper before we go? Or we could go for another ride if the weather holds?"

I opened my mouth to respond, to say I would like that. But Genevieve hurried to say, "But you are welcome to refuse. I know you will be busy with meetings and Drakefield and the horses need to be exercised, of course—"

"Gen," I interrupted. "That would be fine. I shall come to supper at Cawthorn Hall whenever you like."

"Really?" she asked, hopeful in a way that had something going tight beneath my ribs.

I smiled. "Yes, of course. I'm happy to avoid the boardinghouse in the evening."

Genevieve grinned in return. "Because of the feline-obsessed proprietress?"

The pleasant day went quiet all of a sudden. The chirping birds and the clopping horse hooves faded away as Genevieve referenced something I'd only ever told her in a letter. It felt like a secret had been shouted to a roomful of people instead of the innocent question she'd posed to me and me alone.

The intimacy of my written thoughts spoken aloud had my cheeks going hot. I found I could not meet her gaze nor the happy smile that was ever so slowly fading from her face.

"I would enjoy dining at Cawthorn Hall with you and your family," I repeated while completely ignoring the last words she'd spoken.

"You're welcome any time," she stated woodenly.

I closed my eyes, angry with myself and my cowardice. I was being ridiculous. She'd done nothing wrong.

I turned to Gen and opened my mouth, intent on apologizing when she leaned close and whispered, "Viscount Grovewood."

I blinked at the name before noticing the man himself approaching.

She'd saved me yet again.

Our eyes held.

"Thank you, Gen," I murmured before Grovewood joined us.

The remainder of the morning passed much in this manner. Genevieve would whisper names of other gentlemen in my ear and I would ignore her warm breath on my cheek and the shape of the words on her lips. She called upon her elegant manners and kept these conversations going when my own abilities failed me and talking became a trial. Gen even boasted the fine mare she was riding and how the stock at Brightleaf Farms was superior to all others.

We shared secret smiles and teasing when the gentlemen were well out of earshot. I had Genevieve Bartholomew to thank for the success of the outing.

An hour later, when we'd returned to the stables at Cawthorn Hall, Miles passed off their horses to a waiting groom and followed Franny into the house with a smile. I hopped down from Brutus and assisted Genevieve off her mount in the quiet of the yard.

Graceling saw fit to shift around as soon as Genevieve's boots touched the ground. Gen yelped as the horse's flank made contact, pushing her forward and into my arms.

I pulled her close, my hands curving around her shoulders, tucking her against my chest and out of range of the poorly behaved horse. We stayed like that for a moment, Genevieve's forehead resting on my cheek and the only thing between us the sounds of our rapid breaths.

She felt warm and soft pressed against me, and I fought the strange urge to run my hands down her back and up into her long hair. The scent of citrus from her skin enveloped me and I breathed her in.

"I think I can stand," she managed, voice uneven.

I loosened my hold incrementally until Genevieve was upright under her own volition, but she didn't step away and neither did I.

We were still close—so close I could see the striations in her impossibly blue eyes.

"Grace is a menace. I apologize for her behavior," I whispered the words.

"It's no trouble," she answered, a little breathlessly.

My gaze snagged on her lips.

I could still feel the warmth of her body where all her soft curves had pressed against my chest. The lingering sensation was nothing compared to the heat filling my blood. I couldn't explain away the impropriety of my thoughts. This was attraction, pure and simple. But it had been brought about by Genevieve—my friend.

At two and twenty, I was familiar with desire but I wasn't overwhelmed by experience with women. My responsibilities and the life I led didn't afford me the time and opportunity for a mistress. And as a respected business owner, my uncle wouldn't abide anything less for me than a wife. I didn't dally with women my age because I wasn't looking to marry. There had been a few quick and eager encounters with a widow in the village near the farm, but by and large, my own hand saw to my needs.

But in this moment, I wanted to pull Genevieve back to me, feel her again and find out what those teasing pink lips tasted like.

She was my friend. We were trying to reclaim what had been lost to us. I shouldn't be feeling this way. It would ruin this very fragile new beginning.

However, I found it difficult to ignore my confusing and conflicting musings about the woman before me. So much had changed between us, and it was changing still.

I wondered if Genevieve had been well and truly kissed—beyond her girlhood exploration with the insufferable James Madigan. I found myself selfishly hoping she had not. I had no right to these wayward and rebellious thoughts churning within, but with the memory of her warm body pressed to mine, it was easy to forget what was proper.

Genevieve finally said very softly, "Just don't tell anyone I made that embarrassing sound when Graceling shoved me over."

My lips quirked and I finally dragged my gaze away from her tempting lips, muttering quietly, "I make no promises."

"Why are you whispering?" she asked, the words barely there on her tongue.

"I don't know. Why are *you* whispering?" I retorted.

Our grins were matching until Graceling chose that moment to put her pale gray nose over Genevieve's shoulder, eager for attention. Gen's eyes widened at the unexpected contact and I laughed, pulling her to the side and moving to pat the horse's neck.

"I think she likes you," I told Genevieve at normal volume, my amusement lingering even as I fought to control the overwhelming way my body had responded to hers.

Genevieve's gaze was steady as she reached to rub the mare's velvet nose. "I think I like her too."

The dream startled me awake just before dawn.

I'd been in a state of gasping, floundering confusion as I sat up abruptly, the orange cat tumbling from my chest. The animal sent me an affronted glare before hopping onto the tufted armchair by the long-cold fireplace and curling up to sleep once more. But I could not find it within myself to settle.

With concentrated effort, I slowed my ragged breathing before flopping back down onto the bed.

I stared at the ceiling, just barely discernible in the dim gray light.

The dream was loosening its hold, already going fuzzy at the edges. But one thing had been very clear . . . Genevieve Bartholomew—grinning at me and whispering in my ear. We'd been on horseback together. Her backside nestled tightly against me while I'd wrapped my arms around her, holding her close. The surroundings were unclear and even the words our dream selves had spoken were now indistinguishable. But I could hear her laughter—still feel it vibrating against my front.

Now, in my rented rooms, I closed my eyes and placed a staying hand over my bare chest, feeling the thrum of my blood pounding in my veins and the rapid beat of my heart. The echo of her happiness, a tangible thing.

In the dream, I'd taken Genevieve's long brown hair and swept it over one shoulder to place a slow, wet kiss to her neck. She'd made a pleased sound in her throat. I licked my lips recalling the taste of her and catching the scent of lemons on her skin. The memory of it had me glancing down the length of my body. My cock still tented the bedlinens. My discomfort and the confusion of the dream going absolutely nowhere.

With a shaky hand, I palmed my erection and squeezed. My breath gusted out on an impatient sigh remembering the feel of Genevieve pressed against me—both the dream version and the real one.

I closed my eyes and worked myself roughly, searching for relief and understanding amid the muddle of my thoughts. But all I found was overwhelming pleasure when my release seared down my spine, feeling Genevieve's phantom breath in my ear and the illusion of her body under my hands.

My breath was ragged and out of control again. I attempted to wipe away my embarrassment along with the mess on my chest and stomach. I shouldn't have . . .

Thinking about Genevieve while I'd pleasured myself had been wrong.

Hadn't it been wrong?

She was my friend. It was undoubtedly improper to envision her gorgeous blue eyes looking at me with longing. To want to feel her lips whispering sweet words against the shell of my ear. To imagine the feel of her rounded backside tight against my cock.

How could I look at her after what I'd done?

But it hadn't felt degrading and shameful in the moment. I'd felt nothing but warmth and affection. The dream hadn't been a filthy deliberate imagining—peeling off clothes and taking something she'd never offered. It had been companionship and caring and surprisingly innocent touches.

I didn't know why I suddenly found the idea of horseback rides and sweet kisses with Genevieve Bartholomew a temptation.

But I knew I needed to get it under control.

We were in each other's lives for the time being. She was a lady, and I was the furthest thing from an appropriate match for the daughter of a marquess. Gen deserved a respectable husband, not a horse trainer. Not the son of her housekeeper. And not someone who would be forced to walk away.

Nine

GENEVIEVE

Miles was looking decidedly uneasy across the breakfast table. I could tell he wanted to talk to me, but hadn't yet bucked up the courage. Patty and Franny ate their meal, untroubled.

My brother-in-law met my gaze briefly and cleared his throat. I raised my eyebrows expectantly, but Miles looked panicked and glanced away.

With suppressed amusement, I finally asked, "All right, Miles. What is it?"

He appeared unbearably flustered and unable to speak. This was so unlike him. Miles had charm for days and he rarely second-guessed himself this way.

Franny piped up helpfully from my side, "Just ask her, Papa. It will be all right."

After a deep breath, Miles managed, "I wanted to invite Mr. Moore to accompany us to Laurel Park. But I realize that may be difficult for you—to have him there in your home again. So, I shall refrain from asking, if you are in any way uncomfortable. I am eager for his opinion on the stable construction and thought to utilize his expertise before building begins."

There were several emotions tumbling within as Miles spoke. We were set to depart London in four days' time. Seeing Julian back at Laurel Park would be . . . complicated. But not insurmountable.

To the quiet of the dining room, I said, "That would be acceptable. We've been perfectly cordial in recent memory. I don't see any reason that Mr. Moore should not be extended an invitation."

Miles and Patty shared a look.

I didn't know what that was about, but what I'd said was true. Julian and I had been getting along exceedingly well. In the last week alone, we'd shared a productive and pleasant horseback ride through Hyde Park. Ignoring the fact that I fell into his arms and nearly kissed him, of course. And in the days since, Julian had joined us here at Cawthorn Hall for supper. I was still receiving his letters—friendly and informative in nature. Patty had been on her best behavior, even going so far as to engage Julian in pleasant conversation. Franny was growing more and more besotted with every visit. And he and Miles were developing a close friendship.

"See, Papa. Nothing to fret over," Franny offered happily around a bite of eggs. "We'll have a lovely time in the country for our short visit."

"If you're sure, Genevieve?" Miles attempted one last time.

Smiling reassuringly, I replied, "Quite sure. As Franny said, we'll have a lovely stay in Hampshire. I'm sure of it."

Everything was well in hand.

I could compartmentalize my lovesick adolescent memories and current problematic feelings. I would continue focusing my energy on remaining friendly.

If I had to ignore my wildly beating heart and inappropriate thoughts about Julian's thighs, then that was my own problem.

"Miles asked me to accompany your party to Laurel Park," Julian said later that day.

We were walking in the gardens behind Cawthorn Hall as Franny played with her dog nearby. Julian had plans with Miles and Silas at their club that evening and had come by the house early at my brother-in-law's request.

The October breeze ruffled my hair, but at least it wasn't raining.

I tightened my shawl tighter around my shoulders. "Oh, did he? That is exciting news."

Julian cast me a sidelong look, his lips quirking. "You already knew he was going to ask."

I bit my lip, finally admitting, "Perhaps. Did you accept?"

His gaze returned to the path before us, and he said nothing for a moment. We headed left along the tall hedge border of the grounds. I could hear Daisy barking behind us and Franny trying to entice her with a stick.

"It seemed important to him that I come. I owe the earl a great deal for all he's done for me here in London."

I frowned and stopped walking. "It's not payment for services, Julian. You needn't feel obligated to accept. You're not in anyone's debt. Miles has done nothing more than make introductions and welcome you into his home."

Julian sighed and turned back to face me where I stood rooted in the middle of the path. "It's more than that, Gen, and you know it. No one would take a meeting with me before Basilton interceded on my behalf. Believe me, I tried on my own and got absolutely nowhere. He's placed his reputation on the line for me." He looked away. "I feel like an overgrown ward. Or charity. Again."

I stomped up to him, forcing him to meet my gaze. "You have never once been taken in out of pity or obligation or any other such nonsense. Miles has a vested interest in Brightleaf Farms. Consider it business, if that makes it easier to swallow. But he genuinely enjoys your company, Julian. As much as you try to deny it, you have a history with the Bartholomews. You're— you're like family to us. It's not a trial to have you at our table," I finished quietly while his brilliant gray eyes searched my face. Uncomfortable with what I'd admitted, I added, "Except for your atrocious manners when you chew with your mouth open. Then it becomes rather annoying."

His dark auburn brows lowered in irritation before he rolled his eyes at my sudden teasing. "I think we both know whose comportment at the dinner table is inferior. You refused to use your linen napkin until you were at least eleven."

"I still stand by the fact that it was inefficient to wipe my mouth after every bite, Mr. Etiquette. It made much more sense to wait until the end of the meal," I argued, while also fighting a smile.

Sometimes our shared history was a steady ache and other times it was a painful spasm, sudden and sharp. And yet, lately it was wistful and warm, loosening a tight knot that lived behind my ribs.

We still stood staring at one another. I felt the need to say, "Come with us to Laurel Park because you want to. Not because you feel like you should."

Julian nodded, holding an arm out for me as we resumed our stroll. "It might be nice to return."

"Mama and Papa would be thrilled to see you. Mrs. Pennyworth would make all your favorites, I have no doubt."

Another fork in the path had us angling back across the grounds. The silence between us was mostly comfortable when my thoughts didn't get in the way. Like how warm and solid Julian's body was at my side.

With concerted effort, I asked, "Would the horses be all right were you to go away?"

Julian nodded. "There is a stable hand at the boardinghouse who I'm on good terms with. He would see to the care and exercise of the horses. But I would bring Brutus with me."

I smiled. "Because he is your favorite."

Quickly realizing my mistake, I held my breath, fearful that Julian would become tense or awkward at the mention of something he'd written in his letters. I'd learned my lesson last time after drawing attention to the—apparently—secret correspondence. Julian clearly wanted to avoid the topics therein and any acknowledgement of the letters he continued to send on a daily basis.

It had not been my intent to reference them now. It had been a slip—an unfortunate mistake. I fought the sadness and disquiet associated with being Julian's secret—one he couldn't even admit to himself.

But the moment tripped by with a gust of autumn wind. Finally, Julian admitted softly, "Yes, because Brutus is my favorite."

Inwardly, I breathed a sigh of relief.

Our meandering walk through the gardens brought us around to the large stone fountain. Julian pulled us to a stop and simply stood watching the bubbling cascade of water that flowed down the central platforms before splashing into the circular pool.

I noticed his attention was focused on the water but he wore a rather large smile, and I knew exactly what he was remembering.

With an irritated huff, I said, "Go ahead. I know you want to."

Julian's laughter burst out of him, a deep rumble that had him leaning back slightly and placing a hand to his trim stomach. His hand clutched uselessly at the gray fabric of his waistcoat.

His laughter had always been contagious. It was so rare and precious from the serious and practical Julian that it was impossible to ignore his joy.

I shook my head, fighting my own amusement. "Perhaps I should shove you in a fountain and see how humorous you think it is."

That only made him laugh harder.

With righteous indignation flaring, I turned to leave him in the bloody garden, but he snagged my hand and pulled me back around.

Face still bright and happy, he sounded hardly apologetic when he said, "Come back. I'm sorry."

"You're not!" I scolded.

"I am," he managed between residual chuckles, still holding my hand. "But you didn't see it, Gen. Augie helped you out of the water and you had your head held high. It was like watching the Queen exit a fountain."

I let my gaze wander to the water. "I suppose you were at least polite at the time. Not like Silas bent over and behaving like the absolute worst."

When I turned back, Julian was looking down the length of my body. Perhaps he could recall the wet and bedraggled mess I'd been that day, over a month ago. But when his gray eyes finally managed to meet my own, his cheeks were pink.

He cleared his throat. "That's true. I could have been as ill-mannered as Silas."

"I *had* to hold my head high. I was mortified."

"Why?" He frowned. "It was just a small gathering. And mostly family in attendance."

I looked at him incredulously and then huffed an exasperated laugh at how oblivious he was. "Perhaps, Julian, I did not want the first time I'd seen you in seven years to be when I was thrown into a fountain. I was embarrassed and—and soggy. Not my finest moment."

There were layers to my statement. Honesty, bold and bright. And something vulnerable and desperate beneath. An admission. A wanting.

"Genevieve," Julian said softly, squeezing my gloved hand still within his warm grasp. "I'm sorry about what happened in the garden. And . . . just now. I should not have laughed at your expense."

"It's all right," I said, waving away his apology and the way my heart was picking up pace. "Now that I have some distance from the event and some dry clothes, I can see that it was humorous. If it had happened to Emery, I would definitely be laughing."

Julian grinned, just a small, apologetic twist of his lips. And then his eyes lowered, catching my own smile and putting it in his pocket. That was the way it felt. Like he snatched my amused grin and took it for himself. Savoring it. Cherishing it.

I licked my lips reflexively under his attention. And it was like that time back in the stables—days ago—when I'd been drawn too close to a dangerous flame. The pull of my attraction had lengthened the moment, and my body had betrayed me, seeking Julian's warmth and safety. And then I'd been left in the cold when he'd retreated.

This moment burned bright with temptation, but Julian wasn't pulling away this time. In fact, his body was leaning in, all heat and broad shoulders.

Julian took the hand he was still holding and placed it on his chest as our bodies came flush together. When the space between us closed on a whispered breath, his nose brushed softly against mine. I felt my mouth part on a surprised inhale as his eyes closed and his lips met mine.

The kiss was soft and sweet, his upper lip slotting neatly between mine. His hand came up to cradle my jaw and angle my face for his ministrations. The movement deepened our connection and I felt myself shift forward. I made an involuntary sound at the contact, something embarrassingly like a moan. Julian's arm tightened around my waist, anchoring me to him and this moment, lest I become untethered and float away.

My lips parted as Julian's tongue traced the edge of my lower lip. I darted my own tongue out, eager to tease and taste. It was his turn to make a surprised sound low in his throat. The kiss turned from sweet and soft to deep and drugging. I clutched the lapels of his jacket, needing him closer, deeper, harder.

Just . . . *needing*.

The sudden sound of Daisy's barking nearby followed by Franny's breathless laughter had reality washing over us as if I'd tumbled into the fountain once more. Julian pulled himself away from me so quickly that my long hair shifted forward over one shoulder from where his hand had snaked beneath and cradled the base of my skull.

We stood a foot apart, staring at each other as Franny chased her dog around the base of the fountain, paying us absolutely no mind.

My breathing was ragged as I took in Julian's hair, ravaged by my hand and his cheeks flushed pink. I could not begin to say what I looked like in the aftermath of our affections, but I feared I wore my very eager heart upon my sleeve for this man and all the world to see.

Julian blinked as if waking from a dream. He swallowed and looked down to the stone pavers beneath our feet before saying so quietly I had to strain to hear him over the gurgling water, "I should go. That was . . . I should go."

I made no allowances for his departure. I didn't nod my agreement or bid him farewell.

I remained quiet and watchful, refusing to ease his discomfort.

He met my unrelenting gaze once more before repeating, "I should go."

And this time he meant it. Because he turned on his heel and strode across the patio and into the house.

I sat heavily on the edge of the fountain wondering why I couldn't be within three feet of the damned thing without making a fool of myself.

"Gen, you cannot hide in the nursery with the children."

"I'm not hiding," I said without looking up from my truly horrific drawing of sunflowers. "And be quiet. You'll wake the baby."

Beckett was in his crib with his nurse nearby in the rocking chair. Little Reeve was sitting beside me at the children's table, using the charcoal to create a small masterpiece. She must have inherited her artistic abilities from her mother.

"He's a sound sleeper," Emery said simply, coming closer to where I sat with her daughter.

I still didn't look up from the paper.

My sister's emerald skirts entered my field of vision and she was quiet a moment. "Is that . . . supposed to be a . . . lamppost?"

Finally giving her my attention, I glared. "It is a sunflower, if you must know."

Emery's blond eyebrows rose in surprise but she wisely kept quiet.

Reeve giggled before saying in her sweet voice, "It's all right, Auntie Gen. Mama can help you. She taught me how to draw loads of things."

I scowled at my sister as she bit her lip to keep from laughing.

"That is true, my love. I'd be happy to help your auntie draw a . . . sunflower. But perhaps another time. She's expected downstairs and needs to visit with the other adults while you and Beckett play here with your nurse."

"Alright, Mama." My tiny niece had already gone back to her drawing, entirely indifferent to my presence here.

I, myself, was completely uninterested in attending this luncheon.

"Come, baby sister," Emery sang.

With a sigh, I dropped the charcoal to the small box that held the drawing supplies. I brushed my hands together to dispel the dust and rose to my feet. My sister leaned over and pressed a gentle kiss to her daughter's blond curls before hooking her arm through mine and tugging me toward the corridor.

"Tell me what has you hiding with the children."

I made my steps slow and beleaguered. "I don't want to be sociable. I don't want to see anyone."

Emery matched my pace. "Are you sure it's not just one someone you do not wish to see?"

I sighed remembering the kiss in the garden yesterday and the absence of a letter at the breakfast table this morning. It wasn't the kiss that caused my foul mood, it was the cowardly lips attached to it. If he was retreating, well then, dammit, so was I.

I didn't want to go downstairs and be expected to be polite with Julian and his confusing lips. I knew he would be in attendance because Miles had mentioned it on the short carriage ride over to Emery and Augie's home at Kendrick Manor. Therefore, upon arrival, I'd slipped upstairs and hidden in the nursery.

"You know, I never would have invited him if I thought you spurned his advances so thoroughly, Genevieve."

My sister's words had me pulling up short, her arm yanking me forward a step before she'd realized I'd paused. "Whose advances?"

Emery blinked. "Mr. Belham, of course."

"Mr. Belham is here?" I sounded distressed to my own ears. Then I realized my mistake at once.

"Yes . . . Who did you think I was referring to?"

I said nothing, my mind quickly scrambling for a less honest alternative.

My sister's eyes went round. "Wait! Who were you hiding from if you didn't even realize Mr. Belham was in attendance?"

Oh, Lord. Emery was like a hound on the hunt. She'd never let this go. I should just get it over with.

Sighing, I crossed my arms over my chest. "I was avoiding Julian," I replied very quietly.

"Why? I thought you two were getting along with one another?"

I bit my lip and looked everywhere but at my sister. "We may have shared a kiss."

Emery gasped dramatically, drawing my attention. "Why didn't you tell me?"

"I just did," I replied flatly.

She whacked me on the arm. "You know what I mean."

"Ow," I complained, rubbing the spot. "It only happened yesterday."

"And then what happened?"

I could not handle her exuberance. My emotions had vacillated wildly in the last twenty-four hours. First, I'd been angry at Julian's abandonment and withdrawal. And distraught that he had obviously regretted our kiss. For a very small time, I'd foolishly allowed myself to relive the moment and all the warmth and affection I'd felt. Then my mood had swung back around to angry where I'd remained all morning.

Burying my face in my hands, I mumbled, "We kissed and got interrupted by Franny. Then Julian ran away as fast as his boots could carry him."

Emery was quiet, so I peeked between my fingers.

She asked softly, "Did he say anything before he ran?"

I shook my head. "Just that he had to go."

"Did he kiss you or did you kiss him?"

I threw my hands out in exasperation. "Does it matter? We sort of . . . kissed each other."

My sister appeared thoughtful. "Genevieve, listen. He is probably feeling very confused. He's only ever seen you in the light of friendship. Something has shifted or altered his thinking and now he sees . . . possibilities. Give him time. I know it's difficult. You are impatient. You get that from me. But trust me when I say that sometimes men need time to think through new situations. Especially practical men who are not adept at change." I shifted on my feet, uneasy with her assessment. "Julian is a lot like Augie in many ways. Whatever he's feeling for you—and the kiss is evidence of that—has likely transformed his worldview. Give him a moment to regroup."

I nodded, knowing she was right. But just because he needed time to come to terms with whatever new feelings he may or may not be having, didn't mean that *I* did. I'd been waiting on Julian Moore a very long time.

That kiss had ignited something far more frightening than passion. It had sparked hope.

And it had started with his letters. It turned out that their arrival after seven years wasn't too late after all.

My foolish, foolish heart might not survive this.

Whatever expression I wore had Emery muttering "oh hell" and crossing to wrap me in her arms.

I hugged my sister as the vision of the hallway blurred beyond her shoulder.

"You don't have to come downstairs if you don't want to," she whispered. "But don't pull yourself away from him. Not out of misplaced embarrassment or shame or even spite. Let him see your strength and what he'd be a fool to live without."

Breathing deeply through my nose, I managed to keep the tears from falling. "Thank you, Em."

She pulled back, and held me at arm's length. "Any time, baby sister."

I blew out a breath that puffed my cheeks and nodded. "Let's go. I'm as ready as I'm going to get."

It turned out that I had missed the midday meal.

My sister and I arrived as visitors were mingling in the formal receiving room following their luncheon. Emery and I parted ways so she could play hostess.

The guest list had been fairly small for the duchess's gathering— under twenty people. But Augie had requested the event prior to our departure for the country and before he returned to Parliament in the coming weeks. Several influential members of the House of Lords were in attendance for Augie's purposes. I didn't see him in the room, which meant he and his fellow lords had retreated to his study for political discussion.

I caught sight of Julian chatting with Miles and Franny near the window in the farthest corner of the room.

Turning reflexively before I was spotted, I drifted among the guests, greeting those I recognized before finally settling at the side of Mary Lovelace.

"Emery tracked you down like a hound, did she?" Mary murmured for my ears alone.

"She did indeed."

"Your sister has a nose for that sort of thing," she said without malice. "And was she able to drag out of you the reason for your solitude?"

"She did indeed," I repeated.

Mary grinned at me. "Genevieve, you are the perfect combination of all your siblings. Has anyone ever told you that?"

I shook my head, fighting a smile. I enjoyed that assessment. "But only absorbing their finer points, correct?"

"Of course," she said easily. "You have Patty's fierce loyalty and independence. Emery's positivity and willfulness. And . . ." She paused here as if considering including Silas in her analysis.

"And, what exactly did I inherit from Silas?" I teased purposefully. I knew that my brother drove Mary to extremes.

"I suppose," she said reluctantly, "you've developed a bit of Silas's penchant for travel and his—his—humor."

With an obnoxiously toothy smile, I said, "Now, was it so difficult to pay Silas a compliment? He wasn't even nearby to overhear it."

"That," she said pointedly, "is the only reason I admitted it, and if you so much as breathe a word to your pigheaded brother, I will—"

"Breathe a word of what?" Silas asked delightedly from directly behind us causing both Mary and myself to jump a foot in the air. "Were you gossiping about me, Lady Mary? That is frightfully interesting."

Mary's startled expression quickly flattened. "A *lady* never gossips, Mr. Bartholomew."

Silas appeared endlessly amused at having caught us out. "My *lady*, I have a mother and three sisters. I beg to differ."

Before our conversation could transition to bloodshed in the drawing room, Mr. Belham approached wearing a friendly smile.

He greeted everyone and asked after their health, content to converse in this setting. My thoughts turned to Julian whose social capacity had time limits and conditions.

It wasn't fair to compare the two men, but my mind was a wicked place, and occasionally, inappropriate thoughts did prevail.

While Mr. Belham chatted amiably with my big-mouthed brother, I risked a hasty glance to the corner of the room occupied by Julian. He was staring straight at me, gray eyes watchful and serious.

Quickly glancing back to my companions, I felt like *I* had been caught, which was fairly ridiculous. He'd already been looking in my direction. If anyone should feel awkward and look away as a result, it was Jules. Yet here I was, nervously clutching my fingers and unable to focus on the discussion happening right in front of me.

"And, Lady Genevieve," Mr. Belham said while I did my utmost to focus. "I am so relieved to see you in attendance. I was worried you weren't feeling well when you were unexpectedly absent from luncheon."

I smiled, meeting his warm brown eyes. "Thank you, Mr. Belham. I am quite well, I assure you. Simply visiting with my niece and nephew before joining the rest of the party."

"Your brother indicated you would be travelling soon to the country. I had wondered if I would still see you for our standing appointment before your departure."

Utilizing every ounce of my resolve, I didn't allow the alarm or surprise to show on my features. I could not believe that my editor was being so reckless. We were in mixed company and his volume did not demonstrate discretion. Silas didn't know of my secret profession or my identity as G. Everett. I could not fathom why Mr. Belham was being careless with both my reputation and my secret. Even if he assumed that both my brother and Mary were aware of my writing, his references to our regular meetings was highly inappropriate.

Silas turned to me with a quizzical expression. But before he had a chance to speak, I shot Mary a pleading glance.

As my brother opened his mouth, Mary placed a hand dramatically to her chest. "Dear me! I find I am feeling quite unsteady all of a sudden. Mr. Bartholomew, would you care to escort me to retrieve some refreshment."

Diverting his attention, Silas raised an unimpressed brow at my friend. "You just consumed an adequate midday meal, Lady Mary. Surely, you cannot need—"

"I believe I do," she all but growled.

My brother frowned, casting a suspicious look between all of us before sighing and holding out his arm. "Of course, I'd be happy to attend to you, my lady."

They bid us a quick farewell—Silas looking dubious and Mary appearing overly dramatic—but finally they were out of earshot.

My gaze snagged briefly on Julian—now alone—and still watching me.

Mr. Belham—wearing his usual pleasant expression—seemed none the wiser regarding the panic he'd provoked. "I do hope that Lady Mary is quite alright."

I stared expectantly for a moment too long before saying flatly, "I am sure she will be."

Either Aaron Belham was the most oblivious man of my acquaintance or he was simply careless. One of those things was worse than the other. I didn't have the energy to ferret out into which category he belonged. I was too irritated with his behavior. And too raw from Julian's continued attention from across the room.

"Excuse me, sir. I believe I shall go and check on Lady Mary after all. My brother is not the most sympathetic to the female constitution." He wasn't sympathetic to Mary's constitution, so that statement was true enough for my purposes.

I could have told Mr. Belham he would see me tomorrow—at our standing appointment—when I delivered my next several installments of the *Detective Owensby* serial. But I did not wish to encourage that sort of offhand public reference to something extremely private or to acknowledge the mistake he'd already made. Perhaps when I visited my editor in his offices on the morrow, I would remind him of his discretion. But I couldn't do that here in my sister's drawing room.

With a hasty goodbye, I parted ways with Mr. Belham.

I didn't stop to see if Julian watched the quick bob of my curtsy or the undoubtedly insincere smile I managed. I left the room and retreated, plain and simple.

Skirting everyone I knew—including Mary and Silas who had reentered the gathering—I found my way back to the nursery where I never should have bloody left in the first place.

Ten

GENEVIEVE

Julian,

Papa invited you to spend the yuletide with us. This time last year, you'd only been gone for a month, but Papa thought it would be nice to have you home to Laurel Park for a visit. But your mother said it was unnecessary and you were well situated with your uncle and the farm. She said it was an unnecessary expense to send the carriage and the coachman to fetch you. She said it was unnecessary and extravagant to purchase you a coach ticket to travel back to Hampshire. She said it was all so very unnecessary. But it wouldn't be. Not to me and not to my family. Even if your evil mother doesn't wish to see you, we do. We're your family, too, Julian. Did she even tell you of my father's offer to bring you home? I bet she didn't.

Gen

Julian,

   I apologize for calling your mother evil. I was upset.

Remorsefully,
Gen

There were times during my childhood when I felt so overwhelmed by my emotions that I would simply burst into tears —usually at the slightest provocation.

Being the baby of the family afforded me a great many allowances. When I was an infant, Emery told everyone that I was *her* baby and she often took it upon herself to entertain me or care for me the way she thought a mother would. As I grew, Emery and Augie tolerated my presence because I was the youngest. I was able to tag along on their youthful adventures with minimal grumbling, always dragging Julian along with me.

Mama would seldom punish my bad behavior as a child, even though I was terribly stubborn and willful. Emery was usually blamed for our sibling squabbles. Silas was often told not to tease me.

I was Genevieve. I was the baby.

For this reason, I was terribly spoiled. I think my emotions were often demanding as a result. And so, when I felt too angry or too sad or too *much* in general, I reacted dramatically and found myself a teary mess on countless occasions. Julian had always hated seeing me cry, so we'd rarely ever quarreled beyond innocent bickering in our youth. That was probably why he'd looked so stricken, weeks ago, after I'd dragged him into the receiving room to discuss the letters. My emotions had been on full display and he'd reacted much the same way young Julian would have—panicked, uneasy, and helpless.

Therefore it was the kiss, followed by the luncheon yesterday at Kendrick Manor that had my emotions building up. The pressure was increasing and I could feel the snarl of them. One strong wind or minor inconvenience would cause me to break.

While I didn't consider crying a weakness, I hated the way my feelings ruled me in this way. Women had a hard enough time being taken seriously. God forbid I reacted emotionally, allowing myself to appear vulnerable.

The truth was I *did* feel vulnerable. Defenseless and weak. The looming threat of traveling with Julian to Laurel Park compounded by a week-long stay surrounded by our shared history, made all the emotions churning inside me ready to explode.

And that was before the letter arrived.

Dear Genevieve,

Is the aggressively smiling Mr. Belham truly your intended? Your sister indicated as much but I cannot help but notice his absence from your life. Nor can I fathom his appeal. It's not my place to inquire, but I did wonder after seeing you two together . . . does he truly make you happy? Can you envision a future with the man? Do you love him? Perhaps I am being impertinent. No, I know that I am. But that doesn't mean that I'm not curious.

Julian

I smoothed my finger across Julian's signature as I considered what it could possibly mean.

Probably nothing.

The rumblings on the paper likely only indicated that someone had touched Julian's plaything and he hadn't liked the results.

Men were idiots.

He didn't want to kiss me, but he didn't want anyone else to either. He'd much rather mock Mr. Belham's smile and question my choice of supposed companion. Who was this arrogant, self-important man to demand anything of me?

But I had to admit, the thought of a growly, jealous Julian did intriguing things to my imagination. Perhaps Detective Owensby needed a covetous, green-eyed storyline to go with his new ginger cat.

As much as I tried to ignore Julian's questions, I was forced to acknowledge that I'd already considered their answers. I'd never claimed to love Mr. Belham. I'd simply decided to give him a chance. A chance he'd yet to take. No offers, no calls, and nothing beyond conversation and a handful of dances. His intentions were decidedly lackluster.

But the worst part was that I didn't mind. I cared not that his attention had waned or perhaps he'd never held me in the greatest esteem. It didn't matter. Even if there was more between us, Mr. Belham had only ever been a possibility in the vaguest sense.

I was due to his office with my next three serial installments in an hour.

The paper crinkled as I ran my finger across Julian's name one last time before folding the letter and tucking it carefully away in the carved wooden box.

Standing from my dressing table, I pulled on my short lace gloves and straightened the curtain of hair above my eyes.

Then I took a deep breath and decided I'd make the option of a future with Mr. Belham more definitive at last.

"Lady Genevieve! Do come in."

"Hello, Mr. Belham." I smiled at my editor's welcome and entered, ensuring the door remained open to the rest of the *London Post* offices beyond. With a bundled sheaf of papers in my hands, I took the seat Mr. Belham indicated in front of his tidy desk.

His smile didn't waver as he sat. He simply watched me expectantly, hands clasped patiently before him.

"Well, with my upcoming trip to the country, I wanted to drop off my pages for the next several installments." I perched on my chair and passed over the twine-wrapped bundle toward Mr. Belham.

He took the parcel and placed it on the edge of his workspace. "Thoughtful of you, my lady. However, I'm happy to accommodate your schedule."

"Oh." I frowned. "I wouldn't dream of behaving so unprofessionally." In the years I had been publishing with the *Post*, I hadn't missed an issue of *Detective Owensby*. Through illness and travel and time in the country, I'd been adamant about meeting my expectations and deadlines.

Mr. Belham gave me a funny look—somewhere in the neighborhood of indulgent and amused. "Of course not. You are the picture of competence. A valued contributor."

I couldn't pinpoint my reasoning, but those words made me feel as if I was being patronized. I considered his claim of my value and thought once again about writing as myself instead of the mysterious and masculine G. Everett. Perhaps I should broach the subject with Mr. Belham and gauge his reaction.

His pleasant smile seemed so benign.

And yet I hesitated, feeling put off-balance by his previous words and tone. I suddenly felt like a child playing pretend, not trusting the picture he'd painted. My mind refused the compliments as anything genuine.

"Thank you," I replied woodenly.

Unfazed, Mr. Belham inquired, "Are you looking forward to your trip to Hampshire?"

The answer was complicated, but he didn't want to hear that. Our relationship was one of innocuous pleasantries and shallow conversation.

I swallowed down the turmoil I felt, the uneasiness and longing, and said instead, "It will be nice to see my mother and father."

With thoughts of the upcoming journey at the forefront, Julian's presence was invading the space. With his phantom appearance came his accusations regarding Mr. Belham.

As I considered Mr. Belham's perfectly pleasant face, I had to admit that I felt nothing beyond a friendly sort of fondness. Of course I didn't love him. An association with the man wouldn't make my unhappy, but neither would it lead to anything more than the most basic form of contentment.

It made me furious that Julian's claims were entirely accurate.

Therefore it was with heightened emotions, I asked suddenly, "What are your intentions, Mr. Belham?"

His smile faltered. "My intentions, my lady?"

"Yes." I nodded and lowered my voice. "You talk about being ready to settle down. You're kind and attentive. You seem interested and yet you've never called upon me or indicated any sort of attachment. I suppose, I am curious if you have intentions."

Mr. Belham's lips parted in surprise. He was clearly taken aback by my candor. Well, perhaps my behavior wouldn't come as quite a shock if he'd actually taken the time to get to know me.

I felt like I'd left the door open for Mr. Belham to waltz through whenever he got around to it. Well—even without the threat of

Julian Moore and all of my complicated feelings—I wanted to shut that door, firmly and resolutely.

"Actually," I said before he could pull himself together and formulate a response. "You can ignore my ridiculously inappropriate questioning. I simply wanted to clarify my position and say that I would appreciate if our relationship could remain entirely professional from this point forward. You are my editor and I am your writer."

Even if Mr. Belham had never seen a future with me, I couldn't stand the idea of him being unsure of my own feelings. I didn't love him, but I didn't want him wondering and waiting. I knew I didn't owe the man my devotion when no promises had been made. But I didn't like the idea of leaving so much unresolved.

Mr. Belham's shocked incredulity had given way to lowered brows and a corresponding "v" between them. "My lady, I'm afraid I don't know what to say."

I smiled genuinely. "You don't need to say anything."

Standing, I reached out. Mr. Belham followed suit as good manners dictated and cautiously took my offered hand. Using a firm grip, I shook and said, "I value your professionalism. I hope we can continue working together even as our personal lives diverge."

Mr. Belham seemed to finally understand, his frown solidifying on his face as I dropped his hand and stepped away.

"I'll see you in a few weeks, Mr. Belham. Good day."

He said nothing as I stepped out of his office and made my way down to my waiting carriage.

Perhaps it had been foolish of me to make my feelings so boldly known. But I found I could live with that. If Mr. Belham was truly intent on settling down and acquiring a wife, I hoped he could find someone who would make him happy. It would just never be me.

If I was more pragmatic and sensible, I would have encouraged Mr. Belham's suit, but I'd never been very good at pretending to be someone I wasn't.

The truth was that with Julian's reappearance in my life, I couldn't ignore how he made me feel. How he'd always made me feel. It didn't matter if Julian rejected me and denied our kiss and ignored the letters. Despite Julian's clear reluctance, I knew that my interests would never lie with Mr. Belham. And I'd wanted to be honest about that.

It had taken me a very long time to stop mourning the loss of Julian the first time around.

And, in the spring, when he returned to his life in Leicester . . . there wouldn't be enough of my heart left over for Mr. Belham anyhow.

Julian joined us for supper that evening at Cawthorn Hall. Although, by the way he ignored me, one would hardly know it.

The dam of my emotions was holding—just barely, by sheer force of will and my overall annoyance at being so blatantly disregarded.

Julian paid me no mind. He and Miles discussed my brother-in-law's plans for his current building project. Jules asked question after question and kept Miles engaged for nearly the entire meal. I could do more than imagine the social strain that put on Julian, I could see it. His uneasiness showed in the tense line of his shoulders and the way he shifted in his seat from holding himself so tightly. Jules was making quite the effort, and overextending himself as well.

Patty shot me concerned, questioning glances when Franny had to repeat herself for my benefit. I was too focused on glaring in Julian's general direction to maintain the conversational standards of an excitable twelve-year-old.

After our meal, my sister excused herself to accompany her daughter to the family wing. I knew Franny still liked it when Patty plaited her hair before bed in the evening. The little girl had told us over the summer that it wouldn't be for always and she knew that she was growing into a young lady who could do those sorts of things for herself. But Patty had cleared her throat and said she'd braid Franny's hair as long as the child would let her.

I smiled now as I watched the pair walk arm in arm toward the staircase.

Miles shuffled off to his study to retrieve the drawings of the stables from the architect for Julian to review.

And then we were alone in the informal drawing room, just the two of us. Me glaring and Julian studiously examining the curved handle of the iron fireplace stoker.

I sighed and watched him stiffen as a result.

Crossing my arms, I moved toward him. Julian caught the sound of approach and half turned before he remembered he was ignoring me. I watched his jaw clench and a frustrated hand smooth back the long auburn strands that swept rebelliously across his forehead.

"So, you're just going to ignore me from now on. Is that how it is, Julian?" I stood facing him, refusing to back down from this fight.

His glance was dismissive, gray eyes recording my petulance before flicking back toward the fire. "I don't know what you mean, Genevieve."

I scoffed as irritation gathered, forming sharp points on the end of my tongue. "Then I guess we're pretending the kiss didn't happen the same way we're ignoring the letters."

Julian flushed, crimson stripes painting the tops of his fair cheekbones and the tips of his ears. "It was a mistake," he murmured, gaze still pointed down.

I'd known he regretted it, but hearing the admission from his own lips twisted something inside me. That hopeful girl was being crushed under the weight of her own expectations.

"A mistake," I echoed quietly over the sounds of the burning wood, crackling and popping in the grate.

A pause. "It was just a kiss."

"Right," I agreed.

Julian sighed defensively, as if this was an argument, instead of me confirming everything he'd said.

"Stop doing that," he snapped.

I frowned. "What is it I'm doing that displeases you so greatly, Your Majesty?"

Finally meeting my eyes, he gave me a flat look. "You're being argumentative."

"I've literally repeated everything you've said."

"It's not what you're saying, Genevieve. It's *how* you're saying it. Your tone is condescending."

"Well, if you weren't acting like such an idiot, I wouldn't have to treat you like one!"

He held out a hand as if to say, "See. This is what I have to deal with."

"I'm trying to apologize for a regrettable decision on both our parts," he managed primly.

"You didn't apologize. You said it was a mistake. There's a difference."

He glared. "I don't know why it matters so much. It's not as if it was your first kiss. Your lips don't belong to me any more than they belong to James Madigan."

My brain stuttered to a halt as I took in Julian's words. I hadn't thought of my first kiss in a very long time nor the boy I'd shared it with. I hadn't told anyone about that day after the spring festival in the village. Not my sisters, not anyone.

But I had admitted the truth in a letter addressed to Julian.

His head snapped back as if he suddenly realized his mistake.

Anger and hurt flooded my body. "You—you knew."

"Gen, it's not what you're—"

"You lied," I cut him off. My voice was hoarse, barely escaping my trembling lips. Brutal, furious tears were gathering in my eyes.

My letters. All those letters. He'd gotten them after all. And he'd lied about it.

"Genevieve," he said frantically, stepping closer, reaching for me.

In an effort to avoid his touch, I retreated hastily, stumbling over the hem of my skirts before righting myself.

Oh, God.

He'd known all along. He'd read all my adolescent ramblings and foolish, angry diatribes.

Julian knew I'd loved him.

He'd held the evidence of my desperate thoughts written for myself when the boy I'd loved was nothing more than a distant memory.

I wanted to perish on the spot. Instead I turned and ran from the room, Julian calling after me. I didn't stop until I got to my bedchamber. I closed the door and slid to the floor.

The emotions I'd been forcing down deeper and deeper over the last several days freed themselves. They pushed off from the murky bottom, rising swiftly to the surface and joining shame and mortification so profound that I couldn't seem to catch my breath.

My nose started tingling and I knew that I needed to get control of myself. Forcing myself to inhale steadily before forcing the air out, I slowed my panic and blinked tender eyes around my room.

My gaze landed on the carved wooden box on the end of my dressing table.

I rose on unsteady legs before crossing the patterned carpet. Sitting on the narrow wooden bench, I opened the lid and pulled out the letters I'd received from Julian since this madness had begun over a week ago.

I didn't open them. I couldn't look.

All this time, he'd known what was in my heart. And he didn't tell me. He'd lied when he said he'd never received my correspondence.

What if he'd only said those things to spare me the embarrassment? What if he took up writing the letters I held now because he felt guilty? Or worse, sorry for me?

What if he kissed me for those same horrible reasons?

I didn't know. But I felt sick.

He'd said it was a mistake.

Sometimes people said exactly what they meant. It didn't have to be aimless wondering. There weren't always hidden meanings or ulterior motives. Sometimes the truth was just something you didn't want to hear.

Staring down at the folded paper in my hands, I wasn't sure where my gloves had gotten to.

I opened the drawer of my dressing table, and shoved Julian's letters behind my hair brush, stay pins, and a set of blue ribbons.

It felt wrong to put them back in the box. And tonight I lacked the strength and willpower to burn them the way they deserved.

Eleven

JULIAN

Brutus easily kept pace with the slow-moving carriages as we forged ahead to Hampshire.

I didn't know what I was still doing accompanying the Bartholomews and their spouses to the country. A strict sense of obligation was the only explanation.

After the disastrous conversation with Genevieve two days ago and the kiss two days before that, I should have definitely withdrawn from the trip to Laurel Park. A smart man would have bowed out and given excuses. But I owed the Earl of Basilton and he seemed to genuinely desire my input for the stables and surrounding outbuildings being constructed at his neighboring home in Hampshire. If I could lend my expertise—minimal though it may be—then it was important that I paid my debt to the earl.

I wasn't sure which carriage held Genevieve. She'd been inside and ready to depart when Brutus and I had arrived at Cawthorn Hall this morning before dawn to begin the day's journey.

The remembered hurt she'd worn had me shifting uncomfortably in the saddle. I caught myself pressing a hand to a phantom ache in my chest when I considered how my actions had caused Genevieve such pain. I should have told her about the letters straightaway and what my mother had done.

The image of her stumbling away from my touch lingered and had me squeezing my thighs, urging Brutus forward and closer to the line of conveyances.

It didn't matter which carriage contained Genevieve. She wasn't going to talk to me. And I couldn't blame her. I hated that I'd given her reason to run.

After she'd realized I'd read her letters, I'd tried talking to her. She was under the impression that I lied about receiving them and that I'd had them all along.

Needing to explain the full story, I'd tried speaking to her in person. But she'd hidden in her rooms and sent servants to refuse me. Then I'd written to her, outlining what had happened with my mother. She'd had every note returned to me at the boardinghouse by one of the duchess's staff. I'd eventually stopped when the same footman returned for the fifth time in two days bearing a pitying expression and an unopened letter.

In addition to Basilton's invitation, I supposed I was on my horse this morning so I could explain things to Genevieve. She couldn't very well hide from me for a week in the country. Could she?

She was stubborn to be sure, but between the three properties among her family members, surely I could track her down for a single imperative conversation. I'd drag her away from the dining table if she wouldn't see reason. I needed her to understand.

I would have never ignored her letters had I received them. And I wouldn't have pretended as some sort of cruel joke. I wasn't a dishonest person, and I hated that she thought that of me.

A coward? Yes.

But not a liar.

I sighed as I watched the three carriages ahead of us pull to a stop along a wide stretch of dusty road. It was midday and surprisingly dry for late October. The air held the bite of autumn chill as a steady breeze pushed gray clouds across the wide expanse of sky. I took a deep breath. While I'd been enjoying my time in London, it was fine indeed to be back in the country.

Silas Bartholomew stepped out of the final conveyance in the line and waved me over. He gave Brutus a friendly pat before saying, "The horses need a break. We'll stop here and stretch our legs." With a quick glance beyond me, Silas continued, "Actually, why don't you join me for some refreshment? Augie's cook finds me quite charming and packed me my own hamper. I'm willing to share my bounty with you, Mr. Moore."

I eyed Silas warily and decided it would be easier to just go along with him. Arguing wasn't likely to get me anything besides a headache when dealing with the eldest Bartholomew sibling.

"All right. Thank you for your hospitality." I dismounted and Silas passed my reins to a waiting footman.

Lady Mary was climbing out of the first carriage in a tangle of green skirts. Upon spotting us, she called merrily to Silas, "What's wrong, Bartholomew? Needed a break already? It must be terrible to be saddled with such a delicate constitution."

Unperturbed, Silas patted his stomach. "Not at all. I'm fit as a fiddle. Never minded a bit of travel, myself. You're looking a bit green though, Lady Mary. Do take care."

Her eyes narrowed but Emery jostled her from behind as she helped a small child down from the carriage.

With Lady Mary distracted, Silas held the door open for me as Mary eventually called after him, "I've never been carriage sick a day in my life! I'm as hardy as they come."

"My apologies! Perhaps it's simply your skin tone next to your traveling dress making you appear ill." And with that charming rejoinder he ducked inside the carriage and closed the door. With a victorious smile and a much lower voice, he said, "She's too easy to rile. It's like fishing from a barrel."

I nearly laughed at such arrogance. "You know, Lady Mary has sharper teeth than any fish you'll find in England."

He grinned, delighted. "That is a valid point. I shall do my best to keep her mouth away from my more tender parts."

I rolled my eyes but the man was too busy digging through a hamper of supplies to notice.

"Here we are," Silas said, passing me a small bottle of wine while he produced slices of bread and cheese for accompaniment.

Before I'd even removed the cork, Silas cocked his head and said in an oddly flat tone of voice, "Did you hear that?"

I paused but could discern nothing but the sounds of people and horses milling about outside the conveyance.

He didn't wait for me to answer, instead passing over all the food items he'd unpacked and dumping them unceremoniously on my lap. "Yes, that's Daisy, all right. Franny will need some help with her energetic little dog."

What the devil?

I sat in stunned surprise as Silas fairly bounded out of the carriage while I remained seated and covered in bread and cheese.

Removing a handkerchief and spreading it neatly on the seat to my left, I set the wine bottle aside and moved all the food off my person. Just as I brushed crumbs from my brown breeches, the door opened. Emery entered with a baby in her arms.

"Jules, be a dear," she said with absolutely no explanation whatsoever before passing the child to me. I held the warm weight of the boy out in my arms, completely unprepared and entirely confused. Emery made her way inside the reasonably sized carriage, shoving her skirts to the far side as she sat across from me. She called behind her, "Genevieve, can you help Reeve inside, please? She's been asking for you all morning. I'm afraid she's bored of riding with her mother and father and brother and Mary for entertainment."

"Why did Silas want us to ride back here?" Genevieve's irritated voice called from just outside.

I straightened as I realized Genevieve was handing a small girl up into the carriage and following behind her. She hadn't looked up and seen me yet.

I glanced to Emery who was watching me with a wide smile. She said to her sister happily, "He has the largest carriage, of course. And he promised pastries."

When I looked back, Genevieve was glaring in my direction, taking a seat beside her meddling sister. The little girl—Reeve— climbed easily onto her aunt's lap. Gen helped her smooth her skirts before looking back to me, seeming to notice the baby I still held awkwardly in my arms.

"You can set him down, you know," Emery said with no small amount of amusement.

I looked at the child. He had wild brown curls on the top of his head, and he watched me with solemn blue eyes. The very picture of a miniature Augustus Ward. Gingerly, I lowered him to my lap, keeping my hands securely beneath his arms. He seemed to be aggressively chewing on two of his fingers, but then suddenly he withdrew them from his mouth and lunged forward more quickly than I would have thought possible, smacking a wet hand to my face.

"Beckett likes you!" Emery exclaimed eagerly while I extracted another handkerchief and wiped my chin.

Once I'd returned the child to my lap—facing forward this time— I looked up to see Genevieve watching me. The intensity of her glare had receded and the little girl she held played absently with her long brown hair.

I still hadn't spoken. I knew I was being frightfully rude, but honestly I was stunned by the appearance of so many Bartholomews in such a short amount of time.

"Well," Emery said, clapping her hands together. She stood and awkwardly maneuvered, first around my legs and then Genevieve's. "I'm afraid I must see to little Reeve. She gets terribly ill on long carriage rides."

We all looked toward the girl who was giggling happily as her mother retrieved her from Genevieve's lap. She was the very picture of health.

"She may look well now," Emery said after a prolonged silence. "But she could cast up her accounts at any moment. Children are reliable that way."

My gaze flicked uneasily to the boy still in my possession.

And with that, Emery threw open the door and climbed down from the carriage with her daughter. Leaving Genevieve and Beckett and myself within.

"Emery," hissed Genevieve after her. She'd apparently also realized something was afoot on the road to Hampshire.

Emery didn't respond, but before the door could latch, Augustus was filling the space. He cast us both sympathetic glances before reaching in and plucking a gurgling Beckett from my arms.

"I'm so sorry," he murmured around a wince. And I couldn't tell if the apology was for being left with his offspring or for whatever antics were happening around us.

The door closed again.

Genevieve glared at it while I watched her. Her arms rested defensively across her chest. She looked ready to bolt.

I wasn't an idiot. Her family was obviously trying to give us the opportunity to speak to one another in both a highly improper setting and a completely ridiculous way. But I could take advantage of that. I needed to explain so much to her.

Clearing my throat, I drew Gen's attention. Her angry expression focused my way and my bravery nearly wilted under her stare. I opened my mouth, but before I could speak, the door to the carriage flew open again.

"I might need your help with something, Moore," Silas Bartholomew said before looking between myself and Genevieve. As if realizing we were the only inhabitants of the space, he smiled brightly and called, "Never mind!"

The door slammed once more, and then moments later the carriage was in motion.

Gen's eyes widened as she threw back the curtain on the other side, moving toward the glass to peer out. I didn't need to look out the window to see that we'd pulled back onto the main road and were on our way toward Laurel Park once more.

"I cannot believe . . ." she muttered through her clenched jaw.

Just then, Silas came trotting by on *my* horse. I leaned forward to see him raise his hat and shout, "I've been craving the open air!" before he took off at a gallop.

Genevieve and I stayed like that for a moment, both of us perched on the edge of our seats, facing the window. I could feel her soft hair brush my cheek and smell the freshness of citrus. The intimacy of our positions had a not-altogether-unpleasant awareness zipping down my spine.

Breathing in the scent of Genevieve's skin, I watched the trees roll by for another moment before I said softly, "Your family is insane."

She sighed mightily before groaning, "God, I know."

Leaning back against the bench on my side, I faced her and said earnestly, "I'm not going to waste this opportunity, however."

Gen resumed her seat as well but said nothing.

"I didn't lie to you about the letters," I told her, watching her blue eyes harden. "When we first spoke about them and you told me that my mother collected yours to post with her own, I . . . imagined I knew what had happened. She never sent them." Genevieve gasped, a small and wounded sound barely reaching my ears. "And she never gave you the ones I wrote to you, either. I always sent my letters for you along with my mother's until I finally stopped. After our conversation that night, I figured out what she'd done and I went to see her the next day."

I paused briefly, hesitant to admit the truth, knowing how Genevieve would interpret it.

"What happened when you visited your mother?" Her words were soft and plaintive.

"She admitted it. She'd hidden them in her trunk to keep you from finding them. And there they'd remained for years. I was angry and . . ." I found I could no longer hold her gaze. Staring down at my lap, I finally admitted, "She gave me your letters and I read them."

Genevieve made a strangled sound that had me glancing toward her.

"That was how I knew about James Madigan and—and everything else."

She blinked and looked out the window. "I always knew she hated me, but I never thought . . ."

Leaning forward, I spread my knees wide on either side of her dark skirts. I grasped the hand that was absently clutching the bench. "Genevieve, I am so sorry for what my mother did. She was wrong and it kills me to know that you were hurt by her actions—that for so long you . . ." She squeezed my hand when I couldn't find the words. Eventually, I said, "She didn't hate you. I don't think anyone could hate you. It wasn't a slight against you or your family. I think it was just her way of trying to fix me. And her own disappointment in the way I turned out. She thought I was acting above my station, and she was right."

"That's not true, Julian. You were part of our family."

I smiled at her fierce objection. Loyal to a fault was Genevieve Bartholomew. "But that wasn't the way things were supposed to be done, and you know it. My mother thought sending me away to learn a trade would set things to rights. The way it should have been."

Genevieve opened her mouth to argue, but I shook my head. "I'm not making excuses for what she did. Stealing your letters and driving us further apart was wrong. I just couldn't stand you thinking it was about you."

She laced our fingers together and I didn't move away. We stayed quiet as the carriage trundled along the road. I could tell she was thinking, and I was just grateful she knew the truth now. I rested my forearms on my thighs as she stroked her thumb along the back of my hand.

"Were there a lot that your mother saved?"

I fought a wince when I thought of the hundreds of letters sorted and stored in my room at the boardinghouse. So many in the I-hate-Julian stack. "A few."

She sighed, looking pained.

Another heavy silence descended before Gen finally asked, "Why did you write me back? Now, after all this time."

My gaze dropped to our hands and her thumb still moving gently over me. I could feel the heat in my cheeks. I truly didn't know how to answer that. "Can we talk about something else?"

A pause. "Of course. Let's talk about why you kissed me instead."

I shot her an annoyed glance. "Letters it is."

Her lips twisted at the corners fighting a smile.

Sighing, I admitted, "At first I felt like I owed you. It didn't seem fair that you'd been so honest and loyal to me when I didn't bloody deserve it."

Another pause, shorter this time. "And is that still the reason you write to me every morning?"

"I don't know, Genevieve," I confessed, exasperation lacing my tone. I didn't know how to put into words what I was doing—why these letters felt so important. Finally, I managed, "I just like the idea of waking with you in my thoughts."

She sucked in a slow breath.

And since I was being honest, I continued, "I never knew—at the time—that you . . . felt that way about me . . . when we were young."

I risked a glance at her face. Gen glared at me. "Well, I didn't want you to know. I thought you'd eventually grow up and stop being obsessed with horses and notice that I was becoming a woman the same way you were becoming a man. I assumed you'd overcome your shyness and want a life with me."

Frowning, I asking, "You thought, we'd, what? Marry someday? If I'd stayed at Laurel Park?"

Genevieve's cheeks were pink and she shifted on the bench. "Well, yes."

I remained quiet, taking in the blushing heat of her discomfiture and the bashful tilt of her gaze. Just for a moment, I allowed my thoughts to take Genevieve's girlhood daydreams and give them room to bloom. I considered how close we'd been—playmates and companions, confidants and partners in all things. It wasn't forced proximity that contributed to our connection. We'd always simply . . . fit. Like two puzzle pieces that settled seamlessly together no matter which way you turned them. I gave where she pressed boldly forward, and she softened around all my hard edges and rigid nature.

Despite the general hopelessness of a match with the daughter of a marquess, I could see how it might have come about all those years ago. If I ignored my cynicism and my utter unsuitability for someone like Genevieve, I could let myself fall into her notions from the past.

It might have started with comfortable afternoons reading beside one another, thighs pressed warmly in the shade of the magnolia tree she loved so well. Or perhaps her laughter would have drawn my attention, the way it had in front of the fountain at Cawthorn Hall. Small, tentative touches and our connection growing deeper and stronger in unexpected ways. Stolen kisses and sweet exploration. Perhaps I could envision Genevieve's dream after all.

When my silence—and thoughtful imaginings—had gone on too long, Gen rushed to add, defensiveness in her tone, "Sixteen-year-olds are hardly known for having rational thoughts."

I considered the letters where she'd bravely and boldly proclaimed her devotion. They'd been written with the freedom of knowing that no one would ever see them. But at the same time, she'd been so honest and open, as if the idea of loving the boy I'd once been had been simple—a foregone conclusion, an undeniable truth.

I held her gaze and admitted, "Your letters didn't sound irrational to me."

"Those letters weren't the unreasonable thoughts of a sixteen-year-old, Julian. They were my feelings. After a time, they were simply my emotions laid bare."

I considered the distinction and came back to the crux of the issue. The daydream had been lovely in the moment I'd allowed it. "It wouldn't have worked for us," I said very gently, "even if I hadn't been sent away."

Genevieve's thumb paused mid-stroke, but her voice was even when she said, "Because you couldn't see yourself with me?"

Frowning, I met her surprisingly blank features. "No, Gen. Because you would have lived the life you were born into. Seasons and suitors. Your family would have never—I was just the housekeeper's son," I finished, completely baffled.

The careful mask she wore cracked right down the middle and her anger flared bright and beautiful. "Did my family ever make you feel that way? Did *I* ever make you feel that way? As if you were *just* anything. As if you were nothing."

I shook my head, answering her even though I couldn't say the words. "It doesn't matter." It seemed more foolish and painful to give voice to what might have been.

Genevieve yanked her hand out of mine. At some point I'd been the one holding on too tightly.

She straightened in her seat and I leaned back to stay on my side of the carriage.

"It *does* matter," she argued with flashing blue eyes and clipped impatience. "I want to know why you were so sure everything had to change."

"Because that's the way the world works. I'm not titled. Nor am I wealthy. Just because you had some fantasy where we lived happily ever after did not mean that would have been our future."

"Well, you went away and here I am after seasons and suitors—just like you said. Only I haven't been married off to some gentleman against my will. Perhaps my family loves me enough to want me to be happy. Perhaps they would have wanted that for both of us." And just like the girl I'd known, her anger had finally burned itself out and now she just sounded sad and resigned.

I was disappointed too—that we'd never gotten that chance. A future stolen before we'd ever had the opportunity to fight for it.

I watched her swallow down her hurt and absently straighten the fringe above her eyes. I didn't want her thinking about the past. There was nothing we could do about that now. Too much had happened, most of it beyond our control. Too many years had passed, but we were here now. Together. And while I still felt very much like the housekeeper's son, to almost everyone else, I'd grown beyond that.

Shifting forward on the edge of the bench, I slid my fingers into her curtain of dark hair. Cradling her jaw, I closed the distance and watched her eyes widen. My nose slid along hers as I whispered, finally answering her question, "I kissed you because it felt necessary. Like I couldn't go one more moment without knowing what your smile tasted like."

And I pressed my lips to hers.

Genevieve parted for me and I took the opportunity to draw her plump bottom lip into my mouth. After an insistent tug, I felt her hands grasp the lapels of my jacket. I complied easily, needing to be closer. Lowering to my knees before her, Gen wrapped her arms around my shoulders and widened her legs.

I didn't stop kissing her as I inched forward, between her spread thighs.

Slowly and deliberately, I brushed my tongue against hers and —*Christ*—she made that same desperate sound, the one she'd made in the garden. I loved that sound, and wanted to hear it again.

After a time, our breaths grew ragged and our hands restless. Teeth and tongues turned gentle exploration into something more, something vital. This woman felt essential in my arms.

Abruptly, Genevieve pulled away but only far enough to rest her forehead against mine. On a shaky exhale, she asked, "What are we doing, Julian?"

I worked to control my own breath. "I don't know," I admitted, loving the feel of her hand sifting through my hair.

"I don't want you to kiss me because you feel guilty about the past or my feelings for you when we were young."

I opened my eyes and leaned back, needing to see her face— needing her to see mine. Gen's fingers—those that had been absently stroking my hair—tightened on my neck and didn't allow me to get far.

"Gen, look at me."

Reluctantly, she opened her eyes, and I could see that the statement had cost her.

I brushed a dark strand of hair behind her ear before snagging her chin firmly in my grasp. "I didn't kiss you out of pity or shame or any other such nonsense." While I couldn't give her pretty promises or a future fit for a proper lady, I could damn well reassure her in this. She still looked skeptical with her brow furrowed, so I added, "I wouldn't do that, Genevieve. Do you want me to stop?"

In answer, she licked her kiss-swollen lips and urged me forward with the hand still pressed behind my neck. I came willingly as her soft curves molded against me.

Genevieve took the lead this time, parting my lips with her own. Her tongue swept inside and I groaned into her mouth.

She felt so good like this. We were moving together, giving and taking in equal measure. So often, Genevieve and I battled for dominance while arguing our way through our shared history. But here and now, our affections felt effortless—like we were on the same side for once.

The placket of my breeches pressed against the front of the bench, trapping her skirts between us. I was painfully hard as I sought her warmth.

With a shaky hand, I reached beneath Genevieve's skirts, skating gently along the outside of her leg. Slowly, I traced the delicate bones of her ankle up over the curve of her calf, brushing against her stockings until I reached the bend of her knee.

Here I paused and I felt her hand tighten in my hair in response. I smiled against her lips just before she whispered, "Keep going."

At her quiet demand, I shifted uncomfortably against the bench as a surge of desire went straight to my cock.

My thumb traced the outside of her warm thigh, feeling a slight quaver in the muscle there. If she was nervous, I was doubly so.

Flattening my palm against her skin, I stroked up and down— touching the edge of her drawers before retreating along the same path back to the curve of her knee.

Genevieve shifted her hips on the bench. The motion loosened the skirt of her traveling dress and widened her legs even farther in invitation. I kissed lower along her jaw to the delicate skin of her throat. When I reached her collarbone, I walked my fingers to the inside of her thigh. She was unbearably soft. The sound of her sweet little gasp had me pressing my cock to the upholstered bench, searching for relief. I was desperate for harder and faster and the unreal feel of her womanhood at my fingertips.

I found the slit in her drawers and petted the soft skin I discovered as my lips journeyed across her chest to the tops of her breasts.

"Oh God," Gen gasped as my thumb stroked tiny circles around her center. I found the firm little button at the apex of her sex and focused my attention there, adjusting my pace around the sounds she made.

I longed to explore lower, to sink my fingers into her heat, to feel her muscles clamp down around me. But I could sense the sudden tension in Genevieve's body. She was close to release and I wouldn't do anything to alter her course.

My lips and tongue still tended to the tops of her breasts, just visible above her bodice. My lower body moved against the bench seat, eager for friction and encouraged by Genevieve's breathy sounds.

Suddenly, the hand in my hair tightened its hold and Genevieve murmured a broken plea. Her hips shifted restlessly and then she was cresting, pressing herself as close to me as possible while she pulsed against my hand. "Yes, Julian. God." The rest of her passionate utterance had my lips pausing against the swell of her bosom. "I've thought of this—dreamed of this. Your fingers. Your mouth. All over me. Within me . . ." Her words were lost on a long, delirious moan.

Genevieve's admission was so honest and seductive. Hearing of her desire for this—for us—heated my blood. But I could recognize the sincerity beneath her pleasure. She wasn't giving me pretty words to heighten this elicit experience or because she sought to arouse my senses. She'd chosen to bare herself to me— body and mind. I wouldn't make her regret it.

I thought back to the dream I'd had—my subconscious feeding on this new attraction—and how I'd taken myself in hand to sate my need.

My hand was drifting to the front of my breeches now, but before I could grip my hardened flesh, Genevieve was there whispering in my ear, "Let me. I want to touch. I want to feel you . . . the way you felt me."

I leaned back and away from her to meet her determined gaze just as her hand closed around me. With my resolve quickly evaporating, I managed to clutch her wrist in protest. "You"—I swallowed —"you don't have to."

I could see her ready herself for battle, this fiercely willed woman. And despite the absolute lunacy of this situation, something warm and familiar bled through. A challenging twist of her lips that I recognized.

"I know I don't *have* to," she argued. "It's not payment for services rendered. Perhaps I *want* to, Julian. I want to see you lose control."

I huffed a laugh. "Well, I think you can cross that off your list. I should not have taken such liberties in the first—"

She squeezed my erection, halting my speech and forcing my attention her way. "Don't do that. Don't act like you took advantage of me or this situation. We're both adults." Her gorgeous blue eyes narrowed. "I've never cared much for propriety."

I could have argued. I could have tightened my hold on her bare wrist and refused her touch, rejected her offer. But I chose to trust her instead.

There were moments when listening became more necessary than dominating. Genevieve didn't need me to argue our way out of something we both wanted. She needed me to hear her for once—for her voice to rise above my own, and for me to trust that she knew her own mind.

So, I shifted my hips and created enough space to unbutton the falls of my breeches.

Her expression cleared before victory shined behind her eyes.

"It won't take long," I warned. "You felt too good. Too perfect."

Her lips parted at my words before she recovered and said, "Show me what to do."

Unlocking my hold on her wrist, I guided her inside my breeches. I placed my hand atop hers and bit back a groan as she circled my length. With quick and efficient movements, I showed her how hard and how fast to touch me. This was going to be quick.

"So rough," she mused as she matched my punishing pace.

Gen watched my face and catalogued every intimate expression flitting across my features. If I hadn't been so far gone, I would have been embarrassed.

My head dropped back and I released my firm hold, allowing her some independence in her efforts as I lost myself to pleasure.

I didn't notice the burn in my thighs or the rumble of the carriage. There was only Genevieve and the way she was touching me. "Faster," I breathed, fumbling in my coat pocket for another handkerchief.

Gen complied and within moments I was breathing roughly through my release. I used the linen square to prevent a mess and my other hand to slow Genevieve's movements when her touch became too much against my sensitive flesh.

When I finished tucking myself back in and doing up the buttons, I looked up to see Genevieve's curious and fairly triumphant gaze.

I ignored her, focusing on calming my racing heart and producing my final handkerchief. Taking her hand in mine, I wiped the fabric across her palm. I could still feel her eyes on my face.

"Stop staring."

"I can't," she said, unapologetic and incredibly entertained. "Your blush is fierce, Jules. I can hardly see your freckles."

I glared and released her hand, tucking the used handkerchiefs away.

Her smile was radiant—even white teeth and kiss-plump lips stretched wide. "How many handkerchiefs do you have in there anyhow?"

That startled a laugh out of me. "I like to be prepared."

"I'm grateful," she said, blue eyes radiant.

She still had a hand on my neck, and before I could react, she pulled me forward and kissed me soundly. "I mean it. Thank you . . . for letting me."

I kept my eyes closed and fought heroically against unhinged laughter. "You don't have to thank me. *Christ.* I should be—"

"We can thank each other, then." I could feel her smile against my lips. "Come on," Gen said as she tugged me to join her on the bench. "We'll be at Laurel Park soon, and while I assume my family schemed to get us alone so we could work through our differences, I don't imagine they had any of this in mind."

I choked.

Genevieve, unbothered and undeterred, laughed and laid her head against my shoulder.

This, too, was familiar. The warm weight of Gen beside me. Though our bodies had changed in the intervening years, I could still recall her citrus scent and the security of having her close. Comforting and customary. It had been a long time since I'd shared this sort of closeness with another person. It had been since Genevieve herself. When we'd read beside one another on a bench in the garden or sat close in the hay loft, hiding from our governess.

Everything that had happened in this carriage in the last half hour had been unexpected, but this woman wasn't. She was a thousand happy memories and the family I'd acquired by chance.

She was also three hundred unanswered letters and seven years of regret.

Our lives were complex now and one brief encounter wouldn't change that.

As the once-familiar road to Hampshire drifted outside the window, I wasn't sure of the outcome when the past and the present were destined to collide.

Twelve

❦

GENEVIEVE

Dear Julian,

    I have a new one I want you to read----
Detective Barton Owensby couldn't believe his luck. Who could have imagined he'd encounter a murderer while on holiday? The residents of the sleepy, seaside village were not equipped to deal with such a brutal and grisly crime. This wasn't London. There were no detectives, and the closest magistrate was too far away to do any good even if there had been a suspect for the murder of Jacob Mahoney.

    The good detective walked the crime scene again to look for clues. Blood still stained the grass at the edge of the woods leading away from the village square. It was dark but the full moon lent its light, casting long shadows from between the trees.

Perhaps he should simply return in the morning. There was nothing more he could do for Mr. Mahoney on this night.

Just as Detective Owensby turned to retrieve his case from a nearby stump, a howl wrenched the early morning air. The detective straightened. His gray eyes cast about for any sign of a wolf nearby, but there was nothing. The forest had gone utterly still at the horrible cry. No wind rustled the remaining autumn leaves and no small animals scurried about. His horse stood stock-still where he'd been tied to a nearby tree. It was as if the wolf song had frozen everything within earshot.

-----And then I'll have Detective Owensby come back in the morning and find claw marks. Perhaps some dark fur clutched in Jacob Mahoney's poor dead hand. Do you think it's too much to add such an abnormal element as a werewolf to this particular story? I thought it would be a nice addition, something exciting and adventurous and fantastical.

I'll send another installment once I decide how it ends.

Yours,
Gen

When Julian and I were children, reality and expectation occasionally intruded upon our comfortable life at Laurel Park. I'd traveled to London a handful of times with my family before my debut at nineteen. On those occasions, Julian would become unsure and distant. Mama and Papa had invited him to accompany us. But Mrs. Moore refused, and after a while, my parents stopped asking.

There were other instances in which we'd host summer house parties for friends and acquaintances of my mother. No one had ever asked Julian to make himself scarce, but he had regardless. At the time, I'd been annoyed. Irritated that I'd been expected to dress in my finery and mind my manners while Jules had abandoned me to boring adult conversation. He'd typically hide in the nursery or schoolroom, depending on our age, and I'd been forced to seek him out. As a result of the disruption to our normal lives, we were usually in poor spirits—him withdrawn and me bad-tempered—and I suppose I never really understood how difficult those times must have been for him. How confusing and disorienting to be thrust into managing societal expectations when we typically had the freedom to behave however we liked.

But looking at Julian now, a grown man taking in his former home, I could easily recall the quiet and hesitant boy who'd hidden himself away to avoid visitors and the questions they would have posed. For while we considered Julian a part of our extended family, he wasn't a ward or a relation. He was the son of our housekeeper, and what was normal for the Bartholomews was not, in fact, normal for everyone else.

On this chilly gray October day, Julian trailed the loud and boisterous group of my family members as they made their way up the front staircase following our recent arrival at Laurel Park. His gaze took in the newly painted shutters and all the small changes to the structure and the grounds. I could see him comparing the past to the present—how he catalogued all the differences—while his memories fairly shouted from behind tentative gray eyes.

I longed to approach, to take his hand and drag him into the thick of things. I wanted him to know that he belonged and, to me and to my family, he'd never been an outsider. Yet despite the intimacies we'd shared in the back of the carriage, I didn't think I had that right. Julian appeared to be battling demons all on his own, and despite my natural inclination to insert myself into any situation, I thought it best to be cautious.

I didn't know how Julian felt about what we'd done. Oh, I knew he'd liked touching and being touched, but that was just physical. I wasn't sure if it meant anything. And I wasn't quite ready to ask if we could do it again.

My scheming siblings had given me a wide berth since the carriages rolled to a stop in front of the main house at Laurel Park. So, I watched Silas forge ahead to greet our parents while Mary, Patty, Miles, Franny, and Daisy made their way up the stone steps in his wake. Emery and Augustus were slowly herding their energetic children. And I was lingering as the footmen unloaded my things and Julian took uncertain steps behind everyone else.

As Augustus watched his son dash around his legs, he noted my hovering presence still in the middle of the drive. His curious dark brows rose in question and I smiled and shook my head in response. I was fine. Everything was . . . fine.

My brother-in-law's bright blue eyes roamed the vicinity until he found Julian—clad in his black great coat and tan riding breeches —watchful and unmoving near the front wall that lined the path.

Augie smoothly lifted Beckett into his arms and leaned down to whisper into his wife's ear. I watched as Emery's gaze snapped to Julian before she moved swiftly to his side. He startled slightly from whatever internal dilemma had likely been consuming his thoughts. My sister pointed to the side and the rear of the property, likely indicating all the various residences surrounding the estate—those inhabited by my siblings.

Julian nodded through the explanation and didn't seem to notice that Emery was guiding him up the front steps to where my mother was smiling widely at her grandson in Augie's arms.

With boots crunching along the gravel drive, I moved closer, eager for this reunion.

I knew that Patty had written to Mama and Papa. She'd confirmed our quick trip to the country and I knew for a fact that she'd indicated Julian's presence in our party. But watching my parents exclaim in delight at Julian's appearance on the steps of Laurel Park had pressure building behind my eyes. My father pumped Julian's hand enthusiastically before giving in and slapping him gamely on the back. I watched my mother's blue eyes sparkle happily as she cupped his cheeks—the same affectionate way she'd done to Beckett.

His blush was pronounced from the attention and fussing. Julian smiled and cleared his throat, mumbling his gratitude for their kindness and hospitality. My parents could hardly look away, and from my vantage point below, it was easy enough to see the past reflecting in their eyes as well. I dashed a rebellious tear away just as my mother took in my presence at the base of the steps.

"Genevieve, darling, come inside. Both of you," she said, snagging Julian's arm and ushering him through the front entry. "You'll catch your death out here."

My father waited as I approached and greeted me warmly, his features still radiant from Julian's arrival. "Hello, daughter. How was your journey?"

I smiled. "Just fine, Papa."

"Can you believe it? Julian Moore at Laurel Park once again."

"I never thought I'd see the day," I answered honestly, voice cracking on the final word.

My father frowned but I cleared my throat and said, "Mama's right. Let's get inside before we're frozen through."

We found the majority of the others upstairs in the informal drawing room. Silas, Julian, and I would be the only ones staying at Laurel Park with my parents. Augie and Emery would eventually retreat next door to Kensworth Hall, the Duke of Kendrick's ancestral home. Miles and Patty had their own estate that sat just south of Laurel Park that gave their small family a bit of space and privacy. Mary was likely to join them there. I imagined we'd all dine together this evening and then everyone would part ways to get settled following our journey.

Papa broke away to go visit with the children who'd uncovered the new playthings that my mother had undoubtedly acquired solely for this visit.

I looked for Julian among my family. He wasn't in the seating areas nor was he hidden away in any of the corners of the room. Concerned by his absence, I started back toward the corridor but my mother entered, halting my escape.

"Genevieve, would you like to get settled?"

I ignored her question and blurted, "Where's Julian?"

Unbothered, my mother replied, "I've just shown him to his room so he can take a moment to refresh himself after the long journey. I thought you might like to do the same."

For a moment I wasn't sure what to say. My mind stuttered over the fact that Julian was back at Laurel Park. Surely she didn't mean for him to stay in his old room—the small apartment he'd shared with his mother.

"Where—where is he staying?"

My mother frowned in confusion. "Why, the Red Suite, of course. He's our guest."

I breathed a sigh of relief that he would be occupying our finest guest accommodations. Of course. Of course my mother wouldn't expect him to stay in the servants' quarters—the way Mrs. Moore had required in his previous life here. Julian's mother wasn't here to make demands, to persist in keeping the walls firmly between us.

Recovering quickly, I nodded. "Thank you, Mama. That's an excellent idea. I shall rejoin everyone shortly."

"Take your time, darling."

With a final glance toward my family, I proceeded into the hallway. But instead of moving toward the family wing, I passed the top of the staircase and took the first hallway on the right. Perhaps Julian needed some privacy, but I couldn't ignore the obvious uncertainty he'd worn outside. The need to check in on him was overwhelming.

But when I stood in the open doorway of the Red Suite, there was only Julian's unopened trunk to greet me.

I lingered, scanning the opulent surroundings and crimson-themed suite with unseeing eyes. With confidence, I turned back the way I'd come and took the stairs up to the schoolroom on the third floor.

I entered the chilly space and sat down on the short bench next to Julian without speaking.

Wordlessly, I reached for his hand.

His eyes scanned the room, bouncing from the table and chairs in the center of the space to the dormer windows that let in dull gray light. The blackboard was free of writing and chalk dust. The place was lonely with distant memories.

"How did you know where to find me?"

"I know everything," I quipped with a squeeze to his palm.

He snorted.

"In the spirit of honesty, I tried your room first before coming here."

"My room," he said with inflection, "is on the servants' floor."

I looked sharply at his profile. His face was tilted down, staring at our linked hands. My thumb stroked absently along his. "That was your mother's demand, Julian."

He sighed, "I know. But it's difficult to reconcile when standing in a room meant to honor aristocrats and high-ranking guests."

"Can't you see how happy they are to have you back? Of course my mother would want you in the Red Suite. If she'd had her way long ago, you would be returning to your own room in the family wing."

Julian said nothing, so I ventured quietly, "You know, Patty didn't return to Laurel Park for many years. It wasn't until after you left for Leicester that she found the courage to come home again. This place held so many memories for her—of the daughter and the sister she'd once been. It took some time but she eventually grew comfortable here again. She and Miles and Franny actually spend a great deal of time in Hampshire. Miles's mother, too. Some things simply require time, Julian."

He remained quiet but I could tell he was turning my words over in his head. I didn't want to push, but I also did not want this week to be a painful one full of regrets. "Surely there are some happy memories you can call upon."

Finally, he turned to look at me. "Of course there are. I loved my life here. But I never really knew my place. I had my mother on one side and your family on the other. Then I spent years thinking you all so easily cast me from your thoughts. It's a lot to take in."

I felt such anger toward Mrs. Moore for poisoning Julian against us and for misleading her child into misery. And for sending him away in the first place. But I didn't allow my irritation to show nor did I speak out against her. That wouldn't do anyone any good right now.

"Remember the governess who quit because of your abysmal French," Julian said suddenly.

I watched his lips twitch at the corners, but I allowed the insult and the distraction. It felt necessary to combat the heaviness he was dealing with.

"Oui. It was Miss Dandridge and it was a combination of my abysmal French and my attitude."

Julian chuckled. "That's right. She cited both in her dramatic exit."

I smiled. "I hope she's happy wherever she is."

The urge to ask him about what we'd done in the carriage was admittedly strong. I was a fairly straightforward person but I could also recognize that perhaps this wasn't the time or the place. Julian was dealing with a lot of change already, being back in Laurel Park and among the overbearing Bartholomews. Whether he wanted to address it or not, the way we'd touched each other had altered our relationship. I didn't want all the changes to cause him to retreat.

Here and now, Julian needed his friend—the one he'd grown up alongside, the one who knew all his stories and the history we shared in this complicated place.

So I squeezed his hand, offering nothing more than comfort and friendship, and asked, "Remember Miss Ellsworth?"

"Of course. You put a frog in her tea."

I laughed outright and Julian joined me.

"And Miss Hinton," Julian countered.

Another laugh burst out of me. "The one that fell in the pigpen when she couldn't get me down from the railing."

Julian shook his head. "Christ, we were the worst."

I grinned. "We were."

After our smiles had faded, Julian said quietly, "Thank you, Gen. For helping me remember the good times."

I stood and pulled him to standing. "Any time."

Later that night, after a lively dinner where Mrs. Pennyworth seemed to prepare everyone's favorite foods, I found myself dodging the noisiest floorboards as I retraced my earlier steps to the guest quarters.

I recalled the long hours spent with my family earlier in the day. How I'd forced my gaze away from Julian while in polite company. And yet I'd been helpless to stop it.

My parents had claimed much of the dinnertime conversation. They'd spoken at length with Julian, asking questions and devoting their attention to him fondly.

But there had been moments—heated looks and knowing glances from his side of the table—that had me questioning where I would sleep this evening.

I couldn't stop seeing Julian's face in the carriage, ruined from my touch. The anticipation, the temptation, the overwhelming need to see if he felt utterly transformed after our encounter had weighed heavily on me as dinner progressed and the night came to a close.

Would he welcome me in his suite? In his bed? Could I touch him and kiss him and be free with my affections while we were in private?

An afternoon spent trying to avoid detection or rouse suspicion from my nosy siblings had left me nervous and jittery as I made my way through the upper floor in the dark of night.

When I reached the door to the Red Suite, I tightened my dressing gown over my nightdress and fiddled anxiously with my hair. I was being highly presumptuous not to mention reckless and improper. But things *had* changed between us. I needed to see if those changes were merely temporary.

Just as I found my wayward bravery and raised my hand to knock quietly against the smooth wood, Julian pulled the door wide and dragged me inside. "You walk like an elephant."

Affronted, I whispered, "I do not."

His arms were wrapping around me, busy hands ghosting along my back and shoulders. "Your family could catch us."

My fingers sifted through the hair at his temple as our bodies came flush together. "My family is asleep."

His nose nuzzled mine and I loved when he did that.

"What are we doing, Gen?" he whispered.

"I don't know," I admitted. "But I'm not ready to stop."

And then we were kissing, lips moving eagerly as Julian's arms tightened, drawing me against the hard planes of his body.

We shuffled back toward the bed where we landed inelegantly in a tangle of limbs. Julian wore just his shirtsleeves and riding breeches, and I luxuriated in the feel of his lean body beneath the fine lawn of his shirt. My hands roamed his shoulders and arms as we slotted ourselves together, his strong thigh pressed between mine. The pressure of him *there*, against my heated center was both a welcome weight and a delicious tease.

Facing each other on our sides, I took his plump bottom lip between my teeth and he grunted at the abuse.

Julian's hand stroked a lazy path between my shoulder blades and down the line of my spine. Despite our frantic lips on one another, I felt the restraint in his touch, his careful attempt at not going too far or too fast. But I wanted him closer and harder. There was that feeling I'd experienced in the carriage, eager warmth spreading through my middle, an expectant ache at my core.

With a careful flex of my hips, I shifted against Julian's leg. I made a sound at the pressure—something involuntary, both relieved and restless. Julian's hand paused midway down my back before carefully dragging lower to cup my bottom.

I made another tentative thrust and the hand on my backside squeezed, urging me against him. Even through the fabric between us, I felt his strength and the erotic way he pressed against my center. Before long, Julian was guiding my movements, aiding my body's effort to seek pleasure from his own. He never stopped kissing me, using teeth and tongue to layer affection upon my sensitive skin.

That euphoric release that I'd experienced early today by his hand was hovering, just out of reach. I couldn't explain it but I just . . .

"I need more," I gasped out, wrenching my lips away.

Julian never faltered. He trailed his mouth along my jaw, pressing hot, wet kisses while he rolled me onto my back in the center of the bed. My legs widened and welcomed his body as Julian settled his hips against me, so hard I nearly lost my breath. I stared unseeingly at the red fabric of the canopy while Julian paid careful attention to the skin of my neck. His lower body set a generous rocking motion that had my hips chasing, seeking to match the rhythm.

"You feel so good," I murmured.

He groaned quietly against my collarbone. "Keep talking."

I felt a moment of panic at the request. I didn't know what to say, how to be this wanton woman using my words to fuel the intensity between us.

So I did the only thing I could think of, I was honest. I told him exactly how I felt, how I wanted to make him feel.

The pressure and pace Julian exerted against my center had me coiling tight. My muscles grew taut with every thrust and drag of his manhood.

"You feel so good," I repeated. "So hard and hot against me." His lips sucked hard at the juncture of my shoulder and neck. "I love feeling your weight atop me, pressing me into the bed, surrounding me."

His hips moved faster as words kept tumbling unpracticed and clumsily from my lips. And then I could only gasp and cry out as all those tight muscles in my body went loose and liquid all at once. Warmth spread slow and sticky like honey as pleasure pulsed through my core and beyond.

I was aware of Julian's jerky movements against me as his lips pressed to the base of my throat. His low groan vibrated through my skin. I realized suddenly, he'd found his own release as well. We'd taken pleasure from each other in equal measure, and I might never be able to leave this bed.

His weight was welcome and I stroked my hands along his back, nails scratching gently as I repeated the motion over and over through the thin fabric of his shirt.

Finally Julian shifted to lie beside me. His head rested on my chest and his heavy arm draped across my middle.

"I'll go back to my room in a moment," I promised, already drowsy and reluctant.

His arm tightened in response and I smiled.

As much as I enjoyed the way Julian touched and coaxed my body to release, there was something to be said for the comfort and safety I felt now lying in his arms. Why would married couples ever have separate chambers? I could sleep wrapped up in Julian Moore for the rest of my life.

This closeness spoke of familiarity and security and an intimacy that rivaled what we'd just done together on this bed.

I feared for my foolish, eager heart. It had been broken once before.

And as Julian's breathing deepened and he nuzzled even closer in his sleep, I wondered if I'd survive it this time.

The following morning was one of those rare autumn days when the air held the threatening bite of the upcoming winter but the sun shone brightly, not a cloud in the sky. The clear blue heralded a new day, one with possibilities and my very whimsical imaginings couldn't help but run away from me.

I'd woken very early in Julian's bed. The fire was nothing but glowing embers and I'd known it would be wise to retreat to my own rooms. I'd untangled myself from his warm weight and placed a soft kiss to his forehead, brushing soft auburn strands away from his face. Jules had mumbled something unintelligible into his pillow that had me smiling before padding quietly out of his suite.

Instead of attempting sleep in my own chambers, I'd sat down at my desk and written by candlelight. I'd scratched and scrawled my way through two new installments in the *Detective Owensby* serial before the abovestairs maid entered to stoke the fire and deliver some warm chocolate.

I'd dressed and entered the dining room to find Mama, Papa, and Julian enjoying a decadent breakfast spread. Silas was likely to be abed for another hour or two.

Julian and I had shared quiet, knowing looks while I spread marmalade on toast and fumbled my way through the morning meal. I couldn't stop hearing the sounds he'd made the night before. My body remembered his body with equal parts elation and caution. I was distracted throughout, but my family didn't notice. They were too busy and too focused on Julian and his unexpected presence in their lives once more.

Now the sun was high overhead and Julian and I were on horseback enjoying the fine weather with a leisurely ride through the forest and back fields to Patty's home on the rear border of Laurel Park. Julian was eager to see the property and the updated plans for the large stables and building project soon to be underway.

I felt tense and awkward, which was not the typical version of me. Some hopeful part of me wondered if we'd discuss all the things happening between us. I did not kiss men in gardens with any sort of regularity, and I didn't allow men to touch me in the backs of carriages. Perhaps none of this was unusual for this very grown-up version of Julian. I didn't know that part of him. But a jealous, twisted feeling had me shifting in my saddle when I considered the possibility.

Perhaps now was a good time to talk about our changing relationship.

Julian suddenly blurted, "You're not actually betrothed to that Bellend fellow? Are you?"

Maybe we *were* having this discussion.

I looked at Julian's profile while he faced resolutely forward and tried not to feel insulted. I wasn't the sort of woman to be promised to one man while in bed—or a carriage—with another. I'd hoped that was something Julian knew already.

Just then a horrible thought struck. "You don't have a wife in Leicester, do you?"

Julian turned to me, incredulous. "Of course not!" His color was high on his cheeks. He kept staring at me. "You didn't answer my question."

I rolled my eyes and faced forward, urging my mount slightly ahead in my irritation. "Of course I'm not promised to Mr. *Belham*. I wouldn't . . . betray someone that way."

Brutus and Julian pulled even with me easily.

He hesitated before saying, "I know that. It was just something your sister said—"

I sighed, "Emery insinuated a connection to get a reaction out of you. She's meddling, you know that."

"Oh," Jules replied thoughtfully.

Uncomfortable silence descended once more as we entered the tree line between the two properties. The horses carefully picked their way over roots and fallen branches. We weaved in and out of trees but remained near to one another.

Perhaps we *weren't* discussing this after all.

Another thought entered my head and I considered it for a moment, before offering, "Actually, Mr. Belham is my editor. We have a professional relationship and a passing acquaintance."

My heart beat a frantic rhythm in my chest at the admission, warming me even as the wind cut viciously through the trees. I couldn't believe how even my voice was when I could feel how careful and unpracticed the thoughts had been before they escaped my mouth. I hadn't told anyone about my writing in a very long time.

"Your editor?" Julian finally managed, a question in his tone.

I glanced his way once before focusing on the fields of tall dead grass we approached in the distance. I couldn't tell this story and watch his reaction. It was disconcerting to realize I wasn't brave enough to face the possibility of Julian's surprise or indifference, or worse, his disbelief.

My hands tightened on the reins, the leather creaking around my warm gloves. "He's my editor at the *London Post*. I contribute an adventure and mystery serial for weekly publication."

A quiet moment passed where I heard nothing but my own blood rushing in my ears.

"Detective Owensby," Julian said quietly.

My eyes snapped to his before I remembered the letters. He had them now and he'd read them. I'd forgotten the short passages that I'd sent to him when I was plotting and inventing Detective Owensby from my imagination.

"Those were some of my favorite letters," Julian said with a small smile. "That's amazing, Gen. The *London Post*." The name of the newspaper emerged a bit dreamily and awestruck from his lips. I watched as his gray eyes turned soft. "Your family must be very proud of your accomplishments."

I fought a grimace and must have lost the battle because Julian urged Brutus right beside me and questioned, "What is it?"

Swallowing became difficult suddenly. My tongue felt heavy with shame and second-guessing. "It's a secret, Jules. You can't tell anyone."

Confusion furrowed his brows. "What do you mean, it's a secret?"

Irritation with myself made my words clipped. "I mean, no one knows that I am the writer behind the *Detective Owensby* serial. I am published under a nom de plume. Only Patty and Miles and Emery and Augie know the truth."

I braced myself for his reaction and looked over, but Julian was no longer riding at my side. I cast about and found he and Brutus stopped in between two trees a few yards behind me. Julian looked incredulous. I turned my horse so that we were facing and met his gaze.

"Why would you hide this from the rest of your family, Genevieve? From the rest of the world?"

"I don't know about the rest of the *world*. I'm quite sure the *Post* doesn't circulate beyond London."

He gave me a flat look. "You know what I mean."

"I haven't told anyone because—because for the longest time, writing was something I only did for myself. The most I ever revealed were those short passages and ideas I sent to you." I swallowed as Julian crept closer on his horse. "It's just easier if people think the author of the serial is a man. When I was eighteen, Miles used his connections at the *Post* to get my foot in the door. We all agreed that protecting my identity and reputation was the best way forward, and so it has remained."

Julian seemed to consider this, but then said with a fair amount of accusation, "But why keep the knowledge from your parents and your brother?"

I sighed. Of course Julian would easily extract the things I hadn't said, dragging them into the light when I preferred to keep them hidden. "I don't know. At first I worried that my mother would be scandalized and embarrassed, so I kept the secret from my father as well as a result. And Silas . . . he's not exactly discreet."

"He would be if you asked him to be. If he knew it was important to you."

"I know that," I admitted. "But he also thinks his way is best and damn the consequences. He wouldn't be able to tolerate my accomplishment being hidden in such a way. I fear his reaction as much as his disapproval."

We'd started moving again at some point during our conversation, and the horses remained side by side as we stepped away from the tree line and into the tall, wheat-colored grass. In the summer, this field would be dotted with pink and orange and blue—wild-flowers stretching toward the sky.

"You know," Julian said quietly, "I can remember fishing in the pond and you sitting on the bank beside me telling stories about pirates and ship captains and scaring away all the fish." His gaze was distant, squinting against the glare of the midday sun as he recalled our childhood. But it was his smile—completely inward and reflexive—that had a tightness squeezing my ribs uncomfortably. "You've always possessed this grand imagination, Genevieve. I'm happy to know that you're still telling stories." A deliberate pause. "But making yourself smaller—making yourself fit—was not a future I could have ever envisioned for you."

The constriction around my ribs worked its way up to my throat but I somehow managed to say, "I don't know how to go back. It's gone on too long now, and I don't know how to undo it all without hurting anyone. Without feeling like a fraud."

Soft gray eyes touched every part of my face before settling true to meet my own. "You're the bravest person I know, Gen. You'll figure it out."

We approached Patty's home in silence—comfortable this time. The warmth of the sunshine and the lash of the chilly breeze gave plenty of room for my thoughts to breathe.

No longer was I fretting over these new developments between Julian and myself. My admission and our subsequent conversation had muted those worries to a dull ache. For with everything we'd discussed today, Julian had brought our friendship to the forefront once more. His quiet faith in me spoke of a bone-deep knowledge that only a history like ours could allow. His honest appraisal and candid remarks were the sign of a true friend— someone who wanted only the best for me and had known me long enough to know what that was.

Perhaps whatever was happening behind closed doors with our lips and whispered words didn't have to negate our comfortable companionship. Maybe there was a way we could be both— friends and lovers. Ones who remembered how to handle each other's hearts with care because we knew them so well and had for so very long.

Thirteen

JULIAN

"I'm going inside to visit with Franny and Patty. I forgot my bonnet and don't want to return to Laurel Park with pink cheeks. Mother would have a fit."

I frowned at Genevieve's announcement, so bright and suspicious that I narrowed my eyes in her direction.

She stuck out her tongue in response—always the picture of maturity—and walked out of the stable away from Miles and myself. We watched her progress across the yard, toward the grand home a short distance away.

Gen had been quiet since our discussion. The admission about her secret profession as a writer had come as a surprise, while at the same time, I could envision it easily. For most of our childhood, she had been full of life and adventure. She'd read constantly and made up her own stories to go along with those she read. Her imagination had fueled our youthful games and antics. She'd made our childhood fun.

And I knew for a fact that she hated wearing bonnets and she hadn't forgotten anything.

But I'd allow this retreat. She obviously needed a moment to collect herself following the honesty we'd both shared. I worried that I'd offered too much. I didn't want Gen to think I was judging her for her choices. Perhaps my forthrightness hadn't been welcome and she'd fled indoors to escape.

But I didn't think that was it.

Truthful, open, and forthright were things we'd always been in our previous life together. Growing up, it had simply been how our friendship had worked.

I still didn't know what the hell we were doing. What last night in my bed meant in the grand scheme of things. But I knew it wouldn't affect the way we could talk to each other about things that mattered. Our honesty wouldn't stop now because I found myself longing for her touch and her whispered words against the shell of my ear.

"How has it been—being back at Laurel Park?" The Earl of Basilton's words distracted me from my thoughts and the way I'd been staring after Genevieve.

I cleared my throat and fell into step with Miles as he led me in the direction of the land cleared for his stable expansion. "It's been fine." The earl raised disbelieving brows above unusual hazel eyes that called me a liar. "It's been . . ." I trailed off and stared at the landscape as we walked. "Strange. Memories have a way of tucking themselves away when you don't realize it. And now I'm back and remembering things I haven't thought about in years."

Miles nodded knowingly. "I have some experience with returning home after much time and distance. It's difficult to make yourself fit into the space you once occupied. Especially when you spent that time away growing and changing."

That was an apt description. But what I didn't admit was the way my memories had a way of playing tricks on me. I could still easily call upon my bitterness at being forgotten—how I *thought* I'd been forgotten. I'd allowed my mother to poison some of my happiest recollections. I felt like I was training bad habits out of a spirited horse. Only my mind was the reluctant mount and I needed to trust my instincts where the Bartholomews were concerned—not the venom spewed by my mother over the years.

"The marquess and marchioness seem overjoyed at your return," Miles stated easily.

I nodded once more, unsure how to put into words the reception I'd received from Genevieve's mother and father. They'd treated me like a long-lost son, not at all like the fatherless urchin they'd been obligated to support—the way my mother so often made me feel. The kind attention and genuine warmth from both the marquess and the marchioness filled me with so many complicated emotions. They were pleasant reminders of my previous life at Laurel Park but also the source of so much conflict with my own mother. It was difficult to acknowledge that the Bartholomews had been such a source of comfort and companionship, and how little of that I'd had since my departure years ago.

I tried to remind myself that training took time. "Yes, they have been very welcoming."

We walked in comfortable silence until we reached the land intended for Basilton's building project. Trees had been cleared from the space and it looked as if the future stables the earl intended would be substantial—as large as the ones at Brightleaf Farms.

I frowned and held a hand above my eyes to shield the glare from the sun as I scanned the countryside. "This looks expansive, Basilton."

"It could be," he admitted. "I've prepared for that. Wanted it to be an option." Miles reached inside his jacket and produced a small roll of paper. "The more detailed and updated architectural plans are in my study and I'll show you those when we return, but this is a simple sketch of what we could do here."

"We?" I questioned, accepting the paper and carefully unrolling it.

"Yes, Mr. Moore. We."

I didn't know what that meant. Perhaps reviewing the plans would explain.

The drawing was hardly complex but it did accurately outline the earl's intent for building a large stable with a wide central aisle, big enough to house quite the operation. All the borders for the fields and training yards appeared to be to scale. There were even gallops, outbuildings, and housing units included in the plan.

"For the grooms and other trainers who didn't wish to remain in the village," Miles explained from my side, pointing to the row of small structures I'd been reviewing.

"This is more than a hobby farm. Do you want out of Brightleaf?" I asked, still confused. Miles had been an investor with my uncle for many years. I couldn't envision him becoming a competitor.

"No," Basilton said hurriedly, taking back the paper I returned. "I want to bring Brightleaf here."

My shocked gaze snapped to his. The earl appeared calm and entirely sincere.

When I simply stared, Miles explained, "Your uncle deserves to spend his remaining years in comfort. I want to buy him out, partner with you, and move the stock and staff here. You could continue your duties or we could work together to find a farm manager to oversee things. You could go back to being head trainer . . . if that's what you want. I know you've been forced to take on more and more as your uncle's health has declined."

I found I couldn't speak through the jumbled emotions coursing through me. And I couldn't meet Basilton's earnest gaze. Instead, I stared down at the freshly tilled English dirt beneath my boots.

"You'd have options here, Julian. We could be partners. Hampshire could be your home."

"What happened with Miles? You look like you did that time the ice broke and you plunged into water up to your shins."

I had absolutely no idea how to answer Genevieve.

We were back on our horses, hours later, returning to Laurel Park through the woods.

Her description was appropriate. The shock of Basilton's offer left me floundering just as much as that thirteen-year-old boy who'd followed Genevieve across a frozen stream with his much larger body. The ice hadn't held and I'd fallen through a perfect circle into the frigid water beneath. There'd been no cracking sound to prepare me, just the helpful splash and the sting of unbearable cold. Genevieve had laughed at my startled expression before turning back to help me from the water. We'd spent the rest of the day in the library with hot tea and our feet propped up before a roaring fire.

Miles had been true to his word. After we'd walked back to the house, he had reviewed all the plans for his project with me in his study. I'd wordlessly thumbed through the designs from the architect as well as the documents his steward had devised for estimated labor and capital to get the venture off the ground.

The earl had assured me that he'd keep the details of his offer between us. The duchess knew of his plans but that was it. We both knew he was referring to discretion where Genevieve was concerned. The Bartholomews didn't know the extent of our relationship, but Miles Griffin was not an idiot.

I'd asked him what he planned to do if my uncle's answer was no —or if I chose to stay in Leicester. Miles had simply said he'd downsize the project, but he'd wanted me to know that he was committed to seeing this through and that's why so much planning had already been done.

"Jules," Genevieve urged again, bringing her mount even with Brutus and jostling my elbow. "What's the matter?"

"Nothing," I managed, straightening in the saddle. "We walked the grounds and reviewed the plans for the new stable."

"Did you offer your expert opinion?" she teased, blue eyes sparkling.

I nodded. "For as much as it meant anything."

There was a tug on the sleeve of my jacket that had me glancing over. "It did mean something, Julian. Miles values your input. And I'm sure he appreciates you making the trip here to share it."

My thoughts were in a jumble but I managed a jerky nod to acknowledge Genevieve's words, still feeling overwhelmed by Basilton's offer and slightly odd that anyone—much less an earl —would value my ideas.

We made the remainder of our journey with few words spoken between us. I hardly noticed the birdsong or the bright sun descending toward the horizon. I kept thinking about what the future would look like if Basilton's plan came to fruition.

There was nothing tying me to Leicester save for my uncle and the farm. The majority of our grooms and trainers were young men who were similarly untethered by wives or families. I could easily see how they might entertain the offer of employment by following the relocation of the farm to Hampshire. And my uncle —well, he'd been bound to Brightleaf Farms for long enough. The man was plagued by aching joints. Riding on horseback was nearly impossible for him, and while he loved the land and the animals and his status as a respected business owner, I wasn't sure how much convincing he'd require to accept Basilton's offer and enjoy his remaining years free of farm life.

What would it mean for me to become a partner and move my life back to Hampshire?

Inexplicably, my gaze shifted to Genevieve. Could the future Miles had painted so vividly include her?

I forced myself to look away before she noted my abnormal behavior. She'd likely already catalogued my every sigh but was giving me space to think before she pounced and demanded an explanation.

I wasn't ready to talk about this. And neither was I prepared to raise her expectations in addition to my own. I didn't know what Genevieve wanted from me. Our behavior had been reckless. She could be ruined if we were found out. I couldn't imagine she'd want her reputation disgraced by being forced into marriage with a housekeeper's son.

Raising one hand, I pressed it against my sternum where an uncomfortable feeling thrummed. Genevieve caught the movement but said nothing.

When the trees thinned and the fields behind Laurel Park came into view, I looked over and said, "Race you to the stables."

I didn't wait for an answer, I just gave an eager Brutus the freedom to kick into a gallop.

Genevieve shouted, "Cheater!" to my back as the sounds of hooves filled my ears. I was surprised when her mare pulled up even with us, matching Brutus stride for stride. Gen's smile was wide as she bent low over the saddle, competitive in nearly everything she did.

I'd known a race would distract her, and perhaps it was cowardly, but I could not seem to feel remorseful.

The grand house came into view. What would it be like to visit Laurel Park regularly again? To take meals with the entire rambunctious bunch?

I spied the lattice outside the music room on the second floor. Genevieve had climbed out the window and down the woodwork when she'd been ten to escape her lessons. And of course, I'd followed her.

As the horses sped over the tall brown grass, I looked for the wide-limbed magnolia that had always been Genevieve's favorite. We'd spent many afternoons beneath the shade of that massive tree behind the house.

There was so much history here.

As we raced along the perimeter of the hedges in the direction of the stables, I glanced beneath my arm to find Genevieve already looking my way.

And I considered what it might be like to make new memories on this land that I'd once loved so very well.

Dinner that night was another boisterous Bartholomew affair. Mary and Silas were arguing over something at one end while Emery and Franny held a serious discussion about a new pony.

I found that I enjoyed sharing a table with all of these people. They were entertaining and joyful. And it didn't hurt that their constant chatter and playful bickering allowed me to escape notice and simply exist.

This meal was to be Genevieve's birthday celebration. She would be back in London on the actual anniversary of her birth, but she'd told me earlier today to prepare for a celebratory dinner.

"Well, if I can't have a pony, I think I should be allowed to have another dog," Franny said.

Patty wore a small indulgent smile for her daughter, but it was the girl's uncle who piped up. Silas wondered aloud, "I bet Daisy wouldn't like that, Franny. She has all of your attention. She might not like it if you brought a new puppy into the house."

Footmen entered bearing dessert trays. I'd wager a guess that Genevieve still requested blancmange for her birthday.

"But I think she's lonely," Franny argued. "I'm often so busy with my schooling and lessons. Daisy needs a little friend."

Miles said something that had Patty joining the fray, but I didn't hear exactly what they were arguing over because a footman had just deposited an apple cake before me. I stared hard at the domed dessert, deep rich brown and so warm I could see bits of steam rising from the platter.

I looked up to find Genevieve watching me from her place opposite. She looked . . . emotional, but I wasn't sure why. In front of her sat a generous helping of blancmange.

The others were still in discussion, so I had to lean in to hear Gen say, "I told you this evening would be the birthday celebration. Why do you look so surprised?"

I swallowed hard around mounting emotion and that familiar bitterness that clawed at the gate, eager for entry.

I'd been gone for so long, and I was no one. Not really. How could I have assumed they'd remember my birthday as well and celebrate the way we used to? It wasn't logical or rational. But as my gaze swept around the table, I realized neither were families.

"Julian," Genevieve breathed, as if she'd just arrived at the same conclusion and knew exactly what tumultuous thoughts were constricting my airway.

I shook my head, not wanted to explain myself—not knowing how to admit my painful assumptions. The Bartholomews had never done anything to make me feel less than the person I was, and yet it was an old reminder playing through my head. My mother's voice telling me to mind my manners and remember my place.

"Many happy returns on your birthdays, children," the marquess said.

"And blessings for good health and happiness," the marchioness finished with a bright smile.

A short cheer went up from all those assembled before Silas called out happily, "Is that apple cake? Julian, take a slice and pass it along."

I gathered myself enough to turn to the head of the long table and say to the marquess and marchioness, "Thank you both."

"It's good to have you back, dear," replied the Marchioness of Northcutt.

Another brief cheer erupted from the table, with Genevieve's the loudest. I turned to see her smiling face, so familiar and so unexpected at the same time. I was in real danger of wanting things I should not.

Before I could lose myself to simply looking at her beautiful face, Silas's voice rang out once more. "I say, Julian, pass the apple cake!"

Dessert concluded shortly thereafter, followed by tea. And then the Bartholomew family began to branch off with Mary, Miles, Patty, and Franny returning to their home nearby. Emery and Augustus took a short carriage ride back to Kendrick Hall and their children. And after a brief request to an abovestairs maid, I returned to my guest suite.

So entertaining was my reading material that the time passed quickly while I waited. When I heard heavy footfalls out in the corridor, I rolled my stiff shoulders and rose.

I pulled the door open again before Genevieve had the opportunity to knock. I looked pointedly at her bare feet and she rolled her eyes before coming in and closing the door behind her.

The same as the previous night, I felt that urge to wrap her up in my arms. To get her as close as possible, breathing in the citrus scent of her and touching her silky skin. Seeing her like this, late at night, in a dressing gown with her hair loose—the way a husband might see a wife—made me ache at the intimacy.

I wanted to drag her to bed and explore every inch of her, but I resisted the temptation.

Ignoring my desire to touch and take, I returned to my place by the fire. Newsprint was scattered on the low table and I resumed my seat on the small red velvet sofa.

Genevieve followed. "What's all this?"

I pulled the paper I'd been reading back to my lap before looking up at her. "I was curious."

She took in the stacks of newsprint. Her blue eyes widened when she realized just what I'd been reading. She made a valiant lunge for the paper I held, but I was ready for her. I pulled the newspaper safely out of her reach.

"Give me that," she cried, making another grab.

"No," I replied as I clutched the paper and lifted it behind the sofa.

"I don't want you reading that," Genevieve grumbled as she climbed on the furniture with me.

"Too late."

I transferred the newspaper to my other hand and held it away from her.

Undeterred, Gen straddled me before making another desperate grab. "Where did you even get all these?"

Her thighs spread wide before she settled herself neatly on my lap.

I shifted beneath her. "I asked Gretchen if she wouldn't mind to fetch me all the copies of the *London Post* your father had on hand. And what a collection he had. He must be an avid supporter of the paper. This goes back years. I only made it through the last fifteen months before you stomped down the corridor."

Genevieve pressed her center more fully to me and I made an involuntary grunt at the contact. I was getting harder by the second. She used the distraction to snatch away the copy from my hand. I didn't care. The movement had her shifting up and then back along my shaft. I gripped her bottom to still her movements.

"Papa has always sent for the news in London." She flipped the paper around until she found what she was looking for. "Which one is this?"

"It's the one where Owensby finds the severed finger rising in the bread dough at the bakery in Seven Dials."

Her eyes were busy scanning the text. "Oh, right. I liked that one. It was particularly gruesome."

"I like them all."

Her eyes snapped to mine as if to gauge the sincerity of my words.

My gaze remained steady.

"You strike an entertaining balance of mystery, adventure, and humor. The good detective is entirely likeable. You've created something really special with *Detective Owensby*, Gen." She stayed quiet. "I will say, I think your main character is growing a bit lonely. Perhaps a partner or apprentice in his detecting work. Or someone to come home to."

Genevieve laid the newspaper down beside us on the sofa before admitting quietly, "I recently gave the detective a companion."

"What sort?" I asked as her hands came to rest on my shoulders.

"A ginger-striped cat who follows him to crime scenes."

I could feel my smile taking shape, a slow unfurl that softened every tense line on my face. She'd written a piece of me into her story. Something warm wrapped itself around me and squeezed.

She bit her lip to keep from answering my amusement with her own, but it was there in her glittering eyes.

"Something else I noticed," I said, keeping my tone light. "Every week, every single victim has the initials J.M."

Her gaze drifted in the direction of my right ear. "That's an interesting coincidence."

"A coincidence is it?" I squeezed the globes of her ass and she gave a little yelp.

"Alright! I may have been a touch dramatic in the beginning. And then it just became a habit, something consistent that readers always looked for."

I shook my head, my smile still lingering, turning the corners of my lips up. "Murdering and maiming me every week in your daydreams."

"Mostly murdering."

"Some beheadings," I offered helpfully as her grin broke free.

"A strangulation."

"And that dismemberment."

That did it. She collapsed against my chest, shaking with laughter.

I shifted my hands higher, stroking the curve of her back as she settled against me.

"Will you tell me what happens in the next story?" I asked.

She leaned back and shook her head. "No. It's a secret. I don't tell anyone what's going to happen."

"Spoilsport."

She grinned, and with a smile still painting her lips, she pressed her mouth to mine. I could feel her happiness pressed lovingly to my skin—tiny touches all along the seam of my mouth. Her hands cupped my cheeks, rough from the day's growth. Fingernails scratched softly at the stubble along my jaw.

I sucked on her bottom lip, tasting the mint from her tea.

My hands slid back down to the generous curve of her ass as she started rocking against me, just these small questing thrusts that had my cock longing to feel the hot, slick slide of her without all this fabric in the way.

"Can you take this off?" she murmured against my mouth. An impatient tug at my shirtsleeves had me reaching back with one arm to shuck the shirt over my head and onto the floor.

Her eyes traced the smooth lines of my chest and torso before her eager fingertips followed. Her touch was feather-light and teasing. I wanted smooth strokes and scratching nails. I wanted her palms pressed against my chest while she rode me from above.

I mentally shook myself. My fantasies were getting way ahead of themselves. Genevieve was . . . Genevieve. There would be none of that for a lady.

I sucked in a breath as those curious roaming fingers ghosted over my nipples. She watched my face for a reaction before repeating the movement. "Could you do that . . . to me?"

"Yes," I choked out, utterly careless of the consequences I'd just been reminding myself of.

But Genevieve was already untying her dressing gown and gathering her nightdress up and over her head. I wasn't prepared for the sight of a naked Genevieve Bartholomew on my lap but there she was. I wanted to stare and take my time going over every inch of her beautiful body. Her breasts were full and heavy and begging for my touch. The dramatic flare of her hips was emphasized by her tiny waist. The thighs hugging my hips were unfathomably smooth as my hands stroked the skin there.

Gen halted my desperate roaming by taking my hands and placing them on her breasts. I reacted instantly, plumping and squeezing the flesh as my thumbs brushed back and forth across the sensitive skin of her nipples, so rosy and pert.

"Ohhh," Genevieve breathed at the attention as her hips rolled against me.

If she liked that, then she might be amenable to more. Lowering my head, I dragged my tongue slowly over one straining tip. Genevieve arched her back, offering more of herself to me. I savored in the knowledge that she wanted this—wanted me. Even after all this time.

I spanned my hands across her ribs, tucked up just beneath her breasts. And with a hard suck, I used my tongue to swirl her sensitive peak in my mouth.

Genevieve's hands were stroking impatiently through my hair, grasping and releasing as her hips worked her center against me. I could feel her heat and wetness through the fabric of my trousers.

I switched to her other breast in an effort to pay equal attention. And slowly dragged the fingers of one hand to her backside. Gen was moving faster against me and I couldn't believe how good— how right—she felt in my arms. I released her breast from my mouth and pulled her tight to my chest. The feel of her soft curves was unreal.

I dragged my searching fingers over her ass, lower until I found her womanhood. With a single finger, I pressed in to the first knuckle. She was wet and lush, searing my skin with her heat. Her body drew me in, asking for more.

"Is this okay?"

Genevieve nodded hurriedly.

And then my finger was sliding in and out of her in time with her thrusts against my cloth-covered cock. Gen was surrounding me, squeezing me in a relentless pull.

"Tell me how it feels. Tell me . . ." I didn't know how to finish that statement. But Genevieve knew. She heard the honest request in my broken demand. She knew I longed for her filthy whispered words and breathy moans.

She brought her soft lips to my ear before sucking on the lobe. Then her voice emerged, all lush heat and panted breaths. "You feel so hard against me. Impossibly so. I want to take you out and wrap my hand around you again. Feel the heat and the strength of you as you pulse out your release into my hand, on my breasts, my stomach."

I closed my eyes, nearly undone by the image she projected. "Nothing has ever felt this good, Genevieve. I can't—I don't know how to—"

My incoherent rambling broke off as she pressed herself down hard, grinding against my cock as her inner muscles pulsed her release and squeezed my finger over and over. No sound left her mouth but somehow the unstable breaths she panted against my neck conveyed just how overcome she was.

A moment passed before she was recovered enough to whisper in my ear, "I don't want to stop."

She unwrapped herself from me and stood back on shaky legs. I gripped her hips to keep her steady while I searched for answers in her eyes. I knew what she was asking, but I didn't know if I should be the man to take that step with her and take what she offered. I wasn't who she deserved—I couldn't be.

"You have a future to consider, Genevieve," I argued.

"I do," she agreed. "One that is my own."

She pulled me to standing and unbuttoned my trousers. With a firm grasp, she slid them down my legs. We were naked before one another and the rightness of it settled in my soul. This woman was comfort and companionship, desire and temptation. How I'd lived without her friendship for so long, I didn't know.

I threaded my fingers through her light brown hair and admitted, "I don't know how to be what you need."

"*I* know what I need, Julian. Trust me enough to believe it."

She took my hand and led me to the bed, pausing to turn down the red coverlet. Genevieve pulled me down on top of her where I settled between her spread thighs.

"I love feeling you like this. Like I might float away if not for your weight keeping me tethered to the earth."

"Are you sure, Genevieve?"

"Trust me," she urged, drawing her legs up high on my hips.

And so I did. I trusted her to be a woman who knew her own mind and claimed her own pleasure. I pressed forward into her a bit at a time as she tensed and breathed through my advance. By the time I was seated fully within her overwhelming heat, we were both breathing hard.

"I'm sorry," I whispered against the damp hair at her temples.

"I'm all right," she promised, running her fingers up and down my back.

The rightness of the moment didn't go anywhere while I set a pace and found a rhythm that had the base of my spine tingling already.

Genevieve began to move with me in small, tentative thrusts and the push and pull brought me one step closer to losing myself.

And still the feeling of complete and total perfection had yet to fade. Every gasp and sigh we breathed became more proof that what was happening between us was good and true—an inevitable conclusion to the sweetest of stories. I felt it in the press of tender lips to my throat and the scratch of nails across my shoulders.

As my release drew closer, I sat back quickly on my heels working my fist quickly over my hard length. I spilled helplessly over her belly and breasts just like the picture she'd painted with her softly spoken words.

And from lips as familiar and sweet as her own, I knew I could believe whatever story she told. I just hoped there was something bright and hopeful for our future written in the stars.

Fourteen

JULIAN

In the rooms of Laurel Park it was easy to get swept away—to another place and time when long-forgotten memories stepped boldly around corners.

In the countryside, I could feel hopeful about the future, or the prospect of one at the very least. My mother's voice in my head was still loud—telling me I was playing a dangerous game and playing myself for a fool. But the laughter and joy of the Bartholomew family was louder, drawing me in and making me feel like a part of something, the way they'd always done.

In the quiet moments in bed with Genevieve, I lost myself to foolish, reckless wonder. Her skin, her touch, her softly spoken honesty gasped against the skin of my neck. It all came together and made some new and unsteady part of me battle the cynicism I so frequently clung to.

We spent every night together during our stay at Laurel Park. Some nights had been all urgency with grasping hands and frantic breaths. And then others had resulted in slow, desperate lovemaking where we couldn't seem to get close enough.

I could feel myself falling deeper and faster into the pretty illusion. Genevieve in my bed and a future assembled for a worthy gentleman. It was easy to forget who I was—who I'd always been —when we were tucked away and secret in a place that was more dream than reality.

The return to London the following week had been jarring. I felt out of sorts and unused to spending time alone with myself and my thoughts. I didn't know when I'd see Genevieve again and the prospect of a lengthy separation made me irritable. I was in London to do a job, not live out a fantasy where I was courting the daughter of a marquess.

"I'm not sure I want to get in a ring with this one, Bas. He seems strung tight," Daly said, eyeing me cautiously. "And you didn't mention he was so bloody young. We're old men now. I don't want to get trounced by a buck."

Miles laughed from his spot outside the practice ring. I nearly laughed as well. The idea that I could best this behemoth of a man was absurd.

I'd briefly met the Marquess Daly—actually the Duke of Stinton —when I'd arrived in London. Even following the death of his father, Miles and the others still called him Daly out of habit and preference. He'd been at that very first calamitous garden party at Cawthorn Hall and he'd bid me call him Daly as well. The title of duke had been his for years at this point, but he'd said quite plainly that his father's shoes weren't ones he felt obliged to fill. And I could respect that. So Daly he remained, in private—with close friends.

When Basilton had invited me to accompany him and his friend to Langham Boxing Club today, I'd been happy to take him up on the offer. I felt untethered now that I'd returned to London. My business was well in hand with interested buyers and the like, but the prospect of Basilton's plans for Brightleaf felt like a loose thread I'd pick at until I unraveled. I'd written to my uncle days ago about the earl's offer and awaited his decision.

"Speak for yourself, Daly," Miles called good-naturedly, patting his firm midsection. Both men were drawing close to forty years of age, but you'd never know it. Miles had a few silver strands in his dark hair but he possessed the strength and vitality of a much younger man. And Daly—well, he was built like a bull, all broad shoulders and barrel chest layered on muscle and a thick frame. I wasn't eager to accept a punch from the man. I would just hope he wasn't quick on his feet as well.

The duke snorted a laugh at Basilton's assertion before motioning me forward. "Don't look so worried, Mr. Moore. This is just a friendly bout. For exercise of the body and mind. The practice ring is a wonderful place to clear you head."

"Seems like a wonderful place to acquire a brain injury, Your Grace," I mumbled.

Daly boomed a jovial laugh and it was difficult to believe that this hulking brute was more aristocrat than brawler.

Twenty minutes later we were both sweating and breathing hard. The duke's blond hair had darkened and plastered to his forehead. He sported a bruise on the right side of his jaw from a lucky strike.

I clutched my ribs and shuffled out of the ring. Basilton passed me a towel and I wiped the moisture from my brow and neck.

As I struggled to catch my breath, I had to admit, my time weaving and jabbing at Daly in the ring had cleared my mind thoroughly. When I'd been ducking punches, I hadn't been thinking about the farm. As I'd circled the big man, looking for an opening, I didn't have the opportunity to consider the mistakes I was making with Genevieve.

"All right?" Miles asked as he handed over my discarded shirt.

I nodded.

Daly was already dressed when he stepped over and offered me a handshake. "Good fight, youngster."

I grimaced at the moniker and he laughed.

"You'd never know, Julian, but Daly used to be a pathetic, maudlin creature," Miles said with a grin for his friend. "Now you're more likely to hear his ringing laugh and see his broad smile. If you'd been sparring with him ten years ago, he would have pounded you into the mat out of bad temper."

"If I'd been sparring with him ten years ago, I would have been a child."

My dry statement earned hearty laughter all around.

"Fair point," Daly said. "I am indeed much happier now with the love of a good woman."

The duke didn't offer more to that story and I didn't ask. I simply slid on my waistcoat and agreed to join them for a drink at a nearby pub.

When we were settled with cloudy ales in the dim interior of John's tavern, Miles wasted no time in revealing the reason for this little outing. "I want you to bring the horses and come stay with us at Cawthorn Hall. I hate the thought of you in the stuffy boardinghouse and I know you'd feel better with our grooms looking after the horses."

I thought of Charlie, thin and dirt-smudged but always with a ready smile. "I actually have a good lad watching over the animals. The stable boy at the lodgings is adept and I'm giving him extra coin to care for the horses. I think he needs the additional funds."

"Well, bring him with you. We'll find a place for him and certainly better his circumstances."

Daly raised his eyebrows at Basilton's statement but said nothing. He merely sipped from his glass and watched our exchange with amusement.

My cynical nature wanted to balk at Miles's easy suggestion. Only someone with more money than they knew what to do with would be so careless about someone else's employment. Then again, only someone with such a good heart would think to offer in the first place.

A selfish, irrational part of me longed to be under the same roof with Genevieve once more. Almost as if I'd saved every reckless thought for this time in my life, all my typical careful behavior was on the verge of self-assured destruction.

"You'd have your own space. We wouldn't trouble you," Miles encouraged. "Well, Daisy might bother you, but we've all had to adjust when dealing with the Bartholomews."

He didn't even sound cross about it. The earl's wide smile said that the Bartholomews had invaded his life, turned it neatly on its head, and he couldn't be happier.

Could I allow myself to envision the same fate?

"I will begrudgingly accept your hospitality for the time being." Miles patted the table in celebration. "Until," I emphasized, "I hear from my uncle and we figure out the future for Brightleaf Farms. I may need to return to Leicester to set things in motion and I would feel better if the horses remained under your care. I'll talk to Charlie, the stable hand, and see if he's interested in leaving his boardinghouse employment for a position in the duchess's household."

Basilton's smile was victorious as he clinked his glass in toast with mine and then Daly's. And I refused to acknowledge the hopeful dip in my stomach when I thought of being in Genevieve's orbit once more.

"Charlie! Are you about?" I called after dashing through the rain down to the stables behind my lodgings that afternoon.

"Be right down, sir!" the boy called from the loft above.

"I'm sorry to interrupt," I said when his booted feet touched down. Charlie's hair was a tangle with bits of straw clinging to his worn clothes and he held a brown flat cap in his hands. "Were you resting?"

"Yes, sir. One of the other lodgers' horses had a hard time with the rough weather last night. I worried he'd kick himself lame, so I sat with him and kept 'im company through the worst of it. Thought to catch a few extra winks in me room this afternoon while Mrs. Farnsworth was out."

I frowned, "In your room?"

"Yes, sir. I bed down in the loft."

The mild autumn months had long since abandoned us. It was a gray and soggy November, and the cold at night even seeped into my room in the boardinghouse. I couldn't image this young man staying warm in the loft of the stables.

"How long have you been employed here, Charlie?"

"Oh, let's see," he replied easily, unbothered by my intrusive questioning. "My father died six years ago this winter, so about that long."

"You sought employment here after your father's passing?"

A bit of caution entered the boy's blue eyes. He peered over my shoulder in the direction of the main house before he lowered his voice. "I came here when my father married Mrs. Farnsworth. I was just a wee lad. I never knew my ma. She died when I was born, but my father was a good man and said coming here would be for the best. We'd be a family. But after my father's accident . . ." Charlie trailed off, his voice going small.

"She sent you out here to work while she ran the boardinghouse?" I asked gently.

He nodded, looking down at the cap twisting in his grasp.

Indignation flared hot, and I could feel my face going hard at the injustice the boy had faced. That woman should have been a mother to him and instead she'd cast him aside and used him for her own gain.

"I have a proposition for you, Charlie. If you'll hear me."

The boy looked up, the uncomfortable sadness on his face giving way to curiosity.

"I'm leaving these lodgings," I stately resolutely. That woman wouldn't receive one more shilling from me. If I hadn't already made up my mind about moving to Cawthorn Hall, the knowledge I'd learned about the proprietress of this establishment would have easily swayed me. "And I want you to come with me."

~

Two days later, I'd gotten Charlie settled at Cawthorn Hall. The head groom was an older man with white hair and a ready smile. He'd taken a goggle-eyed Charlie under his wing and shown him around the well-appointed grounds, stable, and lodging quarters.

The conversation with Mrs. Farnsworth had been equal parts awkward and enraging, but by the end of it she'd given up her romantic pursuits and accepted that she had an open room on the third floor as well as the stable loft. She'd been unaffected by the loss of her stepson and that only made me more angry.

I'd sent my trunks ahead and brought the horses over the day prior, but now I stood on the circular drive in front of Cawthorn Hall with a satchel in one hand and reservations overflowing in the other.

I wasn't sure how long I stood there contemplating my residence at the opulent manor, but eventually the front door swung open and Genevieve filled the entryway.

"Are you going to stand there all day?" She raised an eyebrow in challenge, and I found it difficult to look away from her mischievous blue eyes. But then my gaze dropped lower to the lace edge of her bodice and the way the creamy fabric clung to her generous curves. I wanted to fit my hands just under the swell of her breasts and run my nose along the column of her throat.

So deep was the well of my distraction that I still hadn't spoken when I heard her delighted exclamation. "Oh, you've brought a friend!"

"What?" I said in confusion before following her line of sight to the ground near my feet. There on the cobblestones was an orange-striped cat. "Oh, for fuck's sake."

The beast sat comfortably on his haunches, his face turned up in my direction. He blinked slowly before bestowing me with his creaky meow.

Genevieve had descended the stairs in her stockinged feet and was making adorable sounds in the direction of the cat. He called back to her and she laughed in delight.

"I'm taking him back," I said firmly.

"No, you are not," she said in her sweet kitty-coaxing voice, scratching the mangy animal beneath his chin. I could hear his purr rumbling for here. "Franny wanted a friend for Daisy. I'd wager they'll get along perfectly. Bring him in."

Reaching down, I hoisted the cat under my arm before glaring in his direction.

"I wish I had a portrait," Genevieve said happily, clapping her hands together. "What are we calling him?"

"Persistent little scoundrel," I mumbled under my breath.

"Percy!" Gen called. "I love it!"

And of course the dog and the cat got on with one another. Franny and Patty and Miles had welcomed Percy with a saucer of milk and many exclamations over his lovely orange pattern, his exceedingly friendly countenance, and his obvious intelligence.

The last I'd seen, Daisy and Percy were snuggled up together in a fluffy dog bed in the library while Franny read aloud to them.

I was uncomfortable enough accepting Basilton's assistance once again. Not only was I a guest in his home, but I'd come with an unexpected animal and brought a boy who required lodgings and a salary. I could not envision a scenario in which I was worth all this trouble as a business partner or family friend.

I'd skipped supper with Genevieve and the others to check in on Charlie and settle in my rooms. My clothing had been unpacked in the wardrobe and I'd just sat down to read Genevieve's latest installment in today's *London Post* when I heard the door quietly opening in the sitting room connected to my bedchamber.

Genevieve walked in carrying a delicate-looking tart. "You missed dessert," she said by way of explanation.

"I wasn't hungry."

"I'd hoped to make some seductive comment about you having me for dessert instead, but that didn't seem like something I could manage."

I smiled thinking of all the words she'd whispered in my ear and how they successfully heated my blood and hardened my cock to the point of discomfort. She could have managed it just fine.

Her gaze was scrutinizing. "Is that today's paper?"

"Yes," I answered without lifting my eyes from the text.

I was aware of Gen sitting beside me and after a few moments she started eating the tart herself while I continued reading about Detective Owensby and the case of the missing woman. It was odd. There had never been a female victim before and something told me the detective was more invested in solving this mystery. The serial ended unresolved, which was not unusual. There was almost always some element of the story to see the reader through to the next episode. What was interesting, however, was the insinuation that the victim might not be dead after all.

"Did you fail to kill off Jane Mathison for any particular reason?"

Genevieve licked lemon curd from the corner of her lip before replying, "I couldn't say."

I folded the newspaper and returned it to the oak side table and turned to Genevieve, folding my arm and propping it on the back of the settee. "Why did you change the dynamic? You've never written a female victim in the story."

"I'm not sure," she replied but didn't meet my eyes. She broke off a corner of the crust and held it against my lips.

I waited a moment, inhaling the butter and citrus scent of the pastry before opening my mouth and sucking the bit of tart and Genevieve's thumb into my mouth.

She removed her hand back to her lap but her eyes darkened as she watched me chew. Her wide pupils followed the movement as I swallowed.

I stretched my hand between us and fingered a strand of her brown hair. "Are you giving Detective Owensby someone to save?"

Gen brushed the crumbs from her rose-colored skirts instead of meeting my gaze. "Perhaps I've tortured him long enough. Perhaps the good detective deserves a happily ever after."

I wondered at this change and at the way she refused to look at me. I could see the beginnings of a blush painting the tops of her cheekbones, but when she replied it was to question my motives instead. "Why did you hide in your rooms rather than join us for supper?"

"I didn't hide," I countered immediately.

I *had* hidden, and Gen knew it. She didn't believe my hastily voiced argument. And I could see it in the careful way she was being with me.

She sighed. "I know you feel strange about staying here at Cawthorn Hall. I realize it goes against your strict Julian code of doing everything yourself and owing no one for anything . . . ever."

"That's not—"

"It is true," she interrupted without heat. "But I want you to know there are no expectations." Her gaze was careful, steady. "It is not my intent to put pressure on you or your time while you are in London. This new development . . ." She waved a hand as if to encompass the intimacy between us. As if it was so easy to summarize the way I felt when she walked into a room. The overwhelming urgency. The warm rush of awareness. And the absolute knowledge that this woman knew me better than anyone ever had. "It could be an extension of our friendship. Nothing has to change. I enjoy being with you and I hope you enjoy being with me. We can continue our intimacies here until you—until you decide to move on."

For as calmly and evenly as she began, her speech ended on a note of uncertainty. Her gaze had strayed over my shoulder at some point and her words had grown quiet, a question mark on the end of each sentence.

I could tell her of Miles's offer of partnership and the possibilities that now presented themselves with Brightleaf Farms. Now would be my chance to put her fears to rest, to admit how much I craved not only her but a future where we were both happy and something more, together.

But in the end, the words wouldn't come. How could I offer her anything—even a choice—when the future was so uncertain? Even if my uncle agreed to the buyout and the transition of the farm to Hampshire, what would that mean for Genevieve and myself?

It would be one more part of me laid bare when I didn't even know what Genevieve wanted. I would never be a gentleman nor a titled lord, someone worthy of a lady. I could love her better than anyone, and I feared very much that that was the path my heart was on.

It was often possibility and hope that did the most damage.

If the partnership with Basilton never came to pass, I would return to Leicester. The prospect of that way forward felt suddenly devastating. I feared I'd already let myself run away with thoughts of a potential future. One with Hampshire and horses and the love of the youngest Bartholomew. At least if I kept quiet now, Genevieve would be none the wiser. What good would it do to raise her hopes along with mine? The fall back to reality might break us both.

"Come here," I whispered, and that had her gaze meeting mine.

I wasn't sure if I trusted her little speech that spoke of a casual relationship with low expectations. But Genevieve had never lied to me. So I would trust her in this. Until I knew for sure that there was a way forward for us, for better or worse.

"We can do things your way," I said, clasping her hands. "Of course I enjoy being with you."

Her relieved sigh plucked an errant string within me. I needed her close. She needed to know.

I pulled her astride before rising to my feet.

"Julian, no." She clutched my shoulders like I might drop her. As if I'd ever let anything happen to her. "I'm too heavy. You'll collapse."

I paused, standing easily and holding her aloft. "You're perfect." My words were paired with a tender kiss to her temple. Then I used the hand beneath her bottom to squeeze and emphasize my point. "But if you don't stop squirming, I might throw you over my shoulder."

Genevieve yelped as I deposited her on the bed. A giggle escaped when she bounced softly atop the bedding. I took her legs and dragged her to the end of the mattress, lowering myself to my knees.

"What are you doing?" she said in a rush, propping herself up on her elbows.

I removed her slippers and peeled down her stockings without answering. When my hands smoothed up her legs and tugged down her drawers, she gave a little squeak that had me hiding a smile against her thigh.

"Julian, what are you doing?" she asked once more, but the question was breathless and expectant this time.

I tossed her underthings over my shoulder and started raising her layers of skirts and petticoats before meeting her gaze. "I'm having my dessert."

Her blue eyes widened as she read my intent. I parted her legs and leaned forward to brush my lips tenderly to the seam of her sex.

Gen made a garbled sound and collapsed onto her back.

I couldn't help the smile that emerged as I used my fingers and parted her. With the flat of my tongue, I gave a long, luxurious lick against her center.

Her breath gusted out as she flung an arm across her face.

She was hot and wet against my lips and so soft that my hands shook.

I took my time with her despite the ache in my cock. I traced her folds gently before focusing my efforts on the little bundle of nerves at her apex.

Genevieve's toes were scrambling for purchase against the red carpet beneath her feet, so I lifted her legs and placed them over my shoulders. The sound she made would haunt me for the rest of my life, fueling erotic dreams and providing the accompaniment to pleasure achieved by my own hand.

"Tell me," I demanded as I put my lips around her and sucked.

"I—I can't," she said, releasing a great gasping breath. "It's like the world is on fire and—and only your lips and your tongue can soothe the flames."

I rewarded her profoundly sensual honesty by sliding a finger within her tight channel.

Her back arched off the bed and she panted, "Julian."

I kept up my pace, swallowing her arousal and thrusting in a second finger. It wasn't long before her intimate muscles pulsed around me, a broken plea reaching my ears. I stroked her tenderly with my tongue as her sensitive flesh recovered from the intensity of her crisis.

Another choked "Julian" had me pulling away and standing. Genevieve surprised me and pushed herself up, hands reaching for me as I removed my shirt and unbuttoned my trousers.

She kissed me hard and groaned into my mouth. Her hands were everywhere, pushing at my remaining clothes while I fought to loosen her bodice and untie her skirts.

Eventually when we'd shed our garments and pulled each other down to the bed, I swept the hair out of her eyes and asked, "Are you all right?"

"Yes," she replied, hitching one leg over my hip as my erection settled right where I needed.

I craved her warmth and her softness and the way she never seemed to be close enough.

Gen reached down and grasped my backside, urging me forward and into her heat. We both groaned at the drag and slide of my cock as I pushed all the way in and then retreated until just the tip remained. Her breasts swayed with the movement and I rested my forehead against hers to glance down the length of our bodies and watch the way we moved together.

For all the ways we'd fought and argued and bickered and teased over the years, we were compatible like this, in tune with one another, open and honest in a way that you could only be with someone you lo—

"Julian," she gasped again as my thrusts approached the edge of wild and inelegant.

Our movements turned frantic and thoughts fled. Release approached for us, both a promise and a threat.

"It's so good," I murmured unthinkingly. "You feel *so* good."

As our bodies edged us beyond reason, I couldn't help but think of Genevieve's assurance. That things between us didn't have to change. The pleasure we sought and the intimacy we shared could be nothing more than an extension of the friendship we'd known all our lives. We could be both friends and lovers and still have this—moments of perfection layered in knowledge of one another so deep and so pure that nothing could alter it.

When the fire had burned low and the sweat cooled on our skin, I begged her with my desperate touch to stay. To just stay with me. And to never let me go.

Fifteen

GENEVIEVE

Dear Julian,

Patty offered to let me stay with her in London. I think she's trying to cheer me up since you left. Perhaps I should focus on the fact that she's actually trying. She was different during her trip to Laurel Park—her first visit in such a long time. You probably don't remember Patty at all. Honestly, I don't either. But I think I'm willing to get to know her again. It was kindness she offered. A distraction. And I'd be a fool not to take it. Perhaps when I return to Hampshire, I'll have a letter waiting for me.

Yours,
Gen

I awoke with a jolt.

Slightly disoriented, I sat upright and looked around the guest suite. It was still dark and painfully early. Nothing was amiss. No servants had entered. Julian lay by my side, hair disheveled, breaths heavy and even, and one pale arm slung across my thighs.

With another scan of the space, I tensed suddenly as I noticed the orange-striped cat reclining at the foot of the bed.

Percy raised his head and blinked sleepy eyes at me as I stared on in astonishment. He hadn't been there the night before.

I could feel Julian shifting, and then a moment later he sat up next to me, propping himself up on one arm. "I don't know how he does it either."

"But I locked the door to keep the servants out." The same as every night we'd spent together since Julian had become a guest at Cawthorn Hall nearly a fortnight ago.

Julian's nose nuzzled against my bare shoulder. "That cat has mystical powers. Best to just accept it."

My eyes narrowed at the lazy feline, but then the sleep-rumpled man at my side placed an indecent kiss to the side of my neck. Jules tugged me back down into the bedlinens, still warm from our bodies, and I didn't worry about the cat again for some time.

Later that morning, when I'd dressed in my nightgown and robe, I stood by Julian's window and shifted the curtains to the side. Peering down into the frost-laden garden, I let the sun warm my face.

The appearance of the bright sunshine and a sudden idea had me turning and asking with little forethought, "Might I borrow Graceling for a ride with my sister? Perhaps she can exercise one of the others for you?" The mare was striking and I had a feeling that with Patty's influence, other ladies in the park today would be interested in purchasing a horse of their own from Brightleaf Farms.

Julian's eyes met mine in the mirror of the dressing table. He was attempting to comb and straighten his unruly hair. Perhaps I'd been too thorough with my attentions last night while his head had been between my thighs.

His brow rose as if he could interpret my amusement at the sight of him. "I have a meeting this afternoon, and I'll ride Brutus. But you're welcome to any horse you like. I'm sure Graceling will appreciate your company. She gives Charlie a hard time."

I smiled at the thought of the young man Julian had arrived with from the boardinghouse. Charlie had settled in nicely and seemed to be getting along well with the other grooms and stable hands. I knew that Julian often visited the boy under the pretense of checking on the horses. I didn't comment on his soft spot for him. I wondered if he'd ask Charlie to return to Leicester in the spring.

I felt a pang at the thought of Julian leaving, but I buried it and turned back toward the window. Julian's keen gaze missed nothing, and I wasn't ready to broach the subject. I wasn't prepared to lose these nights we spent together. We hadn't discussed any part of the future. We were simply going along in secret with our relationship and pretending there was not an end date looming on the horizon.

"Thank you," I said when I could trust my voice again. "We'll take good care of them."

I could hear Julian's footsteps approaching my position by the window. He'd apparently given up on his hair.

"I have no doubt," he said quietly as his arms slipped around me. His touch soothed some of the restlessness.

As he placed a feather-light kiss to my temple, I tried to dispel the remaining uneasiness and worry I felt. We had time. This wasn't the end of anything.

Not yet, anyway.

~

"Patty . . ."

My sister glanced in my direction even as my voice trailed off. One well-manicured blond brow rose but she said nothing.

Patty had always been good at that—giving me space to think. With the gap in our ages and the years we spent apart as a result of her awful first marriage, we didn't get to know each other very well until I'd been mostly grown. I think, as a result, Patty had always treated me like an adult, possessing adult ideas and adult problems. She had never once minimized my trivialities. I loved Emery, but we'd grown up together and she still remembered what I was like as a little girl. She has a tendency to be bossy and presumptuous with me. I would always be her baby sister. We simply had too much history and not enough present when dealing with serious issues.

I wondered if that was also the problem I faced with Julian. Too much of our childhood getting in the way of a future. Of perhaps, there wouldn't be a future in the first place.

"Patty," I tried again. "I am . . . worried."

My sister turned my way again, just a slight tilt of her head from atop her horse. She was riding Cinder while I sat sidesaddle upon Graceling, and we'd been turning heads since we'd entered the chilly park an hour ago. Despite the cool temperature, it was a busy day due to the brilliant sunshine, and we'd been stopping periodically to greet acquaintances who remarked on our mounts.

"What are you worried about, Gen?"

Her statement was simple and held absolutely no judgment, but my face flamed regardless. Patty was not an idiot nor was she oblivious. While we hadn't discussed the bed in which I'd been spending all my nights, I had no doubt that my sister knew. But Patty was discreet and trustworthy. I'd be surprised if she'd discussed my and Julian's relationship with anyone, even Miles.

"I guess, I'm afraid of the future. About what happens when spring arrives."

A telling pause. "Have you asked Julian about his plans or his . . . intentions?"

I shook my head. "No. I suppose I haven't wanted to cause trouble. I've kept my questions to myself."

Patty said nothing for a moment and the hesitation felt purposeful. I noticed only the quiet between us and the horse shifting below me.

Finally she offered, "That doesn't sound like you, Genevieve. I don't think you have to hide your true nature—curious, forthright, honest—just to keep the peace with Julian. He's known you a very long time."

I could feel my features soften, go pleading. "That's the thing, Patty. If I question what's happening between us and where it's going, he'll know how much I—I want. How much I wish for a future. I fear I'm becoming that girl again. The one with stars in her eyes. The one consumed by love for a boy who didn't feel the same. A boy who left her behind so easily." I took a shaky breath and met my sister's sympathetic blue gaze. "I don't want to be left behind again."

"Darling, I think you are making decisions for the both of you based on one-sided information. You need to communicate with Julian. If you're not ready to profess your love, then don't. But it's not outside the realm of plausibility that you'd want to know the future plans of the man sharing your bed."

Subtle panic claimed my features and my stomach tightened with awareness. It was one thing to know that my sister was aware of my nighttime activities, it was quite another to hear it out loud in broad daylight.

I swallowed against my discomfort and forced myself to straighten in the saddle. "Are you mad?"

Patty looked startled, blue eyes going wide. "Mad about what? You're a grown woman, Gen. It would be hypocritical of me to scold you for having a relationship with a man outside of marriage. And so I won't insult you by doing just that."

The tension in my limbs didn't ease so much as dissipate all at once. I didn't realize how much I prized my sister's high opinion of me. Her disappointment would have wounded something deep and precious.

Just then, Lady Gabriella, the Viscountess of Tryton, approached with a maid at her back. She and Patty were friendly. Her husband, Conrad Himmel, was equal parts wealthy and indulgent to his young bride. We ran in similar circles and often interacted at society events. Lord and Lady Tryton were supporters of and frequently mentioned in the society pages of the *London Post*. "Your Grace! Lady Genevieve! My word, look at you both up there."

My sister and I greeted the viscountess warmly.

In truth, I was grateful for the interruption. I needed some time to sit with Patty's advice.

"These horses are gorgeous!" Lady Tryton exclaimed happily. Her large brown eyes kept coming back to Graceling's impressive stature and beauty.

As if sensing a rapt audience, the horse tossed her mane in a move I couldn't have orchestrated with my own hair had I been trying. I smiled as the vain mare garnered delighted applause from the viscountess.

At least the temperamental thing hadn't bitten her.

"Wherever did you find such a fine animal, Lady Genevieve?"

"From Brightleaf Farms," I stated simply.

When the dark-haired woman showed no sign of recognition, Patty added, "Surely you've heard of Brightleaf Farms, my lady."

"Oh, of course!" she replied brightly.

"It's in Leicester," I chimed in helpfully.

Graceling nickered amiably, and I fought a smile.

"We recently acquired both of these gorgeous mounts from Mr. Julian Moore. He's a guest at Cawthorn Hall until the spring. Several of his horses will be participating in the Royal Ascot. Isn't that exciting?" Patty wielded her duchessly influence so masterfully as she gestured to her dark gray mare.

After that it was simply a matter of acknowledging the viscountess's enthusiasm and promising to share her calling card with Mr. Moore at our earliest convenience. She was sure her wealthy husband was in dire need of fine beasts such as these.

The afternoon carried on thusly, and by the end of our outing, the sun was drooping toward the horizon and the tray in the entryway was full of correspondence for Mr. Julian Moore of Brightleaf Farms.

Daly and his lovely wife joined us for supper that evening. The woman was terribly shy but she'd grown comfortable with our circle over the years. The handsome couple made for a lovely distraction, and I was grateful they'd accepted Miles's dinner invitation.

I could feel myself brooding over Julian and replaying my sister's irritatingly mature advice. I wanted to stop pretending. What did it matter if I reached over and took Julian's hand during an informal meal with my family and our close friends? Why should I have to hide my feelings?

A fearful voice whispered that Julian would feel pressured— trapped—were I to acknowledge our private relationship in a public setting. My family was accommodating and understanding, but they wouldn't ignore something so blatant. A declaration on my part would come with expectations for Julian. I couldn't force him into anything even at the cost of my pride. It wouldn't be right and it wouldn't be fair. I wanted Julian's love and affection freely given, not under duress or threat to my reputation. That, in addition to the very real possibility that Julian might pull away, kept my wayward hands to myself.

At one point during the meal—between the soup and fish course —Julian had mouthed, "Are you all right?"

To which I'd responded by jolting as if burned and rattling the glassware on the table.

Julian's eyes had widened in alarm but he hadn't attempted communication again. I'd caught him watching me a few times, gaze wary and concerned.

To punish myself, I'd waited in my rooms—longer than usual. I'd taken a leisurely bath and washed and plaited my hair, adding time to the distance and circumstances that separated us.

Something spiteful and vindictive that lived within wanted to see if Julian would come to me for a change. In these weeks of late night visits, I'd always been the one risking myself and seeking him out in his guest quarters. He'd never come to me.

With the current muddled state of my mind, I was certain I was reading more into that fact. But I still felt an uncomfortable twinge at consistently chasing after Julian. He hadn't escaped my thoughts in all these years, and it seemed he couldn't escape me now with my reliable visits to his chambers after dark.

There was something to be said for feeling wanted and cherished. The pendulum had yet to swing in my favor.

Still, I sat on the edge of my bed with only my thoughts for rather poor company. Finally, I heaved a sigh and stood, intent on finally seeking Julian out. That was when Percy emerged from beneath my bed and scared the life out of me.

"Good Lord, Percy," I said aloud to the animal, placing a hand to my chest. "You are a sneaky devil."

The cat wound himself through my legs affectionately offering his odd, rough reply when I reached down to scratch behind his ears. "Do you think you'll stay with us when Julian leaves, hmm?"

His rumbly purr was my only answer.

"Perhaps he'll want to bring you to Leicester." I paused. "Maybe we could both go with him."

Percy's strange golden eyes seemed to radiate knowing sympathy.

"He'd be lonely without us, I think. But he'd likely never admit it. And Julian would never be the one to ask us. We'd have to show up on his doorstep." I straightened to standing.

"I'm beginning to see why you just presented yourself on the front drive alongside him without warning," I said to the cat.

Percy elected to curl up at the foot of my bed while I donned my dressing gown and slipped quietly from my bedchamber. I moved quickly out of the family wing and toward Julian's guest quarters, feeling as if a weight pressed down upon me making my steps slow and reluctant.

Could I really do as Patty had suggested? Simply tell him my worries and inquire after his intentions? What if all these nights together didn't mean anything to him? What if they didn't spell out a future in the light of day?

He'd been very careful every time we'd made love. Julian always withdrew before his crisis struck. At first, I thought he was being considerate and responsible. But now—in the face of my inconvenient self-doubt—I wondered if instead, he wasn't willing to accept the consequences of our joining.

Would a marriage to me be so awful? Would a child we created be so unwelcome?

I stood in front of his door and closed my eyes in the darkened corridor. I took a deep breath for courage and then one more because I felt like I needed it.

I raised my hand to knock and opened my eyes. Surprise had me stiffening and smothering a yelp. The door was wide open and Julian stood there fully dressed watching me curiously.

"Were you going out?" I whispered.

He ignored my question. "What is going on with you? Did something happen in the park? Did you lose one of my horses? You've been behaving oddly all day."

"I don't know what you mean," I replied stubbornly and brushed by him into the room. "Why are you dressed?" I turned and looked pointedly at his top coat and boots.

When I typically joined Julian in his chambers, he would be down to his shirtsleeves, trousers, and bare feet. I liked the intimacy of that—seeing him unfit for polite company and knowing I was, indeed, *not* polite company.

"I was going to find you," Julian sighed, shrugging out of his layers. "I couldn't very well wander through the Duchess of Cawthorn's halls in my stockinged feet."

"Oh, yes. The horror," I teased as warmth expanded throughout my body. He'd been on his way to me.

"What if Daisy had found me on the landing and started barking? Then Franny would have seen me in such an improper state."

"Yes, that's true. We wouldn't want such an impressionable youth to know that you have an adorable smattering of freckles on the tops of your pale feet."

Julian glared at me but the tips of his ears turned an equally adorable shade of magenta.

With thinly veiled amusement, I directed the conversation. "I was delayed by your cat actually. Percy surprised me from beneath my bed and then I felt bad abandoning him while he was being so affectionate. We had a nice chat."

"That cat is not mine," Julian insisted without heat, now sitting down to remove his boots.

I laughed, the first genuine sound I'd made since I walked in the room. "That cat most certainly *is* your cat. He arrived with you and he'll leave with you. He's yours."

Julian's gaze had snapped to mine at the mention of his departure. But I worked to keep my face impassively benign, and his intense gray eyes eventually melted away to focus on his boots once more.

I'd been absently drifting around the room as Julian and I spoke, but now I wandered to his bed and pulled back the covers, making myself comfortable.

Moments later, Julian sat down beside me. "What's going on? You were quiet at dinner and just now—at the door—you seemed . . ."

"I seemed what?" I asked softly.

"I don't know," he confessed with a furrowed brow. "That's why I'm asking."

This was it. This was my chance.

I scooted up and reclined against the headboard. Jules turned toward me on the mattress, bending his knee and letting it rest against my thigh.

I forced courage into my gaze and my voice. "I was—I was thinking about the future . . ." I trailed off as I watched his face tighten imperceptibly. If I hadn't been focused so hard on boldly making eye contact, I might have missed it. Then again, I knew

Julian better than anyone. His discomfort might as well have shouted to me—and me alone—from the rooftops.

With panic rising along with the beat of my frantic heart, I licked my lips and abruptly changed course. "I was thinking about the future of my writing. I think I'm going to reveal my identity as the writer of the *Detective Owensby* serial. I meet with my editor next week and I'm going to broach the subject."

The faint line between Julian's brows eased and he cleared his throat. "I think that's a marvelous idea. It's time you receive the credit you're due. I'm—I'm so proud of you."

He reached forward and grabbed my hands. I hadn't realized they'd been twisting in the coverlet. "God, Gen," he breathed, stilling my nervous movements. "You've really been worried about this." His thumbs rubbed soothing circles on my palms.

I nodded, the motion jerky and unpracticed.

"Come here," he said as he hauled me to him, embracing me gently and passing a comforting hand across my shoulders and down my back. "I'm sorry this has been weighing on you. But I'm sure your family will support you, and your readers will stick by you. Obviously Mr. Belham is an idiot, but he's sure to see what a valuable talent you are. He should be falling all over himself to keep your work with the *Post*. It will all work out, you'll see."

My chin rested upon Julian's shoulder. I could feel him—warm and solid and comforting—through the thin fabric of his shirt-sleeves. I bit my lip hard to keep the pressure behind my eyes from turning into something far more embarrassing.

What had I been thinking? It was only November. Julian would be in London until the spring races. It was silly to bring up our future so soon just because I was feeling insecure and unlike myself. I could have ruined our remaining months together. We had time to discuss all of this. Perhaps by June, Julian would want more. Perhaps he'd want everything.

Patty's guidance had been sound. Rationally, I knew I needed to be honest and open with Julian. Yet I was ashamed to admit I lacked the courage required to follow through on her suggestion at the moment.

Bravery in the face of defeat seemed somehow kinder. At least then, your warrior heart knew what was coming. Courage when confronting the unknown was the true test. It required faith, and it wasn't for the faint of heart.

My heart felt a bit too tender just then.

When you'd already lost something once, you knew exactly how much it hurt. And you'd do anything to avoid that feeling again.

Later that night, we blew out all the candles and turned down all the lamps. We made love in the darkness, slow and unbearably sweet. All I could hear were our hitching breaths and low sounds of pleasure. All I could feel was Julian moving within me, slow-rolling hips and sweat-dampened skin. We breathed answering sighs as I unraveled in his arms.

This intensity—this sensation—must be love. He couldn't touch me like that so casually. This was an offering. A plea in the darkness. A promise of more—a future. It *had* to be love.

But in the absence of sleep, in the shadow of night, a tiny, persuasive voice—one that lived inside us all—said, "what if it's not?"

Sixteen

JULIAN

There was something to be said for following your gut instinct.

Two days earlier, during an outing with Drakefield and Miles and several others, my gut told me that one of the men who approached for an introduction was nothing more than a shit-stirrer. Viscount Brannigan made me wary with his comical swagger and surface charm that never passed the threshold of sincerity. However, I didn't wish to seem ungrateful or embarrass Basilton and his acquaintances. And I had no proof that Brannigan was a scoundrel beyond his youthful features and permanently cheerful expression. So I shook his hand and, at his insistence, agreed to a quick meeting at the Cawthorn stables on this gray and threatening afternoon.

Drakefield and the others had eyed our exchange carefully, and that had added to the uneasy feeling swirling in my stomach.

At breakfast this morning, Basilton had asked after the meeting with Brannigan and offered to attend, all the while fidgeting with the handle of his teacup. "I know you prefer to handle these matters on your own, so I won't insert myself. But just let me say . . . Brannigan is a snake. His father has indulged him all his life. He comes across all charm and decorum, but once you've served your purpose in his eyes, he'll turn on you."

"You know I don't trust any of them," I'd replied easily.

Miles's expression had been troubled. "Well, trust him even less."

That should have been warning enough.

But now, hours later, I stood in the stable yard showing Lark off to Brannigan and the three gentlemen who'd accompanied him. The other men had been a surprise, but I'd swallowed down my unease and considered the horses I could sell for my uncle and the farm.

That was why I was here—in London—in the first place. To do a job and support Brightleaf. I wasn't here to make friends with these men. Neither was I here to play pretend with Genevieve, no matter how much I felt when we were together. It was easy to get lost in thoughts of a future—especially with Basilton's offer on the table.

I was desperate to tell Gen about Miles's plans for the farm and our partnership. I knew keeping it from her was wrong, but I'd yet to receive word from Uncle Phillip. I didn't know what I'd do if he refused the offer. My hopes were up high enough. There was little reason to involve Genevieve until I knew if I could provide for her, if a future was even a possibility. If she'd even want that . . . or me.

And it was moments like these when I wasn't sure if I could ever fit into her world.

The concern I felt in the pit of my stomach increased as Lark shifted at my side, bored and restless. He'd rather be out with Charlie for a ride, stretching his legs. Instead, the stallion wasted his time with a group of men who were more concerned with hearing themselves speak than with anything Brightleaf could offer them.

"Why can't I just buy this horse, Moore?" Brannigan's brow furrowed beneath his hat. "If he's as fast as you say he is."

"I'm afraid Lark here is racing at the Royal Ascot and we can't part with him. But he's a fine example of the horses we raise at Brightleaf Farms. He's out of Tapa and that brood mare births nothing but racers."

Brannigan eyed me curiously and my stomach gave another uncomfortable twist that had me shifting on my feet.

Lark sighed over my shoulder, losing interest quickly in the conversation as well.

"Would you like to ride him?" I'd assumed that was what we'd be doing this afternoon. Charlie had saddled and readied the horse for that purpose.

"Goodness, no," Brannigan said, horrified and amused. The three other gentlemen scoffed out their amusement in rapid succession. I tried not to let my confusion show as the viscount continued, "I only agreed to this short meeting"—insisted on it, actually—"in my very busy day. Do I look equipped to be on the back of a horse?"

I took in the expensive cut of his trousers and the garishly bright waistcoat that Brannigan sported. The men had all arrived in a carriage together and not on horseback. Perhaps they did have big plans for the day. Although, for an aristocrat, I couldn't imagine what that might be.

Before I had a chance to formulate an appropriate response, Brannigan went on, laughing, "What do you take me for?" He glanced around the yard and pointed over the short distance toward the stable beyond. Charlie was hovering anxiously in the aisle waiting for his charge and to be of assistance if I required it. "Some sort of poor stable hand? Look at that pathetic urchin." Another mocking laugh from the viscount and his friends. "Should I have arrived in my stained and dirty work clothes to try out your horse?"

Blood heated my cheeks in anger as Charlie startled from the unkind laughter and mocking remarks directed his way. He met my gaze quickly before he retreated deeper into the stables and out of sight of the men.

Why would a viscount stand here and mock a servant? And why did that seem to be so humorous to all his young friends? Was this how aristocrats regularly amused themselves?

Would I be expected to accept it if I was part of Genevieve's life? Did living amongst the *ton* translate to feigned humor at cruelty and turning a blind eye to injustice in aristocratic social circles?

I remembered that I was a guest at Cawthorn Hall. Nothing was settled with my uncle and I was not Basilton's partner. I had no power in this situation, and the very worst I could do would be to insult my host and the connections that he and the duchess had facilitated.

So I bit my tongue though it burned my cheeks and soured my stomach.

Brannigan eyed me knowingly.

"My apologies," I gritted out. "I assumed our meeting was for a more specific purpose."

With cruel humor still lining his boyish face, the viscount slapped me on the back. "Ah, Mr. Moore. I have my steward handle all of those things for me. In fact, I'll put him in touch with you and we'll see how many thoroughbreds I can take off your hands."

I clenched my jaw as the three other men made the same loud claims.

They weren't here to buy horses and I wouldn't be hearing from anyone in their employ.

What a waste of time. I could not imagine a scenario in which coming here today served any purpose but their own. Bored aristocrats who needed to feel self-important and keep themselves entertained.

And they'd insulted Charlie while I stood there and did nothing.

As the men shouted their bright farewells and went away laughing to their carriage, I turned and led Lark down the aisle with angry steps.

Charlie was inside, adding a fresh bucket of water and more straw to an already cleaned stall.

"I'll take him, sir." The boy jumped forward at my approach. His blue eyes looked everywhere but at me.

Shame, sharp and jagged, had me tightening my hands on the reins. The leather creaked in my hold and Lark's head jerked against the tension he felt in the line.

I eased my grip and sighed. "Charlie, I'm sorry."

He shook his head quickly, still unable to meet my gaze. "No trouble, sir." He reached for the lead again, but I didn't relinquish it.

"They had no right to come here and behave that way. And—and I should have spoken up." Charlie's eyes darted to mine and then away. "I apologize for their presence here. It was all a horrible mistake."

"No trouble, sir," the boy repeated. "I think I'll take Lark for a ride. I think 'e needs the space to move about."

The anger I'd felt at Brannigan and his spiteful little crew had boiled down, thick and tacky. I felt coated in it, along with burning shame. I'd stood by and done nothing while those men had laughed at a boy who'd been a target for their childishness. Charlie was nothing but kind and hard-working. He'd been so grateful to leave Mrs. Farnsworth and the boardinghouse behind. He loved working with the animals here and he'd settled in with the other grooms. I knew why I felt such kinship with the boy, but I didn't want to think on that too closely.

"Charlie," I tried again.

"Don't trouble yourself, sir. Lark and I will be right as rain." With a smile that didn't reach his eyes, Charlie took the reins from my hands and led the stallion away down the wide aisle.

I stood staring after them for a long while until Percy trotted in from the direction of the house and sat down beside me.

I looked down at the cat and let out a deep breath. "Well, I bollocksed that right up."

Percy's creaky meow of agreement was my only reply.

Later that afternoon, the rain that threatened all day had finally come to fruition and painted lines down the window pane in the library.

I was writing to my uncle again, the lamps glowing brightly to ward off the gloomy weather.

My hand shook slightly as I paused over the paper. I was still unsteady from the encounter with Brannigan and the aftermath with Charlie. A quiet desperation had driven me to inquire after my uncle and ensure he'd received my earlier correspondence regarding the farm and Basilton's offer. It felt as if my entire future—one that wasn't even fully formed in my mind—rested on Uncle Phillip's response.

I must have been staring unseeingly at the fire while attempting to compose a letter that didn't sound quite so anxious, when Genevieve's appearance in the doorway startled me.

She smiled and something grabbed hold of my throat and squeezed.

I straightened abruptly and shifted papers around to cover the half-composed correspondence.

Her smile widened. "You look like me when I think someone might catch me writing."

I could feel my cheeks warm under her amused gaze. "Sorry. I was just writing to my uncle. I don't know why I panicked when I saw you." But I did know. I was keeping a secret and it felt wrong. The knowledge made all my movements fitful and unpracticed.

"Well, don't let me stop you," Gen said easily. "I wouldn't dream of delaying your correspondence to your uncle."

I could feel my features arranging themselves in confusion.

"What?" she laughed. "I miss your letters."

"But you see me every day."

Her expression turned inward—as it occasionally did—and Genevieve looked wounded. "And I enjoy seeing you every day. But there is something about a letter you can hold and return to over again. It's tangible and . . . well, anyway, I'm certain your uncle enjoys your reports from London."

For the second time today, shame made itself known, consuming my thoughts. She wasn't so much referring to the letters she'd received since my appearance in town but all the letters I'd never sent. It wasn't an accusation. I knew that she didn't blame me for my mother's actions, but Genevieve had written to me for years with no encouragement or reason to continue on. As an adolescent, I'd given up after a few months. Even with the discovery of what my mother had done, that knowledge must have hurt.

I swallowed hard against the regret choking me. "Gen—"

"I was just coming to check on you," she interrupted before I could say—I didn't know what. "And see if you'd be joining us for Lady Gabriella's event tomorrow evening."

After today, the thought of being surrounded by more aristocrats was not enticing. "I'm afraid not."

"You'd be entirely welcome. Lady Gabriella is very kind and she was quite taken with Graceling in the park during my ride a few days ago." When I didn't answer, Gen asked, "How did things go with Brannigan this afternoon?"

Lingering irritation and a piss-poor attitude made my reply terse. "Fine."

But Genevieve was unaffected. She moved closer to the desk I occupied and placed her fingertips on the smooth oak surface. "What happened?"

"Nothing, Genevieve. Just leave it," I snapped without looking up from her hands at the front of the desk. She flinched away and I immediately regretted my words and my tone and everything that had happened today.

I rubbed a frustrated hand over my eyes, massaging the ache behind my brows. "Listen, I apologize for my behavior. Brannigan was an arse and an absolute waste of time. And I'm simply trying to get this letter sent off. Can I just see you at supper? Perhaps I won't make such a hash of things if I spend the next few hours alone."

I paused, but no answer came. No reassurances. No excuses for my poor conduct. No gentle teasing for my foul mood.

Smoothing my hand down my face, I looked up and found an empty room. Genevieve was nowhere in sight.

"Gen," I called, just in case she remained in the corridor or had retreated behind a bookcase.

But again, I was left sitting, talking to myself.

Later that night, across the dining table, Genevieve remained quiet and subdued. She didn't meet my eyes and she made no effort to engage anyone in conversation. Emery and Augustus and Silas were joining us and it was easy for her to slip in the background, a shy wallflower avoiding notice.

But that wasn't Genevieve. She'd never been one to hide from anything. I'd made her this way. Snapping out at her and rejecting her attention in the light of day. She'd caught me at a bad time . . . and I'd simply been an arse. There was no excuse.

This woman was a different version of the girl I'd grown alongside. The Genevieve of my past was entirely comfortable wading through my bad tempers. She'd needle me and tease me until I gave in to her silliness. Our fights had been admittedly few and far between. When we were young, I'd hated seeing her cry, and I couldn't tolerate the uncomfortable sensation her tears prompted.

As we grew older, I was typically only ever in a foul mood when Genevieve had plans to go away to London or when the Bartholomews were hosting a house party. Gen's absence or the need to hide myself away from her were the usual reasons I'd become cross and irritable. During those annual summer holidays when aristocrats would descend on Laurel Park, I'd spend my time away from planned outings and common areas. I'd never wanted to put the marquess and marchioness in a difficult position of explaining my presence in their lives. My mother had been more exacting and adamant that I should remain out of sight lest I embarrass her employers. I wasn't their ward, she'd remind me. I was the son of a servant and I should behave like one.

My frustration over Brannigan had melted away in light of Genevieve's standoffishness. Now my irritation was focused entirely inward. I would talk to Gen tonight. I would apologize for my terseness and tell her about the awful meeting and the way I'd handled things with Charlie. She'd know what to say—how to fix things with the boy. I don't know why I'd avoided the topic in the first place. I'd been distracted by writing the letter to my uncle and fretful over his lack of response.

As the meal concluded, tightness was building behind my ribs as I thought over all my worries. They played on a loop, over and over. And if I didn't get away from this table and out of this room, I was going to chip a tooth from how hard I was clenching my jaw.

Finally, I was able to decline drinks with Miles and Augustus and bid everyone goodnight.

When I arrived in my room, I stripped out of my cravat and top coat. With shaking hands, I moved to unbutton the waistcoat that felt like it was constricting my every breath. I don't know how long it took to get myself under control, but eventually I registered Percy's soft fur beneath my dangling fingertips from my seated position on the side of my bed.

His rumbling purr was welcome as he paced under my hands, occasionally rubbing himself along my knuckles.

I forced my jaw to unclench and rolled my shoulders back. The stiffness there and the time on the clock told me that nearly an hour had passed since I'd left the dining room—since I'd fled.

A knock sounded from the hallway and I breathed a sigh of relief.

Genevieve.

I could fix this one thing. Make it right.

But when I opened the door, I found Mr. Pitch standing in the corridor, holding a bundle of calling cards. The butler wore an impassive expression. "Mr. Moore, I wanted to deliver your correspondence and visitor requests."

"Any letter from Leicester?" I blurted in desperation.

Mr. Pitch never faltered. "No, sir. I'm afraid not. These are calling cards from the front entryway, delivered over the past several days. I apologize. I realized you were unaware of their presence."

I frowned in confusion. Why would I receive calling cards at Cawthorn Hall? All my meetings with potential buyers had been set elsewhere or agreed upon during other events, occasionally facilitated through Basilton's club. It never occurred to me to regularly check the tray in the front entryway for visitor requests.

"No, that mistake is mine, Mr. Pitch. Thank you for bringing these to my attention."

He relinquished the fairly hefty bundle of thick card stock and offered a quick bow before leaving.

My eyes followed his movements and looked beyond for any sight of Genevieve, but there was none. Closing the door, I went over to the seating arrangement near the fire. Some kind maid had stoked the flames prior to my arrival and the room was warm. My panic from dinner was receding and I could feel the chill from dried sweat on my back.

Turning over the linen squares in my hand, I noted names—a few I recognized, but none I'd been introduced to or approached about Brightleaf Farms. I flipped over a card from the Viscount of Tryton. A short note indicated that his wife had met several of my horses in the park with the Duchess of Cawthorn and Lady Genevieve and he simply must know where to acquire one for this bride.

I swallowed painfully against a rising awareness. Most of the two dozen calling cards indicated something similar.

Genevieve had asked to ride Graceling several days ago when the weather was fine. I hadn't thought anything of it. Woman and horse got on well and I hadn't realized that Gen had ulterior motives. She'd been showing off Graceling. Illuminating the farm. Gaining interest. Connecting me with buyers.

Helping me.

I hung my head and muttered a timely, "Fuck."

The cards felt heavy in my hands, weighted with the guilt I couldn't seem to escape—the mistakes I couldn't stop making.

Shame kept my feet rooted to the floor, preventing me from marching to Genevieve's room and apologizing outright.

She deserved more from me than a strangled excuse and my untamed emotions.

I flipped back through the cards to the very first one. *Viscount of Tryton* in bold lettering. The name slotted into place and I recalled Genevieve this afternoon, asking if I'd be joining them at the Tryton ball tomorrow. She'd wanted me to attend, and I'd rejected the invitation immediately.

Percy chose that moment to cry for attention.

I looked down at the orange menace.

"I should go to this ball. Join Genevieve and her family. Is that the right thing?"

Intelligent feline eyes regarded me. He offered his rough meow in response and I took that to mean, "of course, you idiot."

"I'll make it up to her. This whole bloody stupid afternoon. I'll tell her I'm sorry and I'll thank her"—I smoothed my thumb over the fine linen squares in my hand—"for all this."

Percy wound affectionately around my legs.

"I should tell her about the farm, too," I mused to a cat and an empty room. "About Basilton's offer and how much I want it—want her."

But bravery only went so far.

And the first step would be owning my mistakes.

I would attend the ball tomorrow and Genevieve would know that I was there . . . for her.

I'd polished my boots to a ridiculous shine. The glaring reflection was impossible to ignore as I focused solely on putting one foot in front of the other as I made my way down the steps of the grand staircase into the Tryton ballroom.

Miles had agreed to take a carriage over with me later and allow Genevieve and the duchess to go on ahead.

Franny was miffed to be left behind, so Basilton had offered a game of chess before the young girl went off to bed and he on to the Mayfair event.

I'd simply hidden in my rooms, keeping my distance from Genevieve and fretting over my appearance like a juvenile. With my very common face staring back at me in the mirror, I couldn't decide if my plan to surprise Genevieve was merely nonsensical or outright idiotic.

"It will be fine," Miles said, grounding me more than my shiny black boots could in this strange ballroom. "Tryton is eager to meet you." And after a cagey glance in my direction, the earl finished, "And whatever is going on with Genevieve . . . you'll work it out."

I released a breath but said nothing.

This wasn't the first event I'd attended as a guest of the Duchess of Cawthorn, but it was the first one that wasn't done under pretense. Despite Tryton's desire to purchase a horse like Graceling for his wife, I wasn't here for him.

I was here for Genevieve.

And there she was.

Standing with the duchess and several others, she looked beautiful in a pale rose gown. Lace lined the sleeves and there was something about the fabric that made it shimmer in the warm glow of the candlelight. Her hair was high, twisting delicately around her crown, leaving her long, elegant neck bare.

I suddenly recalled that very first dream I'd had about Genevieve. The one that had shocked me to my core upon waking. We'd been nestled together on horseback and I'd swept her dark hair aside and kissed her neck. The dream had been so real and unexpected, but my attraction had made itself known.

The sight of her now—after all the ways I'd kissed her beyond my nighttime imaginings—had my fists clenching in restraint. I longed to walk right over to her and scandalize every person in the vicinity. Place my lips against her soft, pale skin and give a gentle suck that would have Genevieve sighing out my name for all these aristocrats to hear.

Genevieve turned then, just as my daydreams were getting away from me. Her face brightened in surprise, but I saw the moment she remembered. The stunned delight gave way to confusion and lowered brows.

I smiled to reassure her but also to say *I'm sorry* and *I missed you* and *I hate that I hurt you.*

Basilton was introducing me to those gathered but I didn't register all the names and faces. My eyes kept flitting back to Genevieve. She eyed me cautiously.

When I'd finished bowing and shaking all the hands that good manners dictated, I settled by Gen's side, allowing the back of my glove to brush against hers.

We looked over at each other as the others resumed their conversation. She gave me a small smile. "I didn't think you were joining us this evening."

"I found it difficult to stay away," I admitted softly, hoping to convey what I couldn't say in front of all these people. That it was *her* I needed. *Her* I wanted to see.

Genevieve's eyes wandered over my face but I couldn't say what expression she read there. I feared I was being too open—too bold. Could everyone see how much I cared for her? Was it written in my eyes, gone soft and warm? Or perhaps in the smile I rarely allowed—the one meant only for her?

After a moment, she murmured quietly, "All right?"

I nodded once, decisively. "I am now."

Seventeen

GENEVIEVE

Dear Julian,

In the immortal words of my eleven-year-old self who still intimately recalls the taste of French-milled soap, "Holy shit, Jules!" I can't tell you the full extent of the secret, but I'm going to be a published author soon. I suppose I could tell you. It's not as if you're receiving these letters or responding to them or acknowledging them. But no matter! I am excited and needed to tell someone. I'm going to be an author, Julian! A wordsmith. No—a word slinger. I like that much better. Can you believe it?

Written by acclaimed author,
Genevieve Bartholomew

Julian was here—in the Tryton ballroom—and I couldn't stop staring at him.

He wasn't doing a very good job at not staring at me either, which, admittedly, gave me a small thrill.

I'd known Julian long enough to know that his presence here wasn't an accident or anything so casual. He'd made a decision, one that meant something. He was here for me.

I knew how difficult these types of events were for him. He was nervous around most people, especially if he wasn't talking about horses or the farm. Julian reverted to quiet observation and hoped to be unnoticed in the face of crowds and strangers. High-society gatherings added another layer of complication and anxiety. I could see it easily enough in his fidgeting and high color, the way he actively fought to achieve absolute stillness.

If Julian attended tonight, it was against all his better instincts.

I hadn't invited him yesterday because I'd wanted to torture him. I'd known that Tryton hoped to conduct business with Julian, and joining us for the ball tonight was the quickest way to earn an introduction. And I thought it would be better if Miles was about for moral support. But then something had obviously been bothering Julian, and he'd rejected the invitation outright and snapped at me to give him space.

The Genevieve of old would have ignored Julian's response and attempted to coax him into a better mood. But now, I felt so unsteady in our relationship. All the secrecy and unknowns made me cautious when my natural inclination was to be bold. I questioned all my actions and was afraid to lose him as a result. So, I'd given him the distance he'd needed, and gotten my feelings hurt in the process.

I couldn't say why I'd taken Julian's bad mood to heart the way I had. That was something *past Genevieve* would have let roll right off her back. Perhaps because everything felt so uncertain and tenuous that I didn't want to overstep and had gone backward as a result.

The old Genevieve had been secure in her friendship with Julian. This new version of us was balanced precariously on the ledge of something more.

Now, in the ballroom, I willed myself not to react too strongly.

When the other guests drifted away and Miles and Patty were talking quietly to one another, Julian motioned me back with him a step.

He spoke quietly at my side, "I'm sorry for the way I acted yesterday. I shouldn't have lashed out at you. And I should have sought you out to explain." Julian's gray eyes were remorseful as he held my gaze.

I nodded. "It's all right. Thank you for apologizing and coming here tonight."

"And I have you to thank for many more inquiries for Brightleaf. It seems several ladies were quite taken by your salesmanship in the park earlier in the week." His stare was intense, meaningful. "I'm grateful, Gen, truly. For your unwavering support. I don't deserve it."

I shook my head, uneasy with his gratitude for something so simple. "I'm happy it worked out in your favor. I'm glad you're here, Jules."

He smiled then, a small and secret thing that had warmth settling in my middle. "As am I."

"Can I ask what happened? Why you were so upset yesterday? Did something happen with your uncle? Is he unwell?"

Julian shook his head. "No, nothing that I'm aware of. Though it was part of my worry. Uncle Phillip hasn't responded to my recent letters. I was—am concerned. And in truth, I had a terrible meeting with Brannigan yesterday that put me in a bad temper. It's no excuse. I should not have taken it out on you."

I knew of Viscount Brannigan's reputation as a somewhat fair-weather gentleman. He didn't keep friends very long and seemed to create drama out of boredom. "What did Brannigan do?"

Julian fidgeted with the buttons of his dark waistcoat. "He never had any intention of buying from Brightleaf. I don't know why he insisted on the meeting in the first place. Showed up with three gentlemen in a carriage and laughed in my face when I asked if he wanted to try out Lark." Julian shook his head in irritation, color rising beneath his cravat in remembered irritation. "He mocked Charlie to make himself seem grand before his friends."

My heart clenched. "Oh, no. Poor Charlie. Is he all right?"

"I don't know. He put on a good mask but I could tell he was upset. Got away as fast as he could. He didn't want to discuss it."

I could understand that. From what Jules had told me, the boy had likely been the subject of plenty of verbal abuse and degradation from his stepmother over the years.

"I didn't say anything." Julian's rough words had me searching his face, but he wouldn't meet my eyes. "When Brannigan mocked Charlie. I didn't tell the viscount to leave or demand an apology or make some cutting remark in return. I just stood there."

I sighed, understanding immediately why Julian had been in a state yesterday. He wasn't upset over Brannigan. Perhaps he was worried about his uncle, but Julian's anger and irritation were focused entirely inward. He was berating himself for his own behavior.

I didn't know how to make this better for him. Reminding Jules that he'd done the only acceptable thing—no matter how distasteful—wouldn't help the situation. His own sense of pride and honor could never agree to that. In his mind, he should have stood up for Charlie and dressed down the viscount.

However, confronting Brannigan for his poor behavior would have never worked in Julian's favor. The spoiled aristocrat would have done whatever he could to sully Julian's reputation out of childish spite.

Finally, I said, "I'm sorry you were put into that situation. With no good outcome." Jules had no reply, so I made my voice soft and kind—in a way that Julian could never be with himself. "Charlie will forgive you. He knows you're not like them."

That had Julian's head snapping up to mine, his expression still vulnerable. "You're right. I'm not."

Something in his tone had my brows lowering in concern. I felt the need to grasp his sleeve to keep him close even though he hadn't shifted away at all. The distance wasn't physical, I realized. But I could feel it all the same.

Before I could question his meaning, Miles stepped over and interrupted, "Come, Mr. Moore. Let's go introduce you to Tryton. He signaled that we should have a chat." With a bow of his head, Miles continued, "Genevieve, please keep your sister out of trouble."

Patty rolled her eyes, but her husband gave her a little wink that had her smiling brightly.

I felt a gentle squeeze to my arm before Julian said in a low voice, "I won't be long."

All I managed was a shaky nod in the face of his departure. I thought, once more, that I was not hiding my feelings very well. I expected Patty to comment on my carelessness but she didn't get the chance. Several other guests approached to seek an audience with the duchess—and myself as a bystander. Our circle grew and shrank over the next half hour as conversation flowed and refreshments circulated.

Julian and Miles had disappeared with Tryton at some point, and I occasionally scanned the room in an attempt to locate them.

Mr. Belham eventually made his way over. He was greeted warmly, and I didn't feel the same sense of disquiet that I usually experienced at his appearance during social events. We'd seen each other several times at the newspaper offices since my return to London and our awkward conversation about his intentions—or lack thereof. I'd submitted pages and Mr. Belham had remained my cordial editor—friendly but professional. But this was my first instance with him at a social gathering. I hoped he would not ask me to dance.

Julian was the only one I wanted to dance with, but I knew that was not likely to happen. It was too definitive. Too much of a proclamation. Too real when we were only playing pretend.

"Lady Genevieve?"

The question startled me out of my wayward thoughts. "Apologies, Mr. Belham. You were saying?"

"I was asking after your plans for the yuletide."

Forcing a smile, I discussed my intent to return to Hampshire next month for my mother's annual house party followed by our family's celebration of the yuletide. I wondered if Julian would come with us to Hampshire. Surely, he would. My brother and sisters and their families would all be joining us as well as Mary and her parents and Daly and his sweet wife.

As if my very thoughts had conjured him, Julian returned to my side as Mr. Belham continued speaking. He seemed to stumble over his words as Jules settled so close to me that our arms brushed. I fought surprise at his boldness and the urge to lean farther into his touch.

"Pardon me, sir. I don't believe we've been introduced." It was the first time I'd seen Aaron Belham's gaze be anything but warm.

Patty stepped in smoothly with an introduction and I noticed that Miles had returned as well. "Mr. Aaron Belham, this is Mr. Julian Moore. He is a close family friend and our guest for the season. Mr. Belham is an editor with the *London Post* and a favored guest of many here in Mayfair."

The men eyed each other and shook hands slowly while Patty, Miles, and I all looked uncomfortably at one another.

"And what business are you in, Mr. Moore, that brings you to London and with the hospitality of such a highly-regarded family?" Mr. Belham asked coolly.

I watched this exchange with horrified fascination—like an animal exhibit at the zoo full of posturing and nostril flaring. Suddenly, I didn't know what to do with my hands or where to look.

Julian's gaze narrowed at the implied challenge in Mr. Belham's question, but it was Miles who spoke up in response, "Mr. Moore represents Brightleaf Farms of Leicester. We've been in partnership and well acquainted for many years. I've been begging him to get down to London for quite some time."

Mr. Belham's dark brows winged high on his forehead as he scanned Julian from head to toe. But instead of acknowledging Miles's explanation in any way or returning his attention to Julian, Mr. Belham seemed to note our proximity and met my eyes instead. "I see. And when did you arrive to town, Mr. Moore?" As if realizing how demanding and awkward he sounded, Mr. Belham smiled with closed lips and looked to Julian, saying brightly, "I do hope it was early enough to enjoy the fine weather before the autumn took hold."

"Indeed," Julian replied cautiously. "I arrived in September and enjoyed many fine days before the weather turned."

"That is illuminating to hear." Mr. Belham's brown eyes flashed to me briefly once more before he took a step back, bowing low. "Well, I will leave you to your evening. A pleasure as always to see you all. Your Grace. Lady Genevieve. Basilton. And of course, Mr. Moore, happy to make your acquaintance."

We joined in with our farewells. And after Mr. Belham retreated, those of us remaining stared at each other in the very odd space recently vacated by the newspaper man.

When all eyes seemed to look in my direction, I panicked and blurted, "Shall we go?"

Patty's blue eyes widened, but she brushed a gloved hand down her emerald skirts and said, "Yes. I do believe that's an excellent idea. Did you finish your business with Tryton?"

Miles and Julian both nodded.

"Perfect," I breathed, grateful for the chance to leave. This night had been strange in so many ways. Julian's unexpected appearance had been welcome, but Mr. Belham's odd behavior made me feel ill at ease and desperate for the comfort of home.

My family said nothing as Julian and I settled into one carriage and Miles and Patty into another. We were all bound for Cawthorn Hall a short distance away.

Julian sat close beside me and threaded our fingers together. "I'm sorry for hurting you," he repeated.

"I know," I said, squeezing his hand. "You're forgiven. Just talk to me next time instead of trying to hide things from me."

Julian nodded, but said nothing else.

And if the ride back home was quiet and tense, I chalked it up to the strangeness of the encounter with Mr. Belham and the unusual end to the night.

And later, when Julian and I collapsed into bed in his guest chambers, we didn't make love at all. Jules simply kissed my temple and drew me snugly to his side. As I drifted off to sleep—secure in his embrace —I fought the notion that something was amiss. Instead, I squeezed Julian tight to me and ignored the voice of warning in my head.

Three days later, I found myself before Aaron Belham once more.

The idea of revealing myself as the writer behind the *Detective Owensby* serial had been growing steadily, a thrum in my chest and an insistent little ache every time I set pen to paper. I wanted to broach the subject with my editor, but his demeanor at the Tryton ball had been so odd that I was slightly nervous for our standing meeting today. I was bringing my pages for this week's installment, as was typical, but I was unsure of my reception.

So, I'd resolved to proceed with caution.

However, when I entered and was greeted by Mr. Belham, it seemed as if all was well.

I sat, arranging my skirts as he resumed his chair behind the desk.

"I have the installment for this week," I said needlessly—nervously—as I slid the bundle onto the glossy work surface between us.

"Wonderful." His tone was friendly, but for the first time in a long time, he accepted the papers and began scanning the words written there and thumbing through the pages.

I frowned at his sudden interest, but resolved to locate my courage and bring up the topic of my identity. "Mr. Belham, I wanted to discuss something with you."

"Of course," he murmured but his eyes hadn't stopped perusing my work.

I cleared my throat and rolled my shoulders back. "Moving forward, I would like to write under my own name." His attention snapped up at that. "And no longer publish under the assumption that I am a man."

"That is an interesting idea, Lady Genevieve, to be sure," Mr. Belham said slowly, gaze narrowed. "But the contract between your sister's solicitor and the *London Post* states that your publication is accepted and printed under the name G. Everett."

Fighting the urge to nervously twist my fingers together, I admitted, "I understand that."

"And I have to admit, the masses are unlikely to appreciate your talents . . . as a young woman. Readers are hardly forgiving and they may feel lied to. They may not be inclined to remain loyal fans of Detective Owensby once they discover they've been deceived by a high-born lady."

I stiffened. Mr. Belham was quick to identify all my fears and call them out. "I've considered that, but I can't imagine such animosity—"

"Change is difficult, I'm afraid, my lady."

"Of course, but—"

"And speaking of change, I did wish to address the direction the serial has taken."

Momentarily distracted from his repeated interruptions, I replied defensively, "What do you mean?"

"Well, in the last month, your writing has changed. The story has become less adventure and mystery and more . . . romantic." I was surprised to see Mr. Belham's eyes so hard and implacable. "Owensby's cases have been pushed to the background so he can what? Find love and marry? He's even settled into a townhouse with a cat. Your readers want action and mayhem. This serial used to be about daring escapades and grisly murders."

I considered the changes I'd made over the last month. Yes, I'd subtly shifted the path my main character was on. Why couldn't Detective Owensby be happy? He could still solve cases and follow clues and then come home to a wife and pleasant household at the end of the day. Didn't the good detective deserve some peace after years of strife? Why was Belham even questioning these changes when he'd never cared what I'd written before? The serial was popular. It made the newspaper money. His concerns were suspiciously timely following our strange encounter at the Tryton ball.

"Perhaps the story needs something different. Readers don't enjoy stagnation either," I argued, my hackles rising further.

"Well, I'm afraid the *Post* will not be prepared to publish the story with the direction you've taken. It's not the kind of tale we signed on for and not the sort of story we're after."

"I see," I said stiffly and things were becoming clearer.

"You've changed," Mr. Belham said, eyeing me bitterly. "And your writing along with it. If you don't get the serial back on track —and soon—I'll be forced to discontinue publication and sever our relationship."

An interesting ultimatum, that.

I'd rejected the man before me outright and found happiness with someone else. And I hadn't hidden that fact very well the other evening. Julian's proximity and my attention might as well have painted a target upon me for Mr. Belham's wounded male ego and chauvinistic aim. His intrusive questions about Julian's stay in London suddenly made much more sense.

Indignation burned through my veins, but I called upon my eldest sister's influence and made myself poised and in control. It wouldn't do to call out Mr. Belham's childish behavior. I had some decisions to make—about several things—and playing the role of hysterical female in this office would not aid in that. I would be untouchable—calm and collected—no matter how much I wanted to shout in his face and call him a prideful coward.

"Your input as my editor has been noted," I said evenly as I stood. "Farewell, Mr. Belham."

I spent the afternoon thinking and preparing for the ball that would take place at Cawthorn Hall this evening. Patty typically hosted two large events during the season—one in the autumn and one in the spring when the weather was fine.

Julian would be attending tonight in his finery. We'd had breakfast together before my meeting at the newspaper and he'd seemed a bit nervous for the event to come.

Now, as I sat at my dressing table, I couldn't help but wallow in my unease from the meeting with Mr. Belham. I stared at my reflection in the mirror and considered what my editor had accused me of.

I suppose I *had* changed.

Not in the usual ways. Despite the elegant hairstyle and beautiful gown, I was still myself in appearance. I took in my plain brown hair, twisted and plaited around my crown as jeweled pins caught the light from the lamps. I was dressed for a lavish affair, to be sure. But it wasn't my exterior that had changed overly much.

I'd spent these weeks happily ensconced with Julian, making love and telling myself I could be casual about all of it. That I hadn't been secretly thinking of weddings and babies and a future where he stayed. A future where he chose me this time.

It wasn't fair and it wasn't rational.

We were of an understanding, an agreement. Our arrangement

was conducted in secret and stemmed from a friendship that we both still wanted.

But in an effort to preserve that friendship, I'd walked delicately around any issue that might drive Julian away. I'd bitten my tongue and watched my words. The honesty that had existed so naturally between us before, as children, was being carefully managed by my constant awareness and desperate fear.

I'd shared my body and done little to protect my heart as it turned out.

But I was tired of hiding my love. Ashamed that I'd allowed something that meant so much to be relegated to the shadows. I'd buried it all in such a way that the influence had sprouted in unlikely places, affecting my work and changing my writing. And I wasn't ashamed. I wasn't going to change it, either. My characters deserved to be happy and so did I.

I wanted to live my life and my work and my love for Julian boldly. He needed to know that we could be happy. And I needed to know that he could love me as myself.

I shouldn't have to make myself small for the *London Post* or for Julian Moore.

If he wanted to return to Leicester, then I could return with him. I could write from anywhere, and while I would miss my family, I would be starting something new with Julian. Something lasting. Something right.

We could figure out all the details. I just wanted to stop pretending. I needed to be myself again—not this muted version who tolerated uncomfortable silences and didn't speak her mind.

With my white satin gloves, I lifted the hand-carved box that sat on the corner of my dressing table. Julian's letters had been returned.

I thought of the young girl who'd written to her friend for years, unwilling to let him go. That Genevieve had been brave. Her actions hadn't been pathetic or pitiable. They'd been fearless and steadfast.

I could take a lesson or two from that bold and willful girl.

I stroked a delicate hand over the edge of the box and met determined blue eyes in the mirror.

I was ready to stake a claim. After seven long years, I was ready for Julian Moore to be mine.

Eighteen

JULIAN

I stared at the letter. Read it again, before the words finally took hold and the implications made themselves clear.

I had been standing when a footman kindly delivered the short missive straight to my suite. And now I was sitting beside the fire and had no recollection of the journey.

Julian,

I'm afraid I cannot agree to the Earl of Basilton's offer. Brightleaf Farms is my life's work. I can't imagine simply selling it off and being nothing again. I'm afraid my answer is no. I'm sorry if that makes you unhappy. I could tell from the tone of your letter that you hoped for a path that led to the success of this venture. But I'm afraid that both you and the farm are too essential to me.

Please understand. I don't know how long I have left on this earth, and one day, Brightleaf will *be yours in its entirety. But until that day comes, I'm afraid I can't share it. Forgive an old man his pride.*

-Phillip

The words didn't change on my third pass, nor the fourth. My uncle wouldn't sell to Basilton. We wouldn't be moving the farm to Hampshire.

And there was no future for me with Genevieve.

The paper held tightly in my hand didn't say that last part, but it may as well have.

I'd remain in London until the Ascot races in the spring and then return to Leicester. Perhaps I'd be the one to return next season to meet with buyers. However, after all the successful connections I'd made, my presence might not be required in London on farm business. She could be married by then. The thought of some nameless, faceless gentleman sharing a life with my—with Genevieve had me inhaling a shaky breath. How could I survive it if Genevieve was someone else's and never mine? A future with a husband who had earned her sweet affection was not a pill I could swallow at the moment. So deep was the pit of my despair.

But I couldn't ask her to wait for me or beg her to come with me. With the arrival of this letter and Uncle Phillip's decision, I was back to being no one. Certainly not someone worthy of Genevieve Bartholomew, the daughter of a marquess, and the sister to two duchesses.

I was simply the heir to Brightleaf Farms.

Forever the housekeeper's son.

It wouldn't be enough.

I was a fool to think being Basilton's partner would somehow elevate my status. It had been a fantasy. I could see that now.

My hand shook and I put the letter down.

How was I going to get through this event in the grand ballroom at Cawthorn Hall?

I rubbed my brows as tension coiled. All those people. And Genevieve. I needed to speak to Miles—to tell him the news of my uncle's decision.

I checked the clock on the mantel. There wouldn't be time for that now. I'd seek him out later.

A cowardly voice within urged me to hide in my room and avoid this spectacle all together, but I knew Genevieve would seek me out. She'd ask what was wrong and I couldn't very well tell her the truth.

Oh, right. I'd hoped to become a respected businessman so that I could marry you. But that's not going to happen now. Let's go have some watered-down lemonade and make inane small talk with strangers.

Christ, how could I even be with her after this?

I'd been reaching and hoping and, God help me, planning for something that was never going to happen. I could not imagine welcoming Genevieve into my bed after this. I'd fall deeper in love with her and destroy us both when I had to end things.

Perhaps Miles would ask me to leave when he found out about the letter. That might be best for everyone. Better if I distanced myself now rather than later.

I pressed the heels of my hands against my forehead as my spiraling thoughts consumed me. With deep breaths, I attempted to center myself and regain control of my mind. I had to get through this event and then I could figure everything out.

Reaching out, I snatched up the letter and folded it neatly into thirds before placing it in the desk drawer.

And then I made my way to the door of my suite to get this night over with.

When I arrived in the ballroom, it was an overwhelming crush. But somehow Silas Bartholomew spotted me and urged me forward with a hearty greeting and slap to the back. He pulled me along until we joined Miles and Augie near a potted fern in what looked like an attempt to hide from guests.

The bodies and heat of the room were oppressive. Something in my expression must have indicated as much because Silas said easily, "Patty's events are always like this. They know she has the best of everything: food, drink, musicians, taste. It's always a mob."

I nodded, not knowing what to say or how to respond. My thoughts were being held hostage in a room upstairs, trapped in the middle drawer of a large mahogany desk.

"We are hiding for the time being," Augustus confirmed.

"The women are over there." Silas indicated with an unsubtle hand in the opposite corner of the ballroom.

My head turned to follow his direction and I spotted Genevieve with her sisters. Lady Mary had joined them, and guests were lingering nearby to seek an audience with the duchess. My gaze stayed on Gen as she smiled politely through an introduction.

I felt covetous. My eyes stealing and preserving every version of her for a future that would be devoid of all this. Was this the last time I'd see her in a gown so grand? Or with her hair up off her neck?

How would I store enough of these moments to last a lifetime?

"Julian," Silas fairly barked and I startled.

All the men were staring at me. Perhaps that was not the first time they'd tried to gain my attention.

"You're being rather obvious," he said before lifting his glass to his lips.

Miles and Augie shot him irritated looks.

My brows lowered in confusion.

"Oh, I'm sorry," Silas said theatrically. "Are we still pretending that Julian and Genevieve are not"—he lowered his voice—"involved?"

My mouth went dry as I realized what he meant. "You know?" I managed to croak in Bartholomew's direction.

Silas stared at me blandly. I looked to Miles and Augie but they could hardly meet my eyes. Augie seemed very interested with the shine on his boots while Miles adjusted the fabric of his cravat and examined a nearby floral arrangement.

"You *all* know?" I whispered incredulously.

Eventually everyone looked my way.

Silas snorted. "Of course we do. Gen has always worn her heart on her sleeve where you are concerned." And then added with a slightly pitying expression, "And you're not quite as good of an actor as you think you are."

I fought the urge to cover my face with my hands. If I'd truly been so careless that everyone knew about my improper relationship with Genevieve, her reputation was at risk. I needed to speak with her—end this before permanent damage was done.

It would all be ending anyway. She just didn't know it yet.

How would I untangle myself from this family?

Augie cleared his throat, drawing my attention. "It's all right. No one else knows anything is going on. And I think we've all"—with a quick, uncomfortable glance to Silas—"been in similar situations and are not intending to shame you."

Miles coughed into his fist, the tips of his ears a bit bright.

Right. We were standing around discussing improper intimacies with someone's sisters . . . all of them.

Silas rolled his eyes. "And we don't have to bring it up again. Just marry her already and be done with all the sneaking about and making eyes at each other across the dining table."

I took a step back against the blow of his casual command. Silas had already turned to an approaching footman for a new drink, but Miles and Augie caught my expression. They both looked confused and concerned.

I wouldn't be marrying Genevieve no matter how much I wanted to. And Bartholomew was right, I needed to salvage her reputation and put an end to the secrets and lies.

With another step backward, I mumbled, "Excuse me."

"Julian," Miles called, but I didn't turn. I was already moving toward her. I had to talk to Genevieve. I needed to end this before I ruined everything—ruined her.

I slipped easily through the crowd. No one hailed me for conversation. I was still very much inconsequential to the majority of the guests here. The only person who thought I was someone was watching me approach with a bright smile on her face.

God, they were right. We weren't subtle at all.

I was too panicked to manage polite greetings for anyone and was relieved when Genevieve stepped a few paces away to join me.

"We need to talk," I said in a rush. "Can we leave? Go upstairs for a moment?"

Gen watched me carefully before determination stole over her features. She straightened and smiled at me again. "No, Julian. I want to dance. Will you please dance with me?"

I could feel the shock on my face and heat blooming in my cheeks. I was so startled by her request that I momentarily forgot my urgent need to speak to her. "What are you talking about?" I whispered, glancing around us.

Her voice rose slightly and I winced. "I would like to dance. That's what I'm talking about. With you. And don't say that you don't know how. My mother taught you when we were fourteen. She had us practicing all around the drawing room while she played the piano for us." Genevieve smiled at the memory. It was one that I'd pushed away in the years since I'd been gone, refusing to allow myself to miss the family who'd accepted me.

But now the recollection rushed to the surface, stepping on Genevieve's toes and laughing together while the marchioness called out steps. It had taken hours but I'd learned to waltz and Gen's cheeks had been pink and happy. We'd both been happy.

It was a near thing, but I couldn't give in no matter how much I might have wanted to take her in my arms and lead her to the dance floor. Drawing attention to us now would be the opposite of my aims.

"We can't, Genevieve. Not here in front of everyone. You know that."

Her eyes turned steely along with her voice. "And why not? Are you embarrassed to be seen with me, Julian? Am I to be hidden away forever? Does it even matter what I want?"

I glanced around and noticed curious eyes and waving fans trained on us. "Genevieve, stop this." My voice was low and absolutely desperate. There would be gossip. People would talk about her after this, and I couldn't allow it.

She opened her mouth to respond, but she never got the chance.

Viscount Brannigan appeared at our side with a bright smile and a pack of men at his back. They took in our exchange eagerly, like wolves awaiting bloodshed. Unease slithered up my spine at the unfortunate attention we'd drawn.

"Lady Genevieve, can I be of assistance?"

Gen didn't even try to hide her annoyance at the interruption. "No, thank you, Lord Brannigan."

"I'd intended to invite you to dance the next waltz with me." With an unimpressed glance in my direction, the viscount finished, "But I'm happy to be of support, if needed."

Our audience had grown. The matrons and debutantes who'd been discreetly watching behind their fans were now staring outright, relishing in the spectacle Brannigan had created.

Genevieve seemed to note the scrutinizing stares and attention we'd garnered. She answered evenly, "No, my lord. We were simply conversing."

"Oh, it's you!" Brannigan said loudly, ignoring Genevieve altogether and focusing his attention on me now. "The horse farmer!"

Several of the viscount's friends chuckled. Two of those men had stood in the yard at Cawthorn Hall earlier in the week.

Heat bloomed aggressively beneath my cravat. I could hear the sound of my own blood rushing in my ears, and I couldn't seem to force my gaze above Brannigan's chin. I did not want this sort of attention for myself nor for Genevieve. The implications and the gossip could be detrimental to her reputation. Simply standing near me was cause for mocking. I needed to get away.

"Is this farmer bothering you, Lady Genevieve?" More laughter from behind Brannigan.

I could not hear the musicians in the center of the ballroom, only the cacophony of whispers erupting around us.

With a glance in Genevieve's direction, I saw her uneasy expression harden and ferocity take its place, and I knew that there would be no end to this display anytime soon. "For the last time, Lord Brannigan. No. Mr. Moore is not bothering me. No. I do not need your assistance. We were in the middle of a conversation before you so rudely interrupted and inserted yourself."

Several gasps sounded from nearby but I didn't look. I simply turned and started shuffling my way through the crowd, escape the only thing on my mind.

Perhaps it was cowardly, but it was all I could do. I was the problem—the reason Genevieve had been singled out by Brannigan. It was my presence in this ballroom causing whispers and negatively impacting Genevieve. If removing myself from the situation would spare her, I would do it.

I passed Silas and Miles, both of whom looked up in concern. Perhaps they'd been too far to hear Brannigan. But I shook my head and continued toward the doorway eager to get to my room and away from everyone here.

Once I entered the corridor, I hurried to the staircase and up to the guest wing of the main house. The plush carpets muffled the sound of my footfalls and I heard nothing but my own ragged breaths.

I'd made it to the closed door of my chambers before I heard a desperate cry. "Julian! Wait!"

Spinning around, I found Genevieve—violet skirts in hand—chasing after me.

"You can't follow me from the ballroom, Genevieve. That will only make things worse."

"I don't care," she said, chest heaving around her words. "I don't care about that idiot Brannigan. I care about you."

"You should care," I all but yelled. "It is your reputation at stake."

I couldn't decide if Gen was being willfully ignorant or purposely obtuse. Her dark brows lowered in confusion. "My reputation?"

"You can't simply argue with a viscount in front of a crowd of people."

"Well, I did. And I'd do it again. He was being awful—talking to you that way and showing off for his friends."

I rubbed a frustrated hand across my forehead.

She put her hands on her hips. "Did you think I would—what—let you run off and then agree to dance with that bastard? Was I supposed to smooth things over and just let him insult you that way?"

I hung my head, cheeks aflame once more. "Christ, Genevieve. Allow a man some measure of pride."

"And why should I?" she hissed. "Why should your damnable pride occupy this space with us—dominate it? Why should it be worth more than me? Is that the cost I should pay? That of your precious pride?"

"Yes!" I exploded, finally finished with her ignorant, moralistic high road. "Yes, Genevieve. Because between the two of us, you are the only one who matters in that ballroom. I am no one. Nothing. Your reputation will be in tatters and no one will even remember my name. That is the way of it. Brannigan didn't say anything that wasn't true. I am a horse farmer. And I'll go back to Leicester and you'll be here, trying to salvage your good standing over a moment of weakness." I swallowed around the emotion clogging my throat, knowing I was no longer talking about the words she'd hurled at Brannigan, but of nights spent in my bed. "For a mistake."

Genevieve was pale, her beautiful face stricken. "A mistake?"

My eyes closed against the expression she wore. "This was never more than a fantasy, Gen. It was never going to be real."

"How—" The word cut off, her pink lips moving silently before she managed, "How can you say that?"

"There was never any future for us. No matter how much I—"

Abruptly, she took a step closer to me. "No matter how much you —what?"

I cursed myself for saying too much and shook my head. "No matter how much I wanted there to be," I finished instead. "You're the daughter of a marquess." I placed a hand to my chest, feeling the frantic beat of my heart beneath clothes too fine to ever feel like mine. "I will always be the housekeeper's son. Can't you see that?"

Tears welled in her beautiful blue eyes, but I knew they were more from anger than sadness. I knew that because I knew *her*.

"No, Jules. You know what I see?" she said, stepping into me, placing her hand directly over mine. "I see your quiet heart. Your loyalty. Your kindness. I see the boy I used to love. And the man who holds my heart."

I shook my head slowly, even as she laced our fingers together. She didn't understand. Genevieve was blinded by our history. She refused to see the truth for what it was—hopeless. Words tumbled from my lips as I stared down at our joined hands, desperate to make her understand. "You saw what happened in that ballroom. I am not a part of your world. I'll never fit in or be accepted. Even when I thought there was a chance, a future worthy of—" I cut myself off, but not soon enough.

Genevieve's fingers tightened around mine. "A future worthy of what? What chance are you talking about?"

I breathed out a sigh, cursing myself for being so foolish. I hadn't been brave enough to tell her before. I might as well get it over with now. "Miles made me an offer. He wanted to buy out my uncle and move Brightleaf Farms to Hampshire. That's what he planned to build—a large stable for a stud farm. He wanted to take on a different role and give my uncle the means to retire. He wanted me to take on a larger role as well, a partnership. I thought if I could achieve that, I could be someone. Not a lord with a title, but someone nearly worthy of a future with you."

"What happened?" Her voice was small.

I untangled our fingers and flipped my hand over, pressing palm to palm, grounding myself in her touch. It was selfish, knowing what needed to be done. But I'd always been weak where Genevieve was concerned. "My uncle said no. I got the letter this morning. He won't sell to Basilton. He won't give up the farm, even to live out his remaining years in peace and tend to his failing health."

"You received word today?"

I glanced up at the accusation I heard in her voice. Gen wore her hurt beneath an angry shroud as her hand slipped out of mine.

I said nothing. It would only make things worse.

"How long have you been keeping this from me? How long have you and Miles been scheming and keeping secrets that affect our future?" Her volume increased with every word. I feared the guests downstairs would be able to make out her angry accusations.

"I didn't want to give you false hope," I explained. "And I asked Miles not to say anything. I needed things to be settled with my uncle before I discussed it with you. I wasn't about to make assumptions, Genevieve. I've been under no delusion that you could want me for more than—"

She was quick to interrupt. "You're a liar, Julian Moore. And a coward. You know me better than anyone. And you know that I love you and want to marry you. Build a life with you, and a family. I always have."

My heart clenched at her words, knowing that it was a future that would never come to pass.

She sniffed and another angry tear fell. "I've been so careful with you. I didn't want to frighten you off. I felt like—" Her voice broke and fractured my heart along with it. "I felt like I just got you back, and I didn't want to do anything that might push you away. I decided tonight I would find my backbone. That was why I asked you to dance—why I insisted upon it. I was tired of hiding my feelings and hiding . . . us. It's not fair. I love you, and I want to be with you. In front of everyone. If that means I go back to Leicester with you, then so be—"

"No," I interrupted, not believing what she'd stated so plainly. "I'm not stealing the only future you'll ever have. I would never ask you to give up so much for me—your family, your reputation, your status. All for a life you're far above. I'm not worth it."

"Well, you don't get to decide that, Julian. I don't have to accept it."

"I'm not asking you to accept it. I'm just not asking you to marry me."

Hurt flashed and her face crumpled. "You'd really punish us both?"

Yes. A thousand times yes. I'd torture myself and live without her for the rest of my life if it meant that I saved her from herself. From the resentment she was sure to feel. The humiliation she'd inevitably face. The loss she'd be unable to escape. I would save her from . . . me.

I took in her tearstained cheeks and wide, pleading eyes. I'd always been helpless in the face of Genevieve's pain. My heart rattled against its cage, pressing forward and seeking her out. But I kept my gaze steady and met hers with unwavering resolve.

Stricken and pleading, Gen backed away from me as if I was dangerous.

And then she turned and ran. Taking every piece of my shattered heart along with her.

I didn't know what to expect the following morning when I stumbled—exhausted from a sleepless night—into the small dining room the family used for informal meals.

But it was not Franny eating alone at a table for twelve with an expectant dog and inquisitive cat at her feet.

"Daisy, you must sit if you'd like me to sneak you bacon from the table. We've had this discussion many times," the girl said, lovingly reproachful.

Francesca noticed me and brightened. "Mr. Moore! Do join me."

I eased farther into the room, cautious, as if Genevieve might pop out from beneath the table. I wasn't ready to face her yet. I didn't know how to pretend like nothing was the matter. Our very careful bubble had burst last night, and I was sick over it.

"Where is everyone else?"

"Mum and Papa were talking in the morning room, taking their breakfast together there. I'm the early riser of the family," Franny stated proudly. And she did look very put together with ribbons in her dark hair at this early hour. "You must be an early riser, too, what with your work with the horses."

I nodded and took a seat across from the girl. I felt Percy nudge against my boots, but when I peeked beneath the table linens, he'd already retreated back to Franny's side. "That's true," I confirmed her suspicions about my morning routine on the farm. "But I've always been up with the sun. Even as a child."

Franny took a bite of bacon and chewed thoughtfully for a moment. I was pouring tea for myself when she finally spoke. "Mum and Aunt Emery said they knew you when you were young. That you grew up at Laurel Park with Aunt Gen."

I took a quick sip from my cup to avoid answering right away and burned my tongue on the scalding liquid. Clearing my throat, I admitted, "Yes, that's true. My mother was the housekeeper at Laurel Park, and my father died when I was very young. We lived in the manor house, and I was raised alongside Emery and Genevieve. Your mum was mostly grown by then. I don't have very many memories of her."

"And you stayed until you left to help your uncle?"

I typically felt so conflicted about my upbringing. When folks in Leicester asked after my history, I could see their judgmental wheels turning when they heard I was raised at the country estate of a marquess. They thought me above my station. It made them standoffish, and me, very aware of my manners. Yet if I told the same story of my background to an aristocrat, they would have pitied me as some sort of orphaned ward and questioned the sanity of the Bartholomews.

However, Franny's innocent curiosity made it easy to answer her questions. "I remained at Laurel Park until I was sixteen. Then I went to Leicester to Brightleaf Farms."

She nodded as if that aligned with what she'd been told. Unexpectedly she murmured, "Mum took me in when I was five—

nearly six. I'd lived at an orphanage in Bethnal Green since I was a few days old. She used to visit once a month and bring gifts and take tea with all the orphans. But one day she came to get me. Promised to always care for me. She said she'd always hoped for a daughter of her own and she thought I could be happy here at Cawthorn Hall. Then she and Papa married and we were a proper family. I've lived with them ever since."

I knew the generalities of Francesca's birth, but it was startling to hear her discuss it so openly, so matter-of-factly.

Her solemn hazel eyes appeared less childlike and more wizened suddenly. "As someone who knows what it's like, I could tell they'd taken you in, too."

My throat constricted at her easy assessment. She went right back to eating bacon and I sat there feeling torn apart. She'd said it so simply, as if there weren't years of complication attached to that statement. As if it was so easy to find your place in the world because the Bartholomews had given you one.

And I realized she was right.

I'd spent so very long after I'd left Laurel Park trying to minimize my time with the Bartholomews. I'd allowed my mother to manipulate me. I'd pushed down my hurt at being forgotten. I'd missed them, but I hadn't allowed those feelings to bubble to the surface. I hadn't believed I'd deserved them at the time. After all, who was I to mourn the loss of a family that had never really been my own?

But they had been. Emery had been like my sister, teasing and jesting and giving me advice. The marquess had taken me hunting and riding and supported my education. The marchioness had doted on me and taught me to dance. And then

Genevieve . . . well, I'd been hers for as long as I could remember.

Franny took a piece of her bacon and slipped it down to Daisy beneath the table. Then she took a spoon and scooped out a small mound of softened butter and delivered it to the cat. She grinned at me.

She met my eyes easily, as if I was not having a painful revelation at the breakfast table and said, "It's not very fair that you had them for longer. But I suppose I can't fault you for being born before me." Her smile was wide and teasing. "We're special, you know. To get a second chance at a family. I'm grateful to Mum and Papa. They accepted me—all of them, really. Emery and Augie and Genevieve and Silas and Grandmother and Grandfather. They took me in and gave me something I never would have had otherwise. It's like we're in a little club, you and I, Mr. Moore."

I swallowed thickly, astounded and shamed that this young girl had figured out how to accept the Bartholomews when I had struggled with it my whole life. Finally, I managed, "If we're going to have our own club, you should definitely call me Julian." Franny smiled. "And we should develop a secret handshake."

She was so wise to be just twelve years old. It was easy to forget her age when she'd just blown my world open with one conversation. But when she laughed, as she was doing now, it was youthful and free. "We do indeed!"

"Franny, could you do me a favor?"

"Of course, Mr.—Julian."

I smiled at her shy use of my given name. "Could you look after Percy for me?"

"I'd be happy to." Her brows lowered in confusion. "But why?"

"I'll be away for a bit. I need to travel to Leicester and see my uncle. And I need to leave today."

The remainder of the morning was quickly spent packing and preparing to depart. During a tense conversation with Miles, I explained about my uncle's refusal to sell and my immediate need to leave. The earl had understood and begged me to take a carriage in order to travel safely, but I knew I'd be quicker on Brutus.

Before departing, I'd sought out Charlie in the stables. I'd asked the young man to look after the horses while I was away and told him that no matter what happened moving forward, he would always have a position and a future. And I already knew what I wanted for him. I just needed to make it happen.

Once I'd packed the minimum I would need for the journey back to Leicester, I carefully wrapped and tucked Genevieve's letters in the bottom of my satchel. I needed something safer to store them in, but I'd figure that out later. Now, I needed to see the woman herself and tell her goodbye.

As I made the unfamiliar trek to Genevieve's door, I realized with a fair amount of shame that it was the first time I'd done so. We'd spent so many nights together, and yet they'd all been in my chambers. She'd always been the brave one. Loyal and determined. Gen had written all those letters and held on to me long past what I'd deserved. She held me still.

I was done being ruled by my fears. I couldn't expect her stubborn, willful heart to carry us through alone. I'd prove my devotion, show her my love if it was the last thing I did.

I took a deep breath and knocked on her door.

"Coming!" Her voice was muffled, but a moment later she was there.

Her brown hair was down and a bit wild. She still wore her pale dressing gown cinched tight at the waist, and she didn't open her door any wider than was necessary. It was very clear that I was not invited within.

I knew I had been silent too long, just standing there, staring at her. But it was difficult to find the words.

"You're leaving," she guessed, blue eyes wary.

I nodded. "I am. I need to speak with my uncle. But I'm leaving Charlie and the horses. I'll return for the Ascot races in the spring at the very latest."

Genevieve said nothing. Her face gave nothing away. But I hated the way she held herself back from me—the cautiousness and restraint that kept her arms crossed and her spine straight. I'd made her this way. Not simply in this moment, but all along. By hiding ourselves away and existing together in secret, I'd leached the life from her. I'd made her less herself and, instead, a faded, hesitant version of the bold and expansive woman I loved.

I wanted to fix what I had broken. I wanted to stitch her back together—to stitch *us* back together.

"I'll return as soon as I can." I felt like a redundant fool, but still she said nothing. "I'll write to you," I promised. And that had her eyes narrowing.

I knew Gen well enough to know that she was biting her tongue. I was sure she wanted to call attention to my failures, reference the past and how I'd let her down the last time I'd promised to write.

But she didn't say any of that. She simply stood, watching me.

"All right, then. Goodbye, Genevieve."

I made it four paces down the corridor before I spun back on my heel. She was still standing in the doorway, right where I'd left her. I wrapped her in my arms and kissed her hard.

She made a surprised sound in the back of her throat. And I told myself that if she didn't kiss me back, I might die but I'd let her go. But then Genevieve's hands fisted in the lapels of my jacket and her mouth moved against mine.

The relief was so stark, I stopped kissing her and brought my forehead to rest against hers. We stood in the entryway to her rooms, breathing the same air and holding on so tightly to one another. Her citrus scent enveloped me, making me ache with longing.

I brushed my lips to hers again and we clung there, suspended in the knowledge that I was leaving London—leaving without her.

With shaky hands, I framed her face and placed sweet kisses on her cheeks, her chin, the tip of her nose. I brushed her hair back behind her ears and murmured against her lips, "This isn't the end."

Genevieve nodded, her eyes clenched tight and kissed my lips goodbye. She pulled away without meeting my gaze and retreated inside her chambers, closing the door with a quiet snick.

I made my way on unsteady legs to the stable yard where Charlie waited with Brutus.

The gray afternoon clouds looked threatening, and the cold seeped right through my layers. But I needed to do this. I couldn't remain in London a moment longer.

I was only taking part of me off to Leicester. My heart would stay right here with the woman I'd love for the rest of my life.

Nineteen

GENEVIEVE

Dear Julian,

I want you to know that this will be the last letter I'll write to you. I have to stop. It's been over three years since you left. This is madness. I can't keep holding out hope. I wish so many things were different. But mostly I hope that you're happy. I love you, but you already know that. I think the worst part is that I can't seem to make myself stop. I'm afraid I'll never love anyone the way I love you. And what a waste that would be.

Gen

I stared at the blank paper on the desk in the library another moment before releasing a frustrated breath and shoving the pages back in the central drawer.

There was something nostalgic about being at Laurel Park without Julian. Like stepping back in time. I was sixteen, seventeen, nineteen, mourning the loss of him all over again.

He was back at Brightleaf Farms. And just once in our relationship, I wanted to be more important than bloody horses.

The one big difference between Julian's repeated departures from my life, was that this time, there were letters. And they weren't mine.

I'd received correspondence nearly every day since Jules had arrived in Leicester, approximately one month ago. One month since he'd told me goodbye outside my rooms. One month since he'd kissed me like the world was on fire.

Dear Gen,

    I reached Leicester safely. I just wanted you to know that I wasn't dead in a ditch somewhere. Sorry. Too soon.

Yours,
Jules

The letters continued even after I'd journeyed with my family back to Laurel Park for my mother's annual house party and our yuletide celebration. We'd arrived three days ago and there had been a note from Julian waiting on the shiny silver tray in the foyer.

Dear Gen,

    Franny wrote to me recently. She gave a full

reporting of Percy's activities. She said he stays with you nearly every night. I hope he's keeping you company. I did not expect to miss the little devil as much as I do. In truth, I miss all of you. Don't tell Silas I said that. He still has high hopes for being the "brother I never had." I miss you most of all, Genevieve. So damn much.

Yours,
Jules

I didn't know what to do about all the blasted letters. I'd decided as soon as Julian had kissed me goodbye at Cawthorn Hall with little explanation for his absence that I would not be writing to him again. It was a decision made out of general stubbornness and spite. I wasn't proud of that fact, but I'd likely inherited those traits from Emery, so I wasn't solely to blame.

I had no idea what this separation meant or why he'd felt the need to go so suddenly. We'd had that awful fight the night of the ball, and part of me worried that he'd fled as a result of our disagreement. I didn't know how to make Julian see that he was worthy of happiness—that he was worthy of me. I could be neither the foundation nor the absence of his self-worth. That had to come from within. He had to stop seeing the housekeeper's son every time he looked in the mirror, and start seeing the man I loved instead. Julian had his own demons to fight.

While I was distraught over this time apart, I believed him when he'd said this wasn't the end.

Dear Gen,

    Charlie wrote to me and said the horses are doing well in my absence. That you visit Graceling every day with a treat. He said she's even more spoiled and bad-tempered as a result. I'm glad she has you.

                        Yours,
                        Jules

Part of me worried that returning his letters would give the appearance of forgiveness. That was why the blank paper had been locked in the desk drawer. I did not forgive him.

I didn't forgive him for choosing his pride over me or for keeping the offer of partnership a secret or for failing to comprehend just how much my family loved and valued him.

But just because I didn't yet forgive him didn't mean I'd stopped loving him.

The part of me that wasn't worried about giving in *was* concerned that he might stop sending the letters without encouragement. It had happened once before. Perhaps that was petty and small of me, but there it was.

Dear Gen,

    Uncle Phillip is having a difficult week. It has been exceedingly cold here, and as a result, his joints are tight and aching. It makes it difficult for him to get out of bed. He is famously stubborn.

And I am fearful that I may have acquired this family trait. I've been reading to him all the Detective Owensby serials that I brought from London. Miles sent through the latest installments since my arrival in Leicester. I was very interested in the most recent story that indicated a thrilling conclusion to the Detective Owensby tale coming next week. I'm sorry I wasn't there to discuss whatever has been going on with your work. I can't imagine it was an easy decision to leave behind your beloved detective. I will be eagerly awaiting the final installment and whatever story you decide to tell next.

Yours,
Julian

I thumbed the edge of the letter I'd received just this morning. It had been the one to tempt me into writing back. I'd pulled the blank sheets out and stared at them for a half hour.

I wanted to tell Julian what was happening with the *London Post* and Detective Owensby. I missed talking to him and seeking his opinion—receiving his advice. He'd been my trusted friend long before he'd ever been my lover. But I missed that part, too. Sleeping had been a challenge without his warm body next to mine. I ached for his possessive touch and gentle kisses in equal measure.

My eyes strayed to the pencil atop the desk.

However, before I could give in to the urge to write out a response to Julian, my father walked into the library with Percy on his heels.

"Hello, my dear!" he greeted me with a smile, his silver-bearded cheeks stretching wide.

"Good afternoon, Papa. I hope you are well."

"I am," he said with a glance toward Percy. "Friendly little thing, isn't he?"

I smiled. Franny had insisted on bringing Percy to Laurel Park. She'd been adamant about her charge. The carriage ride had been a bit dicey, but the ginger cat had eventually settled. Percy was charming the household. He'd made himself at home and I could tell my mother was quite taken with him already.

"He is an unusual feline," I replied. "But we've all grown to care for him a great deal."

My father sat in the armchair facing me and appeared delighted when Percy gave his rough cry and then hopped up in his lap.

"Friendly, indeed," Papa murmured to the cat, stroking his silky back until he settled down comfortably. After a moment, my father met my gaze. His expression became thoughtful and then concerned. "What's the matter, Genevieve? You've been rather quiet since you arrived."

I shook my head quickly. "Nothing at all. Simply tired from the journey."

Papa scrutinized my face before a sympathetic smile tugged the corners of his lips. "Are you disappointed that Julian couldn't spend the holiday with us?"

Was I so transparent? "Julian has his own responsibilities . . . and his own family."

He made a small humming noise. "Is something else bothering you, then?"

My father had always been indulgent with his children. I'd never felt like a liability he needed to unload my means of marriage and a dowry. He'd always taken time with me—with all my siblings. I was fortunate to have a good relationship with both my parents.

Guilt rose swiftly when I thought about the secret I'd been keeping from them. I could tell him. He'd understand and support me. With this chapter of my life coming to a close, perhaps it was time to let go of the secrecy and the shame.

"I have something I need to tell you," I admitted, finally meeting his warm brown eyes. "I'm a writer, Papa. I've been writing under a nom de plume for the *London Post*. The weekly serial is called *The Thrilling Tales of Detective Owensby*. It's an adventure story told in parts, and I've been publishing it for several years." He remained quiet and watchful. "I'm sorry I didn't tell you and Mama. I just knew how scandalized she would be. I didn't want to disappoint anyone."

My father stared at me in amusement before clearing his throat. "Would you prefer that I feign shock or should I tell you that I've known for quite some time?"

I straightened abruptly. "What?"

"Genevieve." He laughed. "Why do you think I have every copy of the *London Post* from the last four years in this very library?"

My mind spun. Julian had found my serial easily enough during our last visit. He'd said he'd gotten them from the library here. "But—"

"You are my daughter. Of course I know about your talents." Papa chuckled again. "Honestly, I don't know what it is with my daughters and their secret identities. First Emery and now you. Is Patricia an actress upon the London stage? Perhaps an accomplished opera singer in disguise?"

That startled a laugh out of me. "I don't believe so, but honestly, that would not surprise me. Patty does have a lovely voice."

"She gets that from your mother," he said, grinning.

That had me wondering. "Does Mama know as well?"

"No, I'm afraid not. And I was not going to be the one to tell her. You must do that on your own."

I groaned and he let out an amused breath.

"I think she will take the news better than you expect, my dear. Your mother has always been a touch more indulgent with you."

"You mean I'm the baby of the family and very spoiled," I deadpanned.

Another chuckle from the man who'd always supported me. "Well, I wasn't going to put it like that. But you are not incorrect." After a moment, he added more seriously, "And mostly, I believe your mother just wants you to be happy."

His words made me feel young again. That familiar nostalgia struck me once more and I felt a stinging pressure behind my eyes. "I'm not sure writing Detective Owensby makes me happy anymore."

"And why is that?"

"There have been some problems with my editor and the requirements of the newspaper. I'd rather end the series the way I want than continue writing only what is demanded of me. I turned in my final installment before we left London. I think—I think my career may be over as a result."

Papa stroked a hand over Percy's back, looking concerned. "Why should your career be over? You've always possessed the keenest imagination, even as a child. Don't you have more stories to tell?"

I bit my lip, keeping my emotion at bay. "I no longer have an avenue to publication, Papa. I'm afraid I've burned my bridge at the *London Post*."

"Tosh! Who needs the *Post*? With your talent and determination, you could approach other periodicals, magazines, or even presses. You could write a novel, Genevieve. You could do whatever you put your mind to. I have no doubt. Don't let others place limitations on you when they have no idea what you're capable of."

I swallowed around the lump in my throat. I knew that not everyone had support the way I did. I was fortunate to have so many people in my corner that it was nearly overflowing. Suddenly, I thought of Julian. His mother had never praised him or supported him or told him to reach for more. She'd done everything she could to keep him down. He was still battling those painful reminders.

I eyed the pencil on the desk, once more desperate to write to him. To tell him the things he needed to hear.

"Thank you, Papa. You're right. Perhaps I do have more options than I thought."

He nodded, expression fond. "Although, whatever you decide, I do think you should confess your secret to your mother. I know she enjoys reading your serial quite a bit. Particularly the last few weeks when the detective gained a sweetheart . . . and a ginger cat."

He looked pointedly at the feline stretched out in his lap and I laughed at my own absurdity.

"All right," I agreed. "I'll tell Mama . . . but you have to tell Silas."

"Oh! Not a chance!" he called, shoulders shaking in such amusement that Percy leapt from his lap in annoyance.

When our laughter had quieted, Papa said sheepishly, "I have been dying to ask what you have planned for the thrilling conclusion of the story."

I gasped in mock affront. "I'm afraid you'll have to find out along with everyone else."

"Come now, Genevieve. I am your father. Surely I deserve special privileges."

I fought a grin, but I didn't think I was very successful.

The conversation with my father had given me comfort and perspective when I'd needed it most. Not just about my writing but regarding Julian as well. Perhaps, I'd put that pencil to good use and let Jules know I was thinking of him too.

With a conspiratorial look around the library, I said quietly, "All right, I'll tell you. But you can't tell Emery."

"I'm afraid I'm not really in the mood to go for a horseback ride in the cold," I groused even though I was already atop my horse and halfway to the building site.

"Oh, come on, Gen. You've been in a foul mood for a month, and it has had nothing to do with the weather," my brother said from his mount.

We were taking a family trip to view the new construction on the stables . . . apparently.

My mother and father had stayed behind with the children, but I'd been forcefully persuaded to join Emery, Augie, Patty, Miles, and Silas for a short ride.

I glared at my brother, but before I could respond that he should mind his own business, Patty cut in, "Leave her be, Silas."

"You're my favorite sister, Patty. Have I told you lately?"

She smiled over her shoulder at me and called, "Not recently."

"Excuse you," Emery said from beside me. "I gave you the last orange cake at tea this afternoon."

"And for that, you were my favorite sister earlier in the day," I said impassively.

Augie laughed as Emery scowled. But then he nudged her thigh where she sat astride and said, "I'll race you." He took off before she could respond. She kicked into a gallop and shouted after him.

The rest of us rode at a more sedate pace over the dead grass. I couldn't believe it was not yet snowing. The sky was layered with gray clouds that hung low on the horizon. The house party guests were due tomorrow and I hoped the weather held as they journeyed from London. No one wanted to get stuck in a carriage on the road.

I pulled my wool cloak tighter against me and felt the paper crinkle in my pocket. I'd been finishing my letter to Julian when I was ambushed in the library by my siblings. Perhaps I could ride into the village and post it after our outing in the fields. I knew I could leave it for the housekeeper, but those old wounds hadn't quite healed. I felt better holding on to the letter and seeing to it myself.

Eventually the land that had been cleared for the stables came into view. It was not far from Miles and Patty's home behind Laurel Park. Straightening in the saddle, I took in the nonexistent progress made on Miles's new venture. I knew he still planned to proceed even without the partnership with Brightleaf Farms. He'd called it a sound investment and refused to back down from the project. Therefore, I was surprised to see that nothing had been done. The weather had been mild thus far this winter with little snow to slow down construction.

I found Miles nearby on his own mount and called over, "Have the crews experienced delays or shortages?"

"Oh—well—they prioritized another project but they should be back to work in the spring." He didn't look upset about this development. Not at all.

So why did everyone want to come out and view the property this afternoon?

Confused, I glanced about for Emery and Augustus. They were still ahead of us nearing the tree line that led to a small hillside. We'd played in that very spot as children. Emery and I had ruined many a dress rolling down the incline and then laughing and scrambling our way back to the top.

"Where are they going?" I asked.

"I don't know," Silas replied, brown eyes bright on his eager face. "I suppose we should find out." And with that he cantered off, his black mare happy for the change of pace.

Patty and Miles both increased their speed and made to follow.

I sat there staring after my family, wondering if they'd lured me out here for some sort of wicked intent. With Emery and Silas, there was no telling.

Alas, the sooner I got this over with, the sooner I could post Julian's letter and then curl up in front of the fireplace and get warm.

When I joined my family, they were picking their way around a few trees before they reached the clearing. My gaze strayed to the short hillside, surprised to see the top cleared neatly and leveled. There wasn't yet a structure but you could see the potential for one. I stood in my stirrups to get a better look and called out, "Were you planning on building here, Miles? Quarters for the grooms or stable hands?"

No one answered, so I turned toward where Miles and Patty had been riding.

They were all motionless on their horses, staring at me . . . and smiling.

"No, Gen," Miles finally answered, voice bright and expectant. "This is not for the stable."

"What is—what's going on?" I said, looking between my family members. Finally, I sought Patty—steadfast and trustworthy— with questions and concern undoubtedly evident on my face.

"Go see for yourself, darling," my sister replied, her expression one of love and encouragement.

I turned back to the hillside and noticed for the first time, a figure at the top, shadowed by the gray sky behind.

Squeezing my thighs, I guided my horse carefully up, my heart was beating hard and urging me onward. When I crested the small knoll, I could see easily where the land had been cleared and made ready for building. And standing among the dirt was Julian and Brutus . . . and Percy.

I dismounted, but he was already there, helping me down from the saddle, sliding his arms around me and kissing my hair.

"Julian," I breathed. "What is this? What are you doing here?"

"I missed you. I missed you so much."

He still hadn't let go of me and I was clinging to him just as desperately.

I kept my hands at his waist and pulled back to see his face. "Tell me what's going on."

"I'm sorry I left, but I had to talk to my uncle. I had to make him understand."

Frowning, I asked, "Understand what?"

Julian ran a finger along my furrowed brow before meeting my eyes. "That I couldn't remain in Leicester. That my life is here. With you, Genevieve. I can't go back to the way things were. I don't want to let you go. I want to be here—in Hampshire—and build a life with you."

"But what about the farm? How will he manage?"

"He's going to keep Brightleaf in his name and all his own. But it will be a much smaller operation—one that can be managed by my replacement. Miles and I will be partners and we'll have our own venture . . . with some of the stock and staff from my uncle's farm."

My heart hadn't quieted, even with Julian's arms around me. I took in his bright eyes. They hadn't left my face. "Are you sure you want this, Julian?"

"I don't want *this*. I want *you*," he emphasized. "And this was the best way to make that happen. To ensure you remained close to your life and your family that you love. To the family we both love. I'm sorry I fought them—and you—for so long. It was so difficult to accept. And I didn't appreciate them before. I heard my mother telling me to mind my manners or I'd be forced to earn my keep, to stop acting above my station, or to put my time at Laurel Park behind me because you'd already forgotten me."

My heart ached for Julian and what he'd endured as a result of his mother's influence. My hands tightened in the fabric at his waist. "Julian, you know that isn't—"

"I do," he said, cupping my face in his hands. "I know it wasn't true. I understand that now. I know I've been given a second chance with this family. I know they care. That's why I asked them to help me—to help make this." He looked around at the fresh earth around us, the space ready for a foundation, for a future. "I want a home here with you, Gen. I love you. I should have told you before I left. But I tried to tell you in all the small ways. I'll write you a letter every day, if you want. I'll make sure you know I love you. Something tangible. Something true. Something you can come back to again and again." I felt tears gather and fall as I nodded along with his words. "Did I fall in love with you or your letters? Do I love Gen from the past or Gen now? I cannot separate the two. You are wholly formed from my memories and my dreams. I love every version of you—and every version of us."

His thumbs brushed the tears from my cheeks so carefully. "But my favorite is who we are together. We were always meant to be in each other's lives. And now, we can make that happen. Will you marry me, Genevieve? Will you be my wife?"

"Yes," I croaked, my throat tightened by emotion.

Julian laughed against my lips. "Yes?"

"Yes," I managed, louder this time.

He slipped his arms inside my cloak and pulled me close. I'd never felt such freedom and surety in his touch. Such blatant devotion in his regard. This was Julian, untethered. And he didn't stop kissing me when we heard horses approach and my meddling family joined us on the small hillside.

I finally pulled back grinning, and whispered, "I love you, too."

Julian's gray eyes were alight.

Suddenly Percy meowed from between our boots and I laughed. "You are never getting rid of this cat."

"I'm done trying. Some things end up right where they belong. No sense in fighting it." He pressed a final kiss to my forehead before we were engulfed by my brother and sisters and their husbands.

When everyone had finally offered their congratulations, Silas declared that it was too bloody cold to stand about and catch his death. The light was slowly leeching away as the afternoon drew toward evening, and I had to admit that it was time we returned.

Pulling my cloak tighter once more, I felt the letter in my pocket and returned to Julian's side. "This is for you. You don't need to read it now. I wrote it this afternoon and was going to send it off —well, before you surprised me."

"Thank you," Julian said shyly, accepting the paper I held. He turned toward his saddle bag and pulled out a carved wooden box, so familiar I nearly snatched it from his hands.

"Where did you get that?" I fairly shouted.

Julian eyed me, confusion lining his brows. "I got it in the village just this morning—from a woodworker there. I wanted something to hold your letters and keep them safe. They'd been hidden away too long. And like you said, they're tangible. Something to hold and return to over again. I wanted a special place for them."

And as he spoke, I could see that the wood grain was lighter than the box currently on my dressing table, brought with me from London to keep Julian's letters safe.

"Is that all right?" Julian asked, still wary. "Do you not like the box?"

I shook my head. My throat suspiciously tight again, I murmured, "No, it's perfect."

Epilogue

GENEVIEVE

Dear Wife,

I cannot believe you contacted the builders and canceled the fountain in our future garden. I had asked for it specifically.

You shall have to make that up to me.

Yours.
Just yours.

Spring, 1864

The June sunshine shone brightly in a cloudless sky.

Julian met my eye from where he was conversing with someone. Probably about a horse. I gave him a saucy wink and his lips tugged up at the corners before he turned back to the discussion. Miles was part of the horsey conversation. And I waited nearby along the railing. The weather was fine and it had been a thrilling week at the racing grounds outside London. Everything was fresh and green as far as the eye could see. Trees wore leaves of bright and energetic green. Flowers bloomed and bees buzzed across the grounds. And people were everywhere enjoying this premiere spectacle in English horseracing.

It was the third day of the Royal Ascot and while Ladies Day had provided ample opportunity to don my most extravagant attire, I was anxious for the outcome of the feature race. The Gold Cup was Lark's big event and Owensby Stud Farm's moment to shine.

Cinder had raced yesterday on the one-mile flat and placed third. Miles and Julian had seen much interest already as a result. But today's event—and a fine performance from the chestnut stallion —could solidify Owensby's future in the market of breeding thoroughbred racehorses.

When I'd given up my good detective just before the new year, Julian asked if we could keep the name as a way to memorialize an important portion of my life. Miles hadn't minded, and so their partnership was christened.

The stables were completed just last month but the farm wouldn't officially open until the summer when the new stable hands and grooms would join us on the property and begin the arduous task of transporting the horses that were acquired from Brightleaf.

Charlie had been tending to Lark, Cinder, Graceling, and Brutus in the interim before the farm really took shape in the off-season. He'd joined us this week for the races and had been making connections and meeting people at his encampment lodgings. I knew Julian was grateful to have him here and eager for the young man to find his place and be successful in his new role as head groom for Owensby Stud.

I felt a hand brush discreetly along my lower back as Julian took his place by my side. He rested his arms along the railing and propped one booted foot atop the lowest rung. The movement stretched the fine material of his trousers and I was momentarily distracted.

It was strange to catch myself staring at my husband. Stranger still, to recall that I had a husband.

We'd been married four months ago at Laurel Park. Our own home was still under construction, but we were comfortable in the small cottage on nearby Kendrick lands that Emery and Augie had offered us. More than comfortable, actually. Living and loving openly was a revelation.

Julian was still adjusting to life as part of a large, meddlesome family. But he was getting there quickly. We were happy. I was writing, and he was preparing for all things farm-related and enjoying his partnership with Miles. They worked well together and I was grateful that Julian had close friendships with the men in our family. Even Silas.

"I can't get used to seeing you in a hat," Julian said quietly near my ear, causing a pleasant shiver. "Your mother would be so proud."

I laughed, touching the smooth brim. "This hat is for fashion alone. Its primary purpose is not protection from the sun." He grinned at my teasing. "You know I enjoy having the warmth on my skin. And I've never minded freckles."

My eyes lovingly traced all the tiny marks dappling his pale cheeks and the bridge of his nose.

Julian grinned shyly. "Were you able to write in the carriage?"

I'd traveled to the racing grounds this morning with my sisters. Julian had needed to be here early to check on the horses and meet with interested parties.

"I did, actually. When Emery wasn't talking the whole time. I was able to focus and get some words on the page."

"I'm glad. I didn't want the disruption of the races to affect your deadline."

Squeezing his forearm, I said earnestly, "I wanted to be here for you. And besides, I can write anywhere."

After my departure from the *London Post*, I'd approached several small presses with an idea for a new story. I'd been lucky to find a good fit, someone willing to take a chance on a former serial writer. My new venture would be published as a triple-decker later in the year.

"True," Julian agreed. "But I'd wager you didn't expect to be finishing a novel with so many distractions."

"Ah, but every wordsmith worth her salt can scrawl dialogue in the back of a moving carriage."

Julian laughed, and my heart still cherished the sound even as I heard it more and more frequently. His gray eyes sparkled, and he corrected, "Word slinger. That's your official title."

My grin was wide as he referenced something I'd written in a letter long ago.

Those old wounds didn't sting like they used to. We no longer stumbled over mentions of the past. It was simply a path we walked together, long and winding. And it was the journey that had brought us to where we were now.

I didn't think in terms of *past Genevieve* anymore. There was just the girl who'd written letters to the boy who would one day be her husband. The constant in her life despite their years apart. And the man who would always and forever be her best friend.

"Miles is trying to subtly get your attention," I said.

Julian glanced over his shoulder to where I was looking. "Well, he was being too subtle." He turned back to meet my gaze. "I'll see you after the race?"

"Of course. Good luck. Lark is the fastest horse I've ever seen. I have no doubt he will succeed and you right along with him."

Heat flooded Julian's cheeks adorably and I bit my lip to contain my joy. It felt boastful to be this happy.

With a swift movement, Julian pressed a kiss to my shoulder before whispering in my ear, "I love you."

"I love you too." It was a relief to say it aloud.

I stood at the railing for a few moments longer, watching Julian make his way to Miles and the other gentlemen gathered there.

With a small smile I could do nothing to dispel, I took my seat and joined my family.

"Oh, there's Mary!" Emery called from my side a short while later.

I leaned forward just as my sister did the same. From her seated position in the grandstand, it was difficult to see beyond her.

"Did you find the largest hat in London, Emery?" I complained as I attempted to see around her feathers and flounces.

She turned toward me—nearly taking out an eye in the process.

Emery replied cheekily, "Do you know? That was the exact set of instructions I gave the milliner."

"Where is she going?" I heard Patty murmur from her place on the other side of Emery.

I went low and Emery went high, and we all managed to see Mary fleeing down the stairs of the grandstand.

"Probably back to her lair," Silas said from behind me as he scanned the race pamphlet in his hand.

Emery snorted, but I whacked my brother on the thigh with my fan and stood. "Be nice, Silas. We haven't seen Mary in months. Don't scare her off."

Emery stood and straightened her hat as we prepared to follow. "That's probably why she ran like that. One look at you, dear brother, and she was off like a shot."

"Just look at her. She could give a racehorse a run for its money," Silas grumbled from beneath his top hat.

Emery was ignoring him and maneuvering her way down the row. Patty was already gliding elegantly down the stairs.

But I turned back to Silas and sat down hard on the bench, drawing his attention. "I don't want to ever hear you say something so disrespectful about a lady—about Mary." My brother's eyes widened in alarm. "I know you two have this ridiculous relationship where you tease and bicker endlessly. But talking that way about her is not appropriate. She is loyal and dedicated and one of our family's closest friends. To mock her appearance—"

"Genevieve," he urged, placing a staying hand on my arm. "I was merely commenting on how she'd bolted out of the seating area. I was not referring to her appearance. Why would you think that?"

I scrutinized his face. It was a rare sight indeed to see my brother serious and earnest. "You really don't know?"

"Know what?"

"Last season, some gossip circulated and rumors spread about Lord Glenfellow calling Mary . . ." I trailed off, glancing around for any eavesdroppers. Lowering my voice, I finished, "Horse-faced. Mary tried to laugh away the moniker but it was repeated several times, usually by idiots. But I could tell it hurt her."

Mary wasn't what gentlemen of the *ton* would call classically beautiful. It was absurd, the way men felt obliged to discuss women's bodies. As if they had the right.

Mary was a few years past thirty. She was tall and very lean, willowy with few curves to speak of. Her hair was a fiery shade of red, so lovely with glinting highlights of copper and auburn. It complimented her porcelain skin, curling wildly around her head no matter how she styled it. But all of those things made her so compelling and interesting to look at. There was nothing plain or common or boring about her. Mary was striking. And when paired with her exuberant personality—well, she was one of my very favorite people.

I hated that anyone made her question her beauty. And if I thought my brother was referencing the events of last season, I would make him regret it.

But Silas's expression turned thunderous. "Who else?" he gritted out.

"What?"

"Who else called her that? Besides Glenfellow, that piece of shit."

I was taken aback by the vehemence in Silas's tone. "I don't remember all of them . . . but Hartley, Westdale. Oh and Brannigan, of course."

Silas looked out across the crowd. The stands weren't yet full. We had a bit of time before the Gold Cup race was run. "Have you seen any of them here?"

He stood as if to get a better look, like he might call out the wooden spoons for what they'd said. Or perhaps commit murder.

"Sit down, Silas," I hissed, tugging the sleeve of his formal jacket. "She wouldn't want you causing a scene. Not for her."

My brother sat with a huff, crossing his arms and crushing the pamphlet in his fist. "Well, someone bloody well should."

"I'm sorry I brought it up. Please don't ever say anything to Mary. I just reacted when I heard your remark earlier."

"I would never, Genevieve," Silas said, still cross.

"I know," I said, patting his arm. "I'm sorry I jumped to conclusions. I really should go after them and see what was the matter."

"Emery was right," he admitted quietly. He scanned the grass flat in front of us as horses were led by riders and spectators milled about. "She saw me and left."

I frowned. "Silas, that cannot be true."

But my brother didn't argue or explain. He simply stared straight ahead.

I left him to stew and I made my way out of the stands and away from the vendors and refreshment stands. Finally I spotted my sisters with Mary well away from the crowds. Mary had her hand braced on a tree and I could see her breathing deeply from here.

"What's going on?" I said as I approached.

"Mary is not feeling well," Patty replied evenly as the woman in question closed her eyes tightly and placed a hand to her lips.

"Oh, God," she moaned before spinning around and vomiting in a bush.

I turned a shocked expression toward Emery who grimaced.

Mary retched for another moment and then Patty handed her an embroidered handkerchief from her reticule.

She straightened from out of the shrubbery with her wild red hair askew. "Dammit, my hat fell off."

"We can get it back," I offered, eager to be of assistance in such a terrible situation.

Mary raised a staying hand. "Don't bother. It fell off as soon as I leaned over. Then I cast up my accounts all over it. It's done for."

"It was a grand hat, Mary. I'm sorry."

"All those feathers," Emery murmured, shaking her head sadly.

Patty shot us both exasperated looks. "Genevieve, will you go and fetch some water for Mary?"

I jolted into motion. "Of course. I apologize. I should have thought of that."

"No," Mary called weakly. "Don't. I won't be able to keep it down. I can't eat or drink anything when it gets like this."

When it gets like this? Did she become ill often?

Patty raised a hand and covered her mouth.

"What's going on?" Emery voiced the confusion I still felt as well. "Was it the carriage ride?"

"Mary doesn't get sick on long carriage rides," I replied automatically, recalling her boasting last autumn on the way to Hampshire.

Mary looked between each of us. She shook her head slowly, tears welling in her dark brown eyes.

We moved forward collectively at the sight.

"What can we do?"

"Should we get a doctor?"

"Do you think you are?"

It was Patty's voice and the final question that had Emery and I staring at her instead.

Emery caught on quicker than I did because she gasped out, "Mary!"

"What? What is everyone going on about?" I demanded.

Now everyone was looking at me. I widened my eyes dramatically. "Why can't you just tell me? What would make Mary sick like this repeatedly and—oh my God."

"Now she's got it," Emery mumbled from my side. "Gets her intelligence from Silas, this one."

I turned to scowl at my sister and tell her she'd just barely figured it out before I had. But just then Mary moaned another, "Oh, God," and promptly heaved into the bushes.

The Bartholomew series continues with Silas and Mary's story!

Last on the List, is LIVE in Kindle Unlimited **Grab your copy today!**

Want more of Genevieve and Julian? Check out a bonus scene for Third Degree Yearn when you sign up for Laney's newsletter **here***!*

If you have trouble with the link above, scan the QR code:

About the Author

Sign up for my newsletter: https://bit.ly/3SbXg2v

Laney Hatcher is a firm believer that there is a spreadsheet for every occasion and pie is always the answer. She is an author of stories both old and new where the HEAs are always guaranteed. Often too practical for her own good, Laney enjoys her life in the southern United States with her husband, children, and incredibly entitled cat.

Find Laney Hatcher online:
Facebook: https://bit.ly/3s6KnuY
Newsletter: https://bit.ly/3SbXg2v
Amazon: https://amzn.to/3IaOwU7
Instagram: https://bit.ly/3s4lRcS
Website: https://laneyhatcher.com/
Goodreads: https://bit.ly/3BD0Gme
TikTok: https://www.tiktok.com/@laneyhatcherauthor

Newsletter sign up

Also by Laney Hatcher

Bartholomew Series

First to Fall: A Friends to Lovers Historical Romance

Second Chance Dance: An Enemies to Lovers Historical Romance

Third Degree Yearn: A Second Chance Historical Romance

Last on the List: A Surprise Pregnancy Historical Romance

Kirby Falls Series

Take It or Leaf It

Smartypants Romance

London Ladies Embroidery Series

Neanderthal Seeks Duchess: A Smartypants Romance Out of this World Title

Well Acquainted: A Smartypants Romance Out of this World Title

Love Matched: A Smartypants Romance Out of this World Title

Find bonus content, reading order, and other news at my website: https://laneyhatcher.com/